THE UNTRODDEN

He answered by catching her in his arms and kissing her on the mouth.

"You know I love every hair on your head."

"You always must," she said under her breath.

"I always will," he said.

"Even," she said with sudden daring, "if you found out that I—"

"That you—what?"

"Oh never mind, I was only being stupid," she added, losing courage.

But she was very silent on the return journey as they slid on the *téléférique* cable across the tops of the snow-powdered trees, down, down to the green valley, thousands of feet below.

**Also by the same author,
and available in Coronet Books:**

The Untrodden Snow

Denise Robins

CORONET BOOKS
Hodder and Stoughton

Copyright © 1958 by Denise Robins

First published in Great Britain by
Hodder and Stoughton 1958

Coronet Edition 1961
Second impression 1967
Third impression 1970
Fourth impression 1971
Fifth impression 1976

———————————————

Printed and bound in Great Britain for
Coronet Books, Hodder and Stoughton, London,
By Richard Clay (The Chaucer Press) Ltd,
Bungay, Suffolk

ISBN 0 340 14985 X

Dedication for my friend, EDITH BERG
who helped to make our holiday
in Crans-sur-Sierre such a perfect one.

1

I T was not until Rowan returned from the funeral and walked
down the garden path of the little cottage in Jordans—the only
home she had ever known—that the full realization of her loss
descended upon her.

At the funeral, itself, she had been in too much of a daze to
think. Everybody had been kind. The Vicar, who had conducted
the burial service. The Doctor, who had been hurriedly called in
when Mrs. Gray had her first heart attack. Mr. and Mrs. Jenkins,
whose cottage stood only a few hundred yards away from Rowan's
home. Ann Jenkins had been wonderful throughout. She was a
nice woman with two children at school. Rowan and her widowed
mother used to see a lot of the Jenkins family. Rowan was so good
with children. Jeremy and Ingrid, the little Jenkins boy and girl,
adored her. Rowan and her mother used to go in two evenings a
week to see the Jenkins' television. Thinking about the television
was one of the things that struck Rowan like a blow as she stopped
midway down the garden path to stare through a haze of tears at
the roses which were just coming into bud. Mummy had had a
passion for roses and theirs were always quite the best for miles
around. They had actually been sitting together, looking at a
Flower Show on the Jenkins' television, and Mummy had been
saying how she was going to try and show her roses this year at the
Chelsea Flower Show, when the first terrible pain attacked her.
Then the frantic rush for the doctor. Then, later, a second attack
and before Rowan could even realize the enormity of it, death had
struck Mary Gray down. Ended Mummy's life just as swiftly and
easily, Rowan pondered, as she could this moment end the life of
the rose she was touching; by pulling off that bud.

Rowan ran into the cottage, shut the door and locked it, and
flung herself down on the sofa in the sitting-room.

It was silent, dreadfully lonely and dim. The early summer sun
had been shut out because Mrs. Jenkins had considered it right
and proper to pull the curtains while the coffin left the house.

Rowan abandoned herself to the passionate grief which she had
tried so hard to check during the funeral. She hated showing her
feelings in public. But she felt the most bitter longing to have her

7

mother back again. She had been so affectionate, so warm-hearted. Now all that warmth and sweetness was gone. She was lying out there in the churchyard under a mound of flowers—tributes from neighbours. The Grays were well known in Jordans but it had been remarked upon that not a single relative had come to the funeral and nobody ever remembered any relations calling at Beacon Cottage. What the district knew was all that Rowan herself knew about her family; that her father was dead and Mummy had brought her up from infancy here, in this little cottage. And that there had been enough money to keep the home going in a modest way, and to educate her. Rowan, as a child, went to a good school in Gerrards Cross. She could speak and write perfect French. Mary Gray had been born a Swiss and often conversed in that language with Rowan. A thing which had always rather mystified Rowan was the fact that her mother never spoke of her own childhood; or her Swiss relations.

"I've taken English nationality," she used to say in her clear precise voice. "I would like you to learn to speak my mother tongue, but I have no wish to return to Switzerland, nor to take you there."

Whatever the mystery attached to the past, it had never entered Rowan's head to probe into it or question her mother further.

On her nineteenth birthday, a fortnight ago, plans for Rowan's future had been discussed. It had always been Mrs. Gray's wish that Rowan should be given the chance to make a career for herself. As the years went by, investments dwindled, money became more difficult and the cost of living had risen. Mrs. Gray must have been forty when Rowan was born. Rowan knew that. Mummy was by no means a 'young mother' and she was always worrying about what would happen to Rowan if anything happened to *her*.

"I simply must be able to feel that you can stand on your own feet," Mrs. Gray had said that day, when they had talked things over, "when I go, you will have nobody in the world."

"I think I'm the only person who hasn't got any aunts or uncles or cousins," Rowan had laughed; then seeing a shadow over her mother's face, had quickly changed the subject. It was not one that Mummy ever wished to discuss. But Rowan went her way quite happily, doing her share of the cooking and the housework, and for the last year she had taken a secretarial course—going into High Wycombe every day by bus.

"With my shorthand, typing and one foreign language, I ought

8

to be able to get a good secretarial job if I ever want one," she had told her mother, more to stop her worrying than anything.

Then *this*—this sudden awful ending of their peaceful tranquil life together in Beacon Cottage.

Ann Jenkins had suggested coming in with Rowan just now but Rowan had asked her not to. She wanted to be quite alone. A deep reserve—amounting almost to shyness—and what Ann Jenkins thought almost an unnatural love of being alone—singled Rowan out from other girls of her own age. She had always been happy here in the cottage just with her mother and their few friends. She had never craved for excitement, parties, boy-friends —the usual interests of the teenager. Books, music, history in particular, interested the young girl. But now she began to see what it would mean to be *absolutely* alone.

It was a terrifying thought.

Death is a thing the young rarely think about. To them it is too remote. For Rowan, her mother's death had come as a horror —a monster that had suddenly opened its jaws and devoured this dearest and nearest creature. She had found it hard to listen to the Christian comfort the Vicar tried to give her. Hers was the all-absorbing sorrow of a young and tender heart. She cried passionately for a long time on the sofa in the darkened sitting-room; not daring to look around, in case she saw the cretonne bag on the table in which there lay the embroidery on which her mother had been working; or any of the familiar objects which they had both loved and shared.

She felt something soft and warm against her foot, and a plaintive 'mew'. She stopped crying for a moment, put out her hand and stroked the ears of Candy, Mummy's tortoise-shell cat whom they had had for eight long years. Poor Candy would be wondering where her mistress was tonight. She would have to find Candy a home, Rowan thought miserably. Rowan was going over to stay with the Jenkins tonight, but she could not take Candy because there was a Boxer dog there who did not take kindly to cats.

"Oh, what am I going to do? *What am I going to do?*" Rowan uttered the words aloud in a voice strangled with grief.

Slowly coming out of her daze, she began to remember all kinds of things that worried her. Apart from Mummy's sudden death— the question of money. Rowan had never had anything to do with the finance of this little household. She did not even know where Mummy's income came from except that she used to go once a month into High Wycombe to visit her Bank Manager; and there always seemed enough to make ends meet, if no more. Tomorrow, Rowan would have to go in and see the Bank Manager, herself; find out how things stood. It was rather a frightening prospect to be nineteen—not yet even of age—and have to make a new life for oneself, she thought.

Of course now she must admit that she and Mummy had led a too solitary existence; that she, Rowan, had been too closely protected from the troubles and difficulties of the world. It would not be easy to face up to realities. Why, she didn't even know if this cottage was actually Mummy's—or mortgaged—or *what*. All these things she must find out tomorrow.

One thing she did know; that was that it wouldn't be possible for her—a young girl—to live alone at Beacon Cottage. She knew nobody who could come and live with her; therefore, there loomed the awful idea of having to leave her home. Yes, sell up and leave; what a bleak, crippling prospect!

Into the young mind that had been so bemused during these last forty-eight hours, crept yet another thought; the uncomfortable and baffling memory of Mrs. Gray's last harrowing moments before she died.

She had been helped back here from the Jenkins' house after the first attack. The doctor had left her in bed seemingly better, quite calm after an injection. But the second and fatal attack had followed while Rowan was in the kitchen boiling eggs for their supper. She had rushed upstairs, seen the terrifyingly altered face of the beloved woman, cradled her in her young strong arms and listened to gasping words:

"*Tin box . . . my diary . . . burn . . .*" she kept saying with her piteous eyes fixed upon Rowan.

Rowan without understanding, had answered:

"All right, darling, all right, *don't worry*."

But Mary Gray's last words on earth had been a reiteration: "*My diary . . . burn . . .*"

It was only now in the silent cottage while the last rays of sunshine struggled through a chink in the drawn curtains and hurt Rowan's swollen eyes, that she again remembered those words.

She stood up, blew her nose and walked to the little walnut bureau which stood by the window. She drew back the curtains and opened the casement windows wide. The tortoiseshell cat leapt up, and like an arch of orange fur, streaked on to the flower-bed below and vanished.

Rowan stood a moment staring at the bureau. It had always

been sacrosanct to her mother; used expressly by her for writing letters or doing accounts. Rowan had her own desk up in her bedroom. Mummy used to be rather odd about this desk, which, for the most part she kept locked. As Rowan grew older, one day she had remarked on her mother's secretiveness; her rather jealous appropriation of the bureau; and Mrs. Gray had received the jest without smiling. In fact, it was the only time that Rowan had ever seen her look angry.

"You must not pry. I must have my own private things, dear," she had said in a cold voice.

Rowan stared fixedly at the desk, still trying to calm her sorrow and think coherently. *What* had been on poor Mummy's mind as she felt the death pangs convulse her heart? *A tin box—a diary—* what did it all mean? Why must the diary be burnt?

'I'll see to it tomorrow,' Rowan thought as she stood there, and she lifted her lashes which were long and sticky with tears and regarded her own face in the oval mirror which hung above the desk. A rather charming little French mirror with two candlesticks.

Rowan was quite shocked to see her reflection. Heavens! How awful she looked!

She was naturally pale but this was a white ghost of a girl. Her cheeks seemed to have sunk in the last three days since tragedy had torn up the roots of her tranquil life, as though by a cyclone. Her eyes which were large and dark, were as pitiful as those of a wounded deer. Her hair, which was extremely fair by contrast, was severely brushed back from her forehead and twisted into a bun. She was without colour. The funereal black of a hastily purchased and ill-fitting suit hid the natural grace of her young figure. She looked quite old, she thought; scrawny and plain.

What was this dreary girl going to do with her life? Once or twice, her mother had talked about her 'meeting the right man' and settling down to marriage and motherhood. It had not been a subject to cause Rowan much excitement.

"I don't think I shall ever get married. I think I shall be an old maid and as I love children, I shall adopt a child," she had laughed.

Her mother had given her rather an odd look and said curtly:

"Oh, you'll fall in love one day. Every woman does."

But Rowan, looking at herself in the mirror this afternoon, decided that there would be no falling in love for her. No man would ever want her. So far there had only been one vague suggestion of a 'romance' in her life. A boy of her own age at the secretarial school in High Wycombe and who lived at Jordans used to travel to and fro on the bus. They both liked music. This boy, Alan Spencer, took her into Slough to hear a concert. It had been quite an experience for Rowan, and Mummy had thought Alan nice and smiled upon the friendship, deeming it good for Rowan. But when Alan had tried a clumsy embrace—as shy and inexperienced as the object of his affections—Rowan had felt herself freeze. She did not want that sort of friendship. She never saw Alan again.

What was she going to do now?

A sudden quite inexplicable curiosity to open her mother's desk rushed over her. Indeed she felt so intensely about it that she was quite shaken by the emotion. Was it a shameful curiosity or a natural one? She did not know. But even to open that bureau seemed an abuse of the trust that her mother had always had in her. In Mummy's lifetime, Rowan had never dreamed of prying.

But now she would have to. She would have to learn more about the business side of things. On the way back from the churchyard, the kindly Mrs. Jenkins had murmured something about a Will and the necessity for a lawyer. Rowan had said that as far as she knew, her mother had never made a Will nor mentioned the name of a lawyer. She must once have had one if she bought the cottage but Rowan, then an infant, would know nothing about that.

'How funny it is,' Rowan reflected as she looked at her sad mirrored face. 'My mother must have *had* a past—a beginning in Switzerland for instance, and I am completely ignorant about it all. I know nothing even about my own father. It's almost as though I never *had* a father.'

How stupid! Of course she must have had a father but she had never even seen a photograph of him. Any time she had begun to question Mummy about him, Mrs. Gray had said:

"He is dead, dear—I don't want to speak about him."

Alan Spencer had been inquisitive about Rowan's parentage. In fact, Rowan recalled now that it was Alan who had made that insinuating remark about 'her birth being shrouded in mystery'.

"Everybody in Jordans *wonders*," he had said.

What did they wonder? Rowan did not know. But sometimes she wondered, too. There were all kinds of possibilities. She never explored any of them. She preferred not to. Sometimes she built up the idea that it was just because her mother had been very unhappy with her father that she did not want to keep his memory alive. So—if that was what Mummy wanted—Rowan wanted it, too.

But now—now that she was alone and the world stretched before her like a wide and terrifying jungle which *had* to be explored whether she wanted to or not—a thousand doubts and queries assailed her mind like invisible enemies.

Suddenly the fount of grief seemed to dry up. Her heart began to race; her pale cheeks to burn; with an expression of mingled curiosity and repugnance, she unlocked the bureau and opened it.

2

ANN and Bill Jenkins, having marshalled their children off to bed, were busily engaged spraying their roses with insecticide when they heard footsteps and turned to see Rowan Gray walking down the flagged path towards them.

Mrs. Jenkins, a tall strong young woman with a thick mop of reddish hair which she never had time to cut, and wearing slacks and a rather grubby jersey, put down her syringe and drew the back of her hand across her perspiring brow. It was the warmest evening they had had yet. Bill had been back from the City some time—he was a junior partner in a firm of solicitors—and they were taking the advantage of the light in order to get on with the gardening which was their pet hobby. Bill, so smartly groomed at the office, now looked as unkempt as his wife, but they were a happy pair. Enthusiastic about life and themselves—they adored their one-time farmhouse which they had bought cheap because it was falling to pieces, and which they had done up without help. They adored their mischievous ten-year-old son, Jeremy, who was now at day school in Beaconsfield. They adored their eight-year-old daughter, romantically christened 'Ingrid' but for ever called 'Scrap' because she was so small for her age. They cared nothing that they had to work terrifically hard. Ann had no domestic help. Bill had to give a hand with the chores and the children when he was at home. School fees were crippling. To run a home nicely even in an economic way meant a drain on modest resources in these days. But the Jenkins continued to adore life—and each other.

They had been saddened by the death of their nearest neighbour. Bill hadn't been able to get away for the funeral but Ann had been there to hold Rowan's hand. This evening, while the Jenkins cherished their roses, they had been discussing Rowan.

"I really don't know what she is going to do. She seems so alone in the world," Ann had just been saying.

"She'll get married, perhaps," was Bill's hopeful opinion.

"Darling, to get married, you've first got to get a chap interested in you and then be interested in him," announced Ann.

Bill, who had just knocked a bud off a rose with his spray, hastily pocketed it so that Ann could not see, and grinned at her.

"Like you were in me, sweetie."

"Like I *am* in you," corrected Ann.

"Honey, shall I stop serious work and come and kiss the dirt off your nose?" asked Bill.

"I'd enjoy that," said Ann, "but I want to talk about Rowan. What *can* we do to help her, Bill?"

"Suggest she sells Beacon Cottage and comes to live at Blackthorn Farm with us. The kids are crazy about her. She might be helpful."

"Bill darling, you *are* an egotistical male. We're supposed to be trying to help *her*."

"Why can't she get married?" persisted Bill.

"She's such a child, still. Could you imagine making a pass at her?"

"I wouldn't make a pass at anybody but you. I'm a respectable married man."

Ann's brown rather charming face with tip-tilted nose and narrow laughing eyes, assumed a satirical expression.

"Darling, Rowan is thin and immature and *not* your type. Don't be so holy."

Bill scratched his head.

"Well, naturally if she had a luscious figure like yours——"

"Oh, be quiet," broke in Ann, blushing furiously. *"What are we going to do for Rowan?"*

"Will Mrs. Gray have left her any money?"

"Nobody knows. The old girl was always so secretive and I don't think even Rowan knew her mother's business. I've always said there was a mystery there. Once I had a natter with her about Rowan and she seemed worried, herself, about what might happen to Rowan if she died an early death—Mrs. Gray I mean. I told

14

her I thought Rowan ought to see more people and get a boy-friend but she said Rowan wasn't that sort."

"I think she's a sweet kid," said Bill, "but a bit shy for my liking."

Ann bent over one of her newest rose bushes and shot an extra vicious load of insecticide at a pink bud which was a green mass of flies.

"Duckie—she's only nineteen. She hasn't developed sexually yet. Maybe she's a 'still water'. That dreamy romantic timid type often turn out to be quite torrid in time."

"Oh, lead me to the torrid zones!" Bill began to sing. It was just then that they saw Rowan coming down the path, stopped talking and waved to her.

"I'm so glad to see you, Rowan," called Ann, "I hoped you'd come. No good sitting by yourself."

Rowan made no answer. She was close beside them now and they saw how deadly pale she was, and that she was trembling.

Ann Jenkins, first and foremost a mother, put down her spray, dusted her grimy hands on the seat of her slacks and looked at the young girl with concern.

"Has anything happened, dear—I mean is anything wrong?" she began.

Then Rowan, who so rarely showed her feelings, crumpled up. She hadn't done so even at the funeral of her mother. She just stood there at the graveside, mute and stiff, looking down with tragic, tearless eyes. Ann had rather wished she would cry and be comforted. But now, Rowan burst into tears. In fact, she began to sob as though in passionate protest of what life was doing to her. To her breast she hugged a leather-bound book—Ann couldn't at that moment see the word 'Diary' that was written on it. Then, regardless of Bill Jenkins' embarrassed gaze, she flung herself into Ann's outstretched arms and gasped:

"Oh, Ann, *Ann*, it's *too* terrible."

Mistakenly, Mrs. Jenkins thought that the girl alluded to her mother's death.

"There, there," she said, "come in with me and have a good cry. . . ." And she led the weeping, distracted Rowan through the lichen-covered portico, into the big cool hall of the farmhouse, farther into a small untidy room filled with books, where the Jenkins usually sat once the day's work was done.

Ann drew Rowan down on to the big settee which was her special pride and joy because she, herself, had made the chintz

15

cover. (It fitted nowhere but she had *made* it and Bill never stopped admiring it.)

She let Rowan cry on her shoulder for a moment, petting her as she did Scrap whenever there was what was known in the house as a 'carry-on'. Scrap was rather emotional and given to 'carry-ons'. She frequently raised her voice in protest against the impish designs of her brother who loved to tease her. In a way, thought Ann, Rowan was rather like Scrap; they were both small and insignificant, yet, surely, full of hidden grace and fire and imagination.

Ann had known Rowan since she was only a little older than Jeremy was now. For it was nine years ago that the Jenkins had bought this dilapidated farmhouse. Scrap had been born here. At that time, Rowan had been going to school in Gerrards Cross. Ann, with her natural *bonhomie* and affability towards the world in general, had soon made friends with the widowed Mrs. Gray, and found her sweet and gentle—but uncommunicative. But the little girl with the long fair plaits and big dark eyes had immediately taken a place in Ann's heart and later in her household.

Rowan grew up to be a bookworm. She loved to come in here to this little room and read all the classics which were actually Bill's. He was the reader of the family—Ann was more domestically-minded. It had become customary through the years for Rowan to wander in and out of Blackthorn Farm as she wished; and later when she took music lessons, to play the old grand piano in the seldom-used drawing-room which had belonged to Bill's mother. Bill always said that Rowan had real talent and that it was a pity that she couldn't take up music as a profession. But there seemed no money for that in the Gray household.

Ann had found that she could get so far with Mary Gray, but no farther. After nine years of being her next-door neighbour, she still knew little about the Grays. On the other hand, lately Mrs. Gray had come more often to the farmhouse. She never spoke of herself but seemed to enjoy the television—the great extravagance indulged in by Bill and presented to the family two years ago.

"The greatest waster of time on earth," he called it, but rushed to his T.V. on every possible occasion, either to see the sports, the news or 'thrillers'. For Ann, her T.V. set was the unpaid mother's help. For in the late afternoons, she could thankfully deposit her screaming pair in front of Children's Hour and know that it meant an hour's peace and relaxation—for *her*.

Now, as she held the sobbing Rowan in her arms, she thought sadly:

'How cruel death is. This funny child was perfectly happy living alone with her old mother. She must feel desperate this evening. I can understand it.'

But she was quite unable to understand, when Rowan suddenly stopped crying, wiped her red-rimmed eyes, drew away from Mrs. Jenkins's arm and said:

"Ann—she wasn't my mother. *She wasn't my mother.*"

Ann stared. For one awful moment she thought that Mrs. Gray's death and the funeral had turned the poor child's head. She began:

"There, there, honey——"

"She wasn't my mother—yet I still can't *believe* it," said Rowan in a loud hoarse voice.

"Duckie—what do you mean she *wasn't* your mother?"

Rowan thrust on to Ann's lap the shabby leather book on which plainly now Ann could see the word 'Diary'.

"It's all in there, I've been reading it. That and some letters which were tied up, which I wasn't supposed to read. I just opened the desk to find the tin box; Mummy had kept muttering about one just before she died, and in the box there was this diary and the letters."

Ann looked at Rowan with the utmost anxiety.

"Let Bill come in and mix you a nice cool drink, darling."

Rowan looked at her with fever-bright eyes.

"You needn't think I'm crazy, I'm not."

"Then, my dear, what on earth——?"

Rowan interrupted and began to talk in that hoarse little voice of hers while Ann listened attentively. As she told Bill afterwards, what the child had found out was enough to send anyone a little off balance. When Rowan walked in with that diary she was suffering from real shock.

Ann Jenkins had always been a practical sensible girl. At thirty-five, she was experienced in mothering both her high-spirited children; the boyish husband whom she called her third child; Luke, the Boxer, who was the household pet, and the farmyard animals which they kept at the back of the house. A goat. The chickens. The geese. She looked after humans and animals alike with a tremendous love and understanding and the pure joy of cherishing. But it took her several minutes in which to decide how best to tackle Rowan's particular problem.

"It's just too fantastic. Like a thriller or a T.V. play—anything

17

but real life," such was her delineation of the affair when she spoke about it in private to Bill.

Bill was finally called in, and husband and wife sat on either side of the young girl, listening to the reiterated story which was on her mind and must come out. They were glad that it could—and did—for this was no time for Rowan's customary reserve. The cool unruffled girl whose life had hitherto been so simple and easy—so calm, that not the smallest breath of drama or passion had disturbed the shining surface, came to life—with a vengeance. To new frightening knowledge. She was no longer what she thought she was. The cyclone that had uprooted her when her mother died, now, like a second tempest, tore across her soul's placidity—her mind's calm. She was no longer ignorant of the past, about which she used to be mildly curious. She had learned everything—and nothing. She knew too much—and too little. She recounted the story to her kind friends while Bill and Ann smoked their cigarettes and somewhat agitatedly sipped some sherry. Rowan, neither smoking nor drinking, for she did neither, sat between them like a slender swan whose plumage has been ruffled and whose innocence of mind and heart is threatened with destruction. A swan with a long slender neck that no longer drooped, and soft eyes that no longer looked coolly upon the world. The young fair head was raised. The big pansy dark eyes were stormy; the mouth a red curve of bitter protest. The nice amiable easy-going Jenkins had never seen Rowan Gray looking anything like that before.

'I can well believe tonight that the child has deep feeling—Ann was right,' mused Bill.

Hers was a startling story.

Little wonder that Mary Gray, in the last convulsions of a stricken heart, hoped that her secret—rigidly kept for nineteen years—would not be divulged; that the diary, mistakenly kept, should be burned before Rowan could read it. Perhaps Mrs. Gray had meant to burn it—and all the other evidence of the past, before she died. Death had come too suddenly and unexpectedly. And her last gasping request was not to be carried out.

"I feel horribly mean, reading what was in that book," Rowan told her friends, the red blood staining her pallid young face. "But at first I imagined it was just a sentimental souvenir—perhaps about Mummy's early life in Switzerland. Then I flicked open a page and *then*——"

And *then* . . . what a fatal page she had opened! Her own name

18

leapt at her—one all revealing dramatic paragraph, like words of fire. A fire too big and hot to put out by just shutting that diary again. *She had had to go on reading.*

The baby was baptized in the little church at Jordans. Nobody knew that she was only my adopted child. She was three months old. Nobody save I was to know that her surname was different from mine. I told everyone that she was mine and that I was a widow. As such, we were accepted. So began my new life in my newly purchased cottage. Never having been married, or had a baby of my own, it was a big responsibility for me to bring up so young a child. But the district nurse was kind and advised me, and I soon learned how to give Rowan her bottle and take care of her. I swiftly became attached to the poor motherless little thing, too. For from henceforward, she would regard me as her mother. . . .

That was the startling and revealing paragraph that had made Rowan's blood turn cold and tempted her to go on reading.

"Do you blame me?" she asked the Jenkins, pitifully. "Could anybody have been human and burnt that diary then and there, without finding out more? Oh, I was flabbergasted and yet fascinated. I *had* to know more. *I wasn't her child!* She said she wasn't even married. What could it all mean?"

"Duckie, of course you had to find out," Ann soothed her. "Don't feel badly about it."

"Devil of a shock," muttered Bill, but his legal mind thirsted for facts—and the fascination of this thing was wound up for him not only in the girl's personal story but the legal angle of it.

They let Rowan pour out her staggering tale—punctuating her own stammered theories and suppositions by occasional quotations from the diary itself. She read the first salient words ever written by Mary Gray (and even that was not her true name). She had been born Marie Thérèse Garnier of Montreux, and had taken that other name with her British citizenship.

3

I T is dangerous to keep a diary and I swore to all those concerned that I would never reveal the story of Rowan's birth. But I have done so much for all the family—I have given my life to those who needed me—for ten long years I have kept silent. Now, on Rowan's *eleventh birthday I feel the urge to begin to write it all down. I dare not speak to a living soul. But I need to write these words and get it all off my mind—and conscience. Maybe when it is written, I shall feel better and some of the weight will be lifted from my shoulders. Then the diary can be burnt. It will be as though it had never been written.*

That was what Mary Gray (*née* Marie Thérèse Garnier) had hoped would happen; but her heart attack had carried her off before she could destroy the revelation.

Bill Jenkins had seen this sort of thing happen so many times. People waiting to make a Will—still young—still feeling they had many years before them. Then sudden death—and chaos. Thus had it happened to the woman who had lived next door—shrouded in mystery—now a mystery no longer.

It was a fascinating story.

Early in 1920 when Marie was a girl of twenty-two, she left Montreux her native town, her elderly parents and a younger brother—and entered the family of some English titled people as resident nurse to their infant daughter, Vivien.

As the years went by Marie became greatly attached to Vivien, her beautiful high-spirited charge, and to the parents who were both handsome, generous and lovable. She was treated as one of the family for she was a cultured girl. She had no wish to return to her own country. She stayed with the Lakers in England.

Sir Charles Laker, who was at one time a regular officer in the Grenadier Guards, had served in France during World War I, been twice wounded and finally returned to spend the rest of his life in his country home in a wheeled-chair—a hopeless cripple.

In her diary 'Mary Gray' described Sir Charles as being a wonderful man who showed angelic patience throughout his tortures; he had one grave operation after another. And Elizabeth Laker as a 'noble and splendid character' who in spite of the fact that she was still young and beautiful, looked neither to the right nor the left, but devoted herself to her wounded husband. Of the child, Marie wrote these words:

Vivien looks a true daughter of both these dear people whom I so much adore and who have been so kind and good to me; treated me always as one of the family. She is petite *and like a Dresden china figure. She has her mother's rippling golden hair. It used to be my pride to wash and curl it, and I was glad they never let it be cut when the first fashion for bobbing and shingling swept England. She had*

her father's large blue eyes. Only her mouth betrayed a slight differ-
ence between her disposition and theirs. It was fine-cut to the point of
thinness. Not a generous mouth. There were moments when she could
be quite frighteningly cold and even callous. For instance, she would
never have an animal about her; she disliked pets. She was jealous
and avoided other small girls. She showed a marked preference for
the boys who were her playmates. Over them she would queen it,
treating the most gentle and kind among them with a selfishness and
disdain which sometimes made me sad and ashamed for her. Yet she
could be so utterly charming, both her parents and I forgave her for
everything. In her eighteenth year, when she was about to 'come out',
she was quite ravishingly beautiful and attractive, even if spoiled.
Her parents gave her everything. I alone, perhaps, saw the grave
twist in her nature and tried to make her a little more unselfish and
kind. It was uphill work but she could melt my heart in two moments
by just one look from her glorious eyes; a touch of her slender hand,
her voice teasing me: 'Darling old Puritan—old Prim and Proper—
I love you. Don't be cross,' she would plead. And of course I couldn't
go on being cross. I had to be as indulgent as she wished.

The diary described how the young Swiss nursery-governess
fashioned her life round the Laker family, in their town house in
Cadogan Square, or their country seat near Aldborough. Once or
twice she returned to Switzerland for a holiday. The third and, so
she believed, final time, was to attend the funeral of her old parents
who had died within a few days of each other. Her brother, Jean,
married a girl from Sierre and settled down to run a small hotel
there. After that, Marie had no wish to return.

Then came a fearful upheaval and change in all their lives.
Vivien—whose mother had always chosen the best friends for her
from the nicest families—fell violently and disastrously in love.

It was her first serious affair. Hitherto she had had only mild
flirtations. She had begun to show herself a coquette—and what
was worse, a hard-hearted little coquette who did not mind whom
she hurt. There were broken hearts strewn right and left of her.
Among the rejected suitors—deeply deplored by her mother—
was a young baronet ten years older than herself, who had a large
estate and a fortune as well as his title to offer Vivien. In Lady
Laker's opinion he was charming and most eligible. But Vivien
was unpredictable. What had seemed a cool even callous young
débutante of the time—fell suddenly from her high estate. The
object of her passion was her parents' chauffeur.

That, wrote Mary Gray, *was I think what caused us all such grief and horror. I admit we were snobs—all of us. My beloved employer, Lady Laker, was such a lady, and we had brought Vivien up as one, yet she became infatuated with* a working man. *As I write this, I know that times have changed. Socialism has swept the world. Perhaps today it would not be thought much of for an aristocratic young lady to marry such a person as a garage mechanic. But in 1937 it still meant social suicide. And what Vivien did was terrible and unpardonable, not only to herself, but to all of us who loved her, who expected her to behave as a young girl* bien élèvée *should do.*

What sort of man was this chauffeur who had inspired such love in the beautiful young girl? 'A physical passion, of course,' wrote 'Mary Gray', 'it could be nothing else.' The young man, Harry Treloar, came from the West Country—a Cornishman—with the dark curly hair and black sparkling eyes which seemed to have been handed down to so many of the Cornish through intermarriage with the people of Spain. He had charm and a soft beguiling voice. Everybody liked him, including the Swiss girl. He was the most trusted member of the Laker staff. But there came that terrible morning when Vivien was taken ill. She had in fact looked ill and miserable for several weeks. Yet so closely had she guarded her secret that not a soul at Lakers Court that warm summer of 1937 guessed the nature of her sickness.

I cannot write in detail about this thing. It weighs too heavily on my heart, wrote 'Mary Gray'. *My beloved child with whom I had stayed as nursery-governess, and later as friend; with whom I conversed in French—to whom I had given my whole life—was* enceinte.

It was Lady Laker who first told Marie the news. The family doctor had seen Vivien. The lovely girl, still a child herself, was going to become a mother.

Harry Treloar was responsible.

Wild with fear and remorse, Vivien confessed. She seemed to have no thought for Harry—only for herself. Three months ago she had spent a few days in London with her godmother, the Countess of L——. Lady L—— was old and deaf and gullible. Whatever story her charming goddaughter told her, she believed. At any rate, Treloar was on forty-eight hours' leave and the two managed to meet continually. The old Countess really did not know whether the pretty Vivien was in or out of the house.

The young chauffeur, off his head with passion and longing, put himself in the wrong and went through a form of marriage by special licence with his employer's daughter—under another name—giving her age as twenty-one. After their marriage they stayed together, but whereas he remained passionately in love, once the excitement of the secret wedding died down, Vivien's ardour cooled. He wanted to tell her parents the truth and be a man about it. She refused to allow him to speak—more especially when she discovered the appalling outcome of her stupid marriage; although when she first consented to it, she told her mother, she had serious thoughts of making her parents accept Harry as their son-in-law. But like everything with Vivien—it had been a whim and little more. She, herself, was not ready to take any blame but quite ready to allow her infatuated lover to suffer.

Our first thought, wrote Marie, *was to have the marriage annulled and bring Treloar to the Criminal Courts as our darling was under age. Oh, never shall I forget how my lady and I talked and talked, trying to make up our minds what best to do, with Vivien imploring us to save her.*

The upshot of it all was that Lady Laker and Marie decided that they could not accuse Treloar. It would be in all the papers. It must never be made public. The scandal would be too shocking. Vivien's life would be wrecked, before her nineteenth year. They would pay Treloar to quit the country and never trouble Vivien again. As for Vivien—it was then that Marie proved her great love and will to repay the Laker family for the long years of happiness she had spent with them.

Between them, she and Vivien's mother hatched a plot. Marie would take Vivien to Switzerland, presumably to see her home, and later announce that they had gone up to the mountains for the winter sports. The child was due to be born at Christmas. Nobody in England would know the truth except the Lakers' physician in Aldborough and he would never talk.

Everything can be done in secret in my native country, Marie had said, *and afterwards Vivien can return to you but I will look after her child. Whatever we say, it will be your flesh and blood, my dear lady, and* hers. *I could not bear that it should be adopted.*

At first Lady Laker had protested. Why should Marie make such a sacrifice? But Marie insisted that it would be her great happiness to mother Vivien's infant.

It was Marie who dealt with Harry Treloar. Lady Laker hated him so bitterly for what he had done to her innocent girl (she refused for one moment to admit that Vivien had driven him crazy and made him act as he did against his better judgment). She would not see him. So it was the Swiss girl, with her calm and imperturbable nature and inborn courage, who interviewed him.

He did not behave like a villain. He was bitterly remorseful yet anxious to do the right thing; he wanted his young wife and the coming child. It was Marie who, after hours of discussion, made the young Cornishman believe that the only way to prove his love was to vanish out of Vivien's life, and forget that there was to be a child.

"You are lucky not to be sent to prison," she said.

But he said:

"If she had still loved me I would have gladly faced prison for her, but as she wants no more of me, I'll clear out."

Later on, Marie told him a divorce must be arranged in secret, but *after* the child was born. Lady Laker was a woman of impeccable virtue. Even under these circumstances she would not have Vivien's child a bastard.

Wrote Marie:

Much as I abhorred Treloar for ruining my beloved Vivien, I had to admire his behaviour when I gave him the cheque that Lady Laker had written for him; more than he had ever dreamed of possessing, enough to take him to Canada and start life there. But he turned to me so proudly. At least, he said, he was man enough not to accept the bribe—if that was how Vivien felt, he was finished with the lot of them. It was his last words I remembered. He said he knew that what he had done was illegal, but what we were all doing was plain immoral—*letting her get away with it, and that he despised us. I told him that her ladyship insisted that he should not try to find out about the child—that if he did, Lady Laker would have him charged. But he told me not to worry, that he wouldn't try to see 'the poor little brute', and that he wanted to be quit of us all.*

He had walked away, packed his things and left Aldborough. The pride of the Cornishman was as great as the pride of the Lakers. They never saw him again. But shortly afterwards, he sent Vivien the evidence required for a 'divorce'. It was granted and nobody ever knew that the young Mrs. Treloar 'deserted' even before her child's birth, was the daughter of Sir Charles Laker, D.S.O. And Vivien was free.

But Marie, if not the rest of them, felt her conscience smite her yet again when, in the Second World War, she saw the chauffeur's name in the papers among the list of killed.

Captain Harry Treloar, R.A.S.C., won the Military Cross for conspicuous gallantry on the beaches of Normandy on D Day.

Now Marie's diary skipped over the months that followed and described briefly how she took Vivien to Lausanne to stay with an old blind aunt of Marie's. There, Vivien, sullen and fretful, seemed far more concerned with the discomfort of her pregnancy and banishment from home than the wrong she had done both to Harry Treloar—and her mother. All she wanted to do was to end it and return to England for her 'coming out'.

I was greatly saddened, wrote Marie, *by Vivien's exhibition of callous disregard, not only for her sin and shame, but the strain and grief her mother had to bear. The lies that had to be told. The letters that Vivien had to write, pretending to enjoy Switzerland—fully deceiving her father, her relations, her friends.*

Even the Swiss woman who so much loved Vivien had to admit that she was heartless.

Early in December, Lady Laker made an excuse to leave her husband with a sister-in-law and his attendant, and go out to Switzerland 'for her health'. But it was, of course, in order to be with her daughter when her 'time' came.

And there in my old aunt's house on the outskirts of Lausanne, in a little room looking upon the snow-clad mountains, Rowan was born. The child was registered at the British Consulate and once legally adopted as Mary Gray's child she became British by adoption, so there was never any question of her being Swiss.

Vivien never saw the baby; never wanted to see it. She was interested only in recovering her health and her figure.

The grandmother looked once and once only on that tiny unwanted mite. With the tears pouring down her patrician face, she said to Marie:

"God have mercy on the poor little thing, for she is my own flesh and blood. She has hair as fair as Vivien's. But her eyes are Treloar's. *I never want to see her again.* Oh, Marie, my dear loyal Marie, let us send her to an adoption home. There is no need for you to be further involved!"

But Marie Garnier had fallen in love with that tiny child whose great dark eyes were like Harry Treloar's. Perhaps—who knew—she had, in her stiff reserved way, herself, loved the young chauffeur a little. When the small perfect fingers of the infant clung convulsively to her hand, she knew she could not abandon the child.

It meant that I would spend the rest of my life looking after her. But to care for her ladyship's granddaughter, that for me would be like holding Vivien in my arms all over again. Only in later years have I begun to think of those words that poor Harry Treloar said to me in his hurt pride—about the immorality of the thing that we were doing. Sometimes my conscience smites me. I wonder if he was right? If we should have let her discard, so easily, the grave responsibility that was hers, as well as Harry's. Supposing that all that I and her ladyship did in our frantic wish to save Vivien, might in years to come have a reverse effect, and lose her her soul! *Who is to know?*

There followed a brief summary of Lady Laker's return to England with Vivien. A return to the old life, as though the terrible thing had never happened, plunging Vivien into a round of gaieties suitable to her age—her Presentation at Court, the parties, the dances; *this time* all under a strict maternal vigilance. There must never be another Treloar.

However, it seemed that Vivien, having paid a price for her one reckless passion, now became cool and unapproachable. Just before the outbreak of the Second World War, Sir Charles died. Shortly afterwards Lady Laker followed. Vivien's father never knew the facts. Marie Garnier faded out of the Lakers' lives and was not seen by any of them again.

But she did not stay in Switzerland. Both Lausanne and Montreux were small towns. Her family was well known. She could not 'disappear'. It was necessary for her to return to England in order to start a new life under a new name—among strangers.

She applied for a British citizenship, finally taking the name of Mrs. Mary Gray. Lady Laker had settled enough money on her to bring her in a small income, and bought her the tiny cottage in Buckinghamshire.

Perhaps if Elizabeth Laker had lived she might have been tempted to visit Vivien's child, but death claimed her and Vivien neither knew nor asked where the faithful Marie had gone, nor seemed interested whether or not her infant had lived. With her remarkable lack of heart, she flung off all memories of that early indiscretion. But just before her mother's fatal illness, Vivien repaid her as Lady Laker wished to be repaid. She made a brilliant marriage. At St. George's in Hanover Square—a radiant white bride—she was married to one of the richest men in England, a man fifteen years older than Vivien.

Edward Ripsdale, 'Rip' to his intimate friends, was a well-known figure in Society. One of the eligible bachelors whose name had been linked with that of several women and whom all the match-making mothers had tried to catch in vain. At thirty-five he had inherited a fortune from an American aunt and become almost an international figure. Grey-haired long before forty, tall, good-looking, exceedingly amusing, with a passion for fast cars; a yacht; a castle, which he had bought and restored in Wales; a pent-house in Grosvenor Square; a villa in Mentone. A young man who had never done a stroke of work in his life, nor had need to.

And into the lap of Vivien Laker, fell this much-prized plum. With her slenderness, her long amber hair and her violet-blue eyes that could look so dewy, so shy—Vivien captured the seemingly unattainable. Other matrons, envious of Elizabeth Laker, fell back sighing on the day of the big wedding. 'Rip' was no longer available. Vivien was the envy of one and all. Rip's men-friends smiled a trifle wryly. There was old Rip, devil of an amusing chap, absolutely on his knees, eating out of little Vivien's slender hands. A 'gonner'—that's what they said about him.

And the thing that Rip prized most in Vivien was what he thought to be her essential sweetness and purity.

Wrote Marie:

I used to devour the Society journals, see many photographs of Vivien, first with her fiancé, then her husband, on the honeymoon. Later, those taken when she came back to her first Season in London as Mrs. Edward Ripsdale. She always looked so beautiful, so starry-eyed, sometimes it did more than hurt me to look on her face. I even began to feel something like nausea. She had no conscience. *Never did she give one thought to the past. And it was doing a wrong to Ripsdale to marry him under such a cloak of deceit. How horrified he would have been to hear that his 'child-bride' had already gone through a form of marriage and borne an infant.*

Shut away in Beacon Cottage, the quiet widow 'Mrs. Gray', brought up 'her' fair-haired, dark-eyed baby, and who on earth could ever dream that she had any connection with the beautiful Mrs. Ripsdale whose name appeared so frequently in the papers?

Among the best-dressed women in Great Britain; among the social lights of society; and when the war came, there was Mrs. Edward Ripsdale in Red Cross uniform, looking even lovelier and so touching with that brave dutiful expression in her big long-lashed eyes.

She had been incredibly lucky. And her luck seemed to hold. Rip joined the Army and came out of it with decorations and not a scratch. After Vivien had been photographed with the Red Cross, she flew out to America and spent the rest of the war in sunshine and peace with some of Rip's American relations.

She had none of her dead mother's or father's nobility of character; that was obvious. Yet Marie—faithful to the end—tried to think of her with tolerance—was unable to tear the old allegiance and affection completely out of her heart.

Little mention was made of Vivien in the years that followed. The diary was all about Rowan and life in Beacon Cottage.

I christened the baby Rowan, wrote Marie, because I've always loved the rowan tree; the mountain-ash, some call it, so graceful and colourful with its bright-red clustered fruit. At first life seemed lonely for me and I missed the family life with the Lakers but my own parents were dead and my dear English employers, too; my life now centred wholly around little Rowan. I felt that she was absolutely mine, and it has been a wonderful thing to me to receive in return her tender affection and companionship. I have been thankful that none of the wildness in Vivien's blood—nor the hard streak—seem to lie in Rowan. She has always been a gentle child, incapable of hurting anybody. Perhaps at times too withdrawn and reserved for one so young, and I blame myself because I have allowed her to lead such a hermit's life. But she seems to want nothing else. She has a lot of her maternal grandfather in her. He was a studious man who loved books and music in a way that his own daughter never did. And Rowan is generous and proud—maybe with the pride of the Cornishman that runs in her veins. I admire my darling's character. I am grateful to her for her devotion to me. Yet sometimes I am afraid for her. If I were to leave her—what would she do—where would she go? I would not want her to shrink like a man from the outside world. I should, I feel, have stirred myself to take her abroad; or send her to travel and broaden her outlook. But lack of money after the war, has made it difficult, and perhaps I have always been afraid that she might yet have something of her mother in her. I want to protect her from that! . . .

28

Here the diary ended abruptly, with only one more entry that appeared to have been made a year ago. And it concerned Rowan's mother.

June, 1957.

My poor Vivien seems destined for a stormy life. Ripsdale has been killed in an air crash—flying his own plane, apparently, near Le Touquet. So Vivien is a widow. And she has no children to comfort her. Somehow I do not think she will ever have another child. She never liked them. Yet she is still only thirty-seven—so young. Of course she will marry again. I must watch the papers. . . .

There were no further entries. Maybe Vivien's former nursery-governess and loyal friend read no further news about her. And assuredly, the Swiss woman who had posed for so long as Rowan's mother, must have thought she had many years left yet of life and that the diary into which she poured her heart and recollections would remain safely under lock and key.

The story—so far as she could recount it—had ended.

Now Rowan sat between her cheerful kindly friends at Blackthorn Farm, looking at them with her dark dazed eyes.

"It can't be true," she kept saying, "it can't be true. Mummy must have imagined it all."

The Jenkins exchanged glances. Bill lit a pipe; Ann, another cigarette. With a slightly shaky hand, she poured out two more glasses of sherry and tried to make Rowan drink one.

"You need a stimulant, duckie, drink this—for heaven's sake!"

Rowan shook her head.

She got up, her diary under one arm, and walked to one of the side windows from which she could see the red roof of Beacon Cottage through the trees in the violet dusk. Like one in a dream, she stared.

"That has been my home all my life—and *she*—was my mother—my dear, good kind mother. I am *not* the daughter of that terrible cruel woman whom she calls *Vivien*. I won't be. *I refuse to be.*"

Ann exchanged another look with her husband, put down her cigarette and glass, walked to the girl and put a firm arm around the young trembling figure.

"Poor kid—this has been the second awful shock for you, today. It's too much. What with the funeral *and this*—it's *too* much."

Rowan swung around to Ann, breathing hard.

29

"Tell me I'm just Rowan Gray and not the daughter of that cruel heartless girl who didn't want me."

"Oh—just burn the diary and forget it," said Ann rather stupidly.

Bill Jenkins rose and put in his say with an awkward attempt at comfort.

"Anyway I shouldn't worry too much, Rowan, for that chap, your father, he sounds rather a nice guy to me. Proud and so on, not a money-grabber. Got decorated in the war."

Rowan put a hand to her throat. She felt suffocated. She felt as though every word she had read in that diary to herself and aloud to the Jenkins just now, beat into her brain in a precise and deadly fashion, and that the echo of those drum-beats would go on and on for the rest of her life, without respite or remorse.

It was all so incredible. She could not reorientate herself. Twenty-four hours ago she had been just Rowan Gray, the daughter of a widow, with some slight mystery attached to her father that had never been revealed, but hadn't really seemed important. She and Mummy had been complete—a unit in themselves—armed by their mutual love and trust against outsiders.

But this dear creature whom she had called *mother*, was no relation to her at all. She, Rowan, had only been granted the name of Gray, by deed-poll. She had been born Rowan Treloar, and she was the child of Vivien Laker. The granddaughter of the late Sir Charles and Lady Laker. Good people—noble-minded—according to the diary. Poor grandfather, crippled in the First World War, had never known of her existence. But Elizabeth Laker had known and rejected her—and encouraged her own mother to reject her.

Rowan's dazed mind, flooded and tormented by these revelations of her beginning, fastened on to that one point. In her young fervent way, she had always been an idealist, without much tolerance, perhaps, or understanding of the more dark and tortuous paths that the erring human being can tread.

Nevertheless she was not a prig. Her existence with Mummy had been narrow, but she was not ignorant. She was well-educated and they had read much together; and laughed together, too—far from being without humour. But such things as hot passions running in the veins of reckless youth, love between the sexes without respect—those things had never so far touched Rowan's life.

Now she felt as though the white page of that life had been suddenly scorched, and was crumpling at the corners. She felt nothing but scorn for her real mother. As for the 'hero' father—there seemed only a little more, perhaps, to love and admire in him, the lowly-born Cornish chauffeur. More, certainly than in those others to whom wealth and position had meant so much; more than the love of humanity. Pathetically, she clung to the memory that *he* had died a hero's death. At least *that* blood ran in her veins. But as for her mother . . .

"I would never have left my baby. If I had had one, I could never have left it!" Rowan sobbed the protest aloud.

"No, darling, I am sure you couldn't and neither would I," said Ann.

"Of course, there were extenuating circumstances. One mustn't judge," came from Bill, looking upset and embarrassed.

"But I can't think of that *other one* as my mother, I can only think of Mummy, lying out there in her grave," came from Rowan in an anguished voice.

"Forget it all—at least, no more soul-searchings tonight," counselled Ann. And she motioned to Bill to leave them alone, and held the distracted weeping Rowan in her strong arms, trying to help her.

But she looked down rather gloomily at the diary which had dropped from Rowan's hands to the floor. For she knew that Rowan could not forget—or wipe one single word of it from her memory.

4

ONE morning in the following January, a young slender girl, with a dark blue beret on the side of her fair head, and wearing a Jaeger coat with a navy blue scarf tucked into the collar, followed a plump cheerful Swiss porter down Platform No. 2 on Geneva station. He carried her two suitcases, and kept peering into all the second-class compartments. They appeared to be full. The train which was marked *Lausanne—Montreux—Sierre*, was packed with winter-sports enthusiasts. Dozens of young people, men and women, carrying their skis—some of them already attired in heavy ski boots and sweaters—thronged the train. There was the usual sprinkling of business men from Geneva and of elderly couples of all nationalities seeking to get away from fog and rain and find the sunshine in the higher altitudes.

The porter with the two suitcases at last put them down and looked doubtfully at one of the labels.

Miss R. Gray, c/o Garnier, Hotel de Montagne, Sierre

"Sierre, *hein*? Train full—maybe you stand—you so late, *mademoiselle*," he said in tolerable English.

Rowan looked anxious. She knew that on account of fog at home, the plane had been late leaving London Airport. She had been warned that she might not be able to catch this express which was due to leave Geneva at half past one. She had no particular wish to stay alone in Geneva for another hour and wait for the next train. She was very anxious to get on.

Now the kindly porter, seeing that the young English lady looked so troubled, motioned her up the high steps of a first-class carriage.

"Better get in, train going. *Vite, mademoiselle!*" he said.

Rowan climbed up on to the train, her breath rising like vapour in the air, for it was bitterly cold and raw, almost as foggy in Geneva as it had been in dear old London, she thought. She longed for the sun.

Now the porter, in true Swiss fashion lifted her cases and thrust them through the open windows into the hands of a tall young man already there leaning out, smoking. He took the cases in. The next moment Rowan found herself also in the compartment, and the train was moving smoothly out of the station.

She looked with dismay at the young man. He lifted her cases on to the rack. He seemed to be alone in the carriage. The papers, bags, clothes and skis strewn on the seats were all presumably his.

"I haven't a right . . . I've only a second-class ticket . . ." she began to stammer, then repeated the words in her excellent French. Whereupon the man gave a faint smile and said in an unmistakably English voice:

"It's all right. I understand."

She blushed hotly, her cheeks bright red with confusion.

"Oh, I should stay here," he said, throwing himself into a corner, "the train's absolutely packed—mostly with Swiss and French—not many English, as far as I can see. They're the only ones who spend the money travelling first class these days."

"But, I can't afford——"

For the third time he interrupted, giving her a slight ironic smile.

"Oh, we can tell the inspector when he comes round—that you can't find a seat. Anyhow, you can't stand all the way and it isn't all that much extra, you know."

A little helplessly, Rowan dropped into the window-seat opposite this rather masterful young man who seemed to want to organize her journey. She was not really sorry to be organized. She felt very strange. She was not used to travelling and now that she had actually left England, she was a trifle apprehensive.

She wondered if she ought to have taken this step. But then she had been wondering that ever since Bill Jenkins fixed things up for her, bought her tickets, and saw her off from Victoria this morning.

'I must learn to be independent—to make my own decisions and stop being so shy of everybody. I must not worry about everything,' she reflected.

She was sure she used not to be like that. She was once quite cool and self-possessed, even if never very sociable. Perhaps it was the shock of all that had happened after Mummy died that had changed her.

She stole a brief and rather unhappy look at her travelling companion. Silly of her to have imagined him a foreigner—he wore black ski-trousers and a black thick sweater with a yellow scarf. Of course the sports outfit was deceptive but so many people, even English, seemed to travel like that—not only for warmth, but in order to reduce the weight of luggage, when coming by air.

This man was rather striking in his black sports outfit, she thought. He was of medium height and slimly built. He was not exactly handsome. His face was too bony and his mouth too big. But he had thick warm hair the colour of horse-chestnuts, and just now when he had looked at her she had noticed that he had remarkable eyes—of a clear cool grey. Brilliant eyes, thickly lashed, and the only soft feature in an otherwise hard face. Now that he was holding a newspaper up in front of him, she also noticed his hands. They, too, were brown from the sun and looked very strong. On the small finger of the left hand there was an onyx signet ring.

Rowan picked up her bag. She began to rummage in it, vaguely anxious in case she had lost or forgotten something. No—everything was there. Passport, tickets, her red leather wallet with the Swiss money and travellers' cheques, all of which dear kind Bill had got for her; and her powder-compact with the initial 'R' on it which Ann had given her as a parting present. She opened the

33

wallet and extracted a snapshot from it. The one of the entire Jenkins family. Jeremy and Scrap with the Boxer, sitting on the lawn with Ann and Bill at Blackthorn Farm. Rowan had taken it in the summer. How sweet they all were! How wonderful they had been to her.

Then she took out another snapshot—an older one. And as she looked at the short thin grey-haired woman with the cat in her arms, standing in the doorway of Beacon Cottage, Rowan's eyes filled with tears. Dear Mummy! *Dearest* of mothers—for as such she would always think of her. (Never, *never* of that other one!)

But she mustn't shed any more tears or grieve too much over Mummy, thought Rowan, nor work herself up continually over the facts about which she had learned from that fatal diary. She *must* try to remember what Ann had said as she kissed her goodbye.

"Try to be happy, dear Rowan, and for goodness sake don't hark *back* all the time. At your age, it's ridiculous. It's the *old* who like churning over memories. For them it's permissible, but not for a young girl. You're pretty even though you won't admit it. You've got charm when you choose to exert it. You're cultured. And you've got bags of guts. So make a go of things, and no matter how hurt or upset you have been—forget it. It's the only way you'll find peace of mind again."

Rowan knew that Ann was right, and oh! how badly she needed that peace of mind. It seemed to have been temporarily destroyed. Since that day, six months ago, when she had first learned the true facts of her birth, Rowan had felt that she would never be happy or tranquil again. It was because she had loved Mummy so much that she had resented the revelation which had, in a way, separated them even more completely than death, itself.

But because Mummy had sacrificed her entire life in order to give her the love and care her own mother had denied her—Rowan had felt an urge to visit Switzerland and Mummy's relatives.

She could not have stayed on at Beacon Cottage. Bill found out that the pension paid from Lady Laker's estate to 'Mrs. Gray' had ended with her death. Presumably Rowan's grandmother had not bargained for the fact that Marie would die before sixty, and that the child would be left without home or means of support.

Rowan looked back to the day that Bill had first taken her to the Bank in High Wycombe and clarified the position. Then she had still been in a state of shock; too dazed and unhappy to care much what happened. But as time went on, staying under the kindly

34

Jenkins' roof, she had been nursed back to normal by Ann, comforted by the children who loved and laughed with her and given sound and sane advice by Bill. She felt she owed the Jenkins a debt of gratitude she could never repay. She disagreed with them only on one point, and over that one she had shown a dogged obstinacy that had quite surprised her friends. They had admitted that they had not thought that the shy retiring young Rowan would stick her toes in quite so firmly. It was about her own mother. Bill had suggested that armed with the diary and a bundle of letters which had been written many years ago to Marie by her parents when she first went to live with the Lakers—she should seek out her mother and produce the evidence.

"Your father is dead; no use to look for his people, and I don't think you'd want to, anyhow. But I don't see why that egotistical mamma of yours should not be given a rap," Bill had said. "Mrs. Edward Ripsdale ought to be fairly easy to trace. She's a wealthy, well-known woman. She ought to be made to provide for you, at least till you're of age."

"I agree," Ann had said. "And I for one would enjoy seeing Mrs. Ripsdale's face when confronted by Rowan. I don't see why such a woman should get off scot-free. Her runaway marriage wasn't the crime. It was abandoning the little baby, even though to the care of a kind woman like the late Mrs. Gray. It was the callous way in which the whole Lakers' family seemed to behave to Rowan, just in order to give that girl a chance to make a splendid match. I think it was *sickening*."

"So do I," said Bill.

But Rowan would have none of it.

"I don't want to see my mother, nor will I admit that I've ever had a mother other than darling Mummy," she said. "I'd rather starve than ask for a penny from *her*!"

And she was not to be moved. Bill Jenkins, however, prevented her from burning the diary and all evidence of her true identity.

"I wouldn't do that," he said. "Being the cautious lawyer, I strongly advise you to hang on to those papers."

And when Rowan argued that Mummy's last wish had been that the diary should be burned, he argued that it was too late. Rowan had read it. She knew the facts. It was advisable for her to keep the proof securely under lock and key—even if at this precise moment she felt she would never make use of it.

In the long run, Rowan gave the diary and letters to him to put in a strong-box.

Beacon Cottage went up for sale and fetched a little over £3,000. After settling income-tax, outstanding bills and paying for the storage of a few treasured possessions which reminded her of her old happy life with Mummy and which she refused to sell—Rowan found herself with nothing much left. A little over £2,500, perhaps, in the world.

It was then that she thought about Mummy's native land and the brother whom she had mentioned in the diary. Why not go to Sierre and find 'Uncle Jean'?

The Jenkins offered her a permanent home with them—she could help look after the children and assist Ann in the house in return—they said. Rowan thanked them gratefully but declined.

"I don't want to be dependent on anybody and much as I love you all at Blackthorn Farm I think I *must* get away from Jordans. I'd *like* to meet Mummy's people if they are still alive."

Bill had reminded her that Jean Garnier would certainly not know of her existence, nor of his sister's change of name. Whereupon Rowan decided that if he could be found, she would write to him; tell him that she was Marie Garnier's adopted daughter, and ask if she could go out to stay with him in Sierre for a while.

It did not take Bill long to discover that Mrs. Gray's brother *was*, indeed, very much alive (he had been younger than Marie) and that he and his wife and son were still running their hotel—the Hôtel de Montagne in Sierre.

In her perfect French, Rowan wrote to Mummy's brother:

I have such a great wish to meet one of Maman's *relations. If I could get some kind of work in one of the hotels—it would also be a wonderful thing for me. As you see, my French is good and I am qualified in shorthand and typewriting. . . .*

Within forty-eight hours came the reply from Jean Garnier. Quite a charming and enthusiastic letter.

For years I have wondered what happened to our beloved Marie. I was much grieved by the thought that she had vanished out of my life, for she was my only sister. There is nothing I would like more than to see you, my dear Mademoiselle Rowan whom I might regard in the nature of a niece, and my wife, Elise, agrees with me. We will give you a warm welcome. For the moment pray come as our guest—our relative—later we can see about your work.

He was obviously a man of heart and generous impulse. He assured Rowan that she would have no expenses whatsoever once

36

she got to Sierre and enclosed a photograph of himself and his wife for her to see. One look at Monsieur Garnier's face reduced Rowan to tender tears. He was so like Mummy—the rather thin aquiline features, and the shrewd kindly eyes, the gentle mouth. Mummy all over again.

She felt that she could be fond of this man. He would seem like a real uncle to her. He was Mummy's flesh and blood. Doggedly she clung to the old loyalties. Never, she told herself with passion and resentment, would she ever think of herself as *that other woman's child*.

She had looked forward to this, her first visit to the Continent, yet it had been such a break. Almost she had thought at the time, it was like dying—as Mummy had done. A long good-bye to the old familiar ties and faces. She had even felt a pang when she gave Candy, Mummy's tortoiseshell cat, to old Mrs. Pelly from the housing estate, who used to come and help with spring cleaning; and who loved cats.

She had felt quite guilty, too, because of all this expense. She had been forced to buy new clothes. Ann Jenkins had helped her. Ann could not, herself, ever be called 'chic'. When she had gone up to London to shop with Rowan they had bought nothing spectacular, nothing black—Mummy disliked mourning. Just this blue suit—a couple of sensible dresses, some woollies and an evening skirt and chiffon blouse which Ann had thought Rowan ought to have in case the Swiss relations changed for 'an occasion'. The real extravagance was the ski-ing trousers and heavy ski-boots, and the white waterproof coat and hood combined. It was Bill who had plugged for them.

"You can't go to Switzerland in the winter and not take part in the Sports," he had told Rowan. "Whether you work for your living or not, everyone skis in Switzerland at week-ends. You don't have to buy the skis. You can hire them out there. But you *must* have a suitable outfit."

So Rowan had bought the things and the children had been amused when she dressed up for them, and been wildly envious when she showed them coloured photographs of people at ski-resorts in the brochures collected from tourist agencies.

It was all rather exciting . . . and yet . . . so strange. Something she had never dreamed of or ever discussed with Mummy. She felt terribly alone in the train this afternoon *en route* for Sierre.

The train quickened speed. They were now well on their way

through the neat clean-looking countryside, already white with snow. The distant mountains were half hidden behind a lowering mass of heavy cloud.

Rowan tried to stop thinking. She stared out at the passing scene—still finding it hard to believe that she was so far from Jordans and actually on Swiss soil.

'The land where you were born, Mummy,' she thought. 'Perhaps it will bring you back close to me again——'

Mrs. Gray was assuming more than the memory of a fond, good mother to Rowan. She was rapidly becoming a saint—a martyr who had given up everything that a normal young woman might have desired, in order to give *her*, Rowan, mother and home.

The door of the carriage was rolled aside. A nice-looking uniformed inspector made his appearance and asked for tickets. At this juncture the young man in black ski clothes began to explain about the packed second-class compartments and '*Mademoiselle's* plight'; why she was here with a second-class ticket.

Rowan suddenly felt annoyed. She could manage her own affairs without help from strange men. She gave the interfering stranger a cold look and addressed the inspector in her flawless French. The young man grinned and returned to his newspaper.

'Snubbed,' he muttered. 'Put in my place. Well, well, how deceptive appearances can be. One would have thought she was just an inexperienced schoolgirl, scared to death.'

Which was precisely what Rowan felt like, but she wasn't going to show it. She paid the extra francs on her ticket. The inspector withdrew. The young man cocked an eyebrow and smiled at Rowan again.

"I must apologize. I didn't mean to interfere."

The colour flooded Rowan's face. She said primly:

"Oh, please—that's quite all right—it was nice of you."

'Glacial,' the young man decided. 'And much too young for me anyhow. Not at all my type.'

Then he found the page he had been looking for in his newspaper and fastened on it. A review of last night's *première* of *Summer Song*, a new operetta produced at a West-End theatre. He had already seen that one and all the other reviews. But it made pleasant reading.

This particular paper said:

Summer Song is one of the most refreshing and delightful operettas we have had on the English stage for years. It deserved all the ap-

plause that it got. The lyrics, by Simon Cottar, are witty and the music by Ashley Moore is of an unusually high order. In Mr. Moore, who is twenty-seven and whose small amateur revues were such a success when he was still up at Oxford—we have a real musician.

The review went on to describe the story and ended with this paragraph:

I went away humming the haunting melody of the theme song: 'The Summer Song', itself, so beautifully rendered by Greta Norman.

The young man in black ski-clothes stretched out his legs and smiled with a little natural satisfaction.

'Ashley, my boy, you've hit the jackpot at last,' he thought.

Everybody he knew seemed to think so, anyhow.

He hadn't had much sleep last night. First the production itself—himself in the author's box—a bundle of nerves he had to admit—with Simon Cottar who had been at university with him, the nervousness gradually changing to relief and gratification because the audience received the show so well.

Ashley had spent the whole of last year working on *Summer Song*. At the supper-party on the stage with the entire cast fêting and flattering him, Ashley had realized this meant no more struggles to make enough money to pay the rent for his two-roomed flat in Chelsea. He could sit back and smile. He was a success. His backers were well satisfied.

Ashley felt almost sorry that he had no family with whom to share the glory. He had lost his parents in an air crash when still a boy at Public School. The uncle who had brought him up was also dead. Ashley had many friends but no close ties now except for one uncle—Laurence Moore, ten years younger than Eric, Ashley's father, who had been a studious, music-loving man.

Eric Moore had started life as a teacher of pianoforte in a big London College of Music. In later years he had embarked on a business career, running a small shop for pianos and musical instruments. Lack of money had necessitated that he did so and he had shocked his rather snobbish and aristocratic family by the enterprise, which incidentally, before he died, had failed. After his untimely death, his equally musical son, Ashley, had been taken care of by his mother's brother, Geoffrey Holworth, headmaster of a small boys' preparatory school in Seaford. Mr. Holworth, recently a widower, had no children. He had done his level best to keep Ashley at Sherborne, and even managed to send him up to Oxford. But it had soon been apparent that Ashley cared only for music and would never make a business man. He consistently disappointed his uncle by merely scraping through maths in every exam he tackled. It was a pity that Uncle Geoffrey had not lived to see his nephew's name in the papers after the launching of *Summer Song*. But he, too, had died, before his sixtieth birthday, while Ashley was still a struggling composer.

There remained now, only Laurence Moore. Laurence was the 'different' one of the Moores. Unmusical but artistic and deeply interested in painting, Laurence had also a strange flair for things financial. The two rarely go together but in his case he started life in a stockbroker's office, and was determined to make money. Later he was able to indulge his passion for collecting art treasures. Ashley always said that fortune fell into Uncle Laury's lap. He had made a lot of money during the boom years. Recently he took a long holiday in America. While out there with friends, he had met a rich widow who, to Ashley's surprise seemed to have wooed Uncle Laury from his state of confirmed bachelorhood, for he had suddenly got married.

He had written a brief line to his nephew to say that his future wife was *petite and beautiful as a Tanagra figurine* and that he would soon be bringing her back to England and retiring from the Stock Exchange in order to continue with his search for beautiful *objets d'art*.

He had ended the letter by advising Ashley not to go on wasting his time as a composer.

Get into the world of finance and make some money first, he wrote.

But money could not come first and foremost with Ashley. It was artistic achievement that satisfied his spirit and he would have been just as exhilarated this morning if he had known that he would make nothing out of the show, but had those reviews.

However, he reflected, he was only human and it was pleasant to become rich overnight. His producer and manager had told him that he and his lyric writer, Simon Cottar, should be able to count on a fat income for some time to come. It was prophesied that *Summer Song* would run for years.

Ashley could have stayed on in London to enjoy being under the fierce light of publicity but he had not allowed success to interfere with his plans for coming out to Switzerland.

He had a two-fold reason for taking the holiday now. First of all, some very good Swiss friends of his (the son had been up at Oxford with Ashley) were going to South Africa for a couple of months, and had offered him the use of their chalet in Crans-sur-Sierre. He could live rent free there with a cook-housekeeper to look after him.

The Swiss friend, André, was musical. There was a piano in the chalet. That was one of the things that tempted Ashley. For a couple of months he could combine business with pleasure, work on a new show in absolute peace—in Crans (which he could not do in London)—and he could ski. That was a sport he particularly enjoyed and had not been able to afford since his undergraduate days. The uncle who had given him a home had managed to educate him well, but most of his income was derived from his job and a pension which had ended with his decease. There had been little left for Ashley. For the last five years Ashley had struggled to make ends meet by writing popular songs and incidental music for television and radio shows; none of which he enjoyed doing. However, now *Summer Song* would place him right at the top. He could compose the music he most enjoyed, and Simon had already given him a new idea.

This time, the opera would be half fact, half fantasy—set in a sports-hotel in the mountains (with an avalanche, perhaps, thrown in for dramatic measure). They had decided to call it *The Snowbird*.

Between them Ashley and Simon had agreed that the story should mostly concern the love romance of a girl (the title rôle, of course) who had lived all her life in the mountains and could skim down the snowy slopes like a white bird. (Always in white.) She would be a strange, aloof, unawakened sort of girl. They had had the story in mind some time, and Ashley was brimful of inspiration for the music. A chalet in the Alps would be just the right place in which to write such a show.

Last night when Greta Norman, flushed and excited from her triumph, had kissed him good night, she had looked at him with sparkling eyes and said:

"Go away and compose some wonderful music, darling, I shall be your 'Snowbird', shan't I?"

"Of course," he had said, full of champagne and enthusiasm.

But, dreamily thinking things over on the plane this morning bound for Geneva, he was not quite sure that Greta would be at all suitable for the part. She was perfect in *Summer Song*; as a warm-blooded passionate young woman, all Mediterranean glamour and provocation, but the Snowbird would be a very different character. If not Greta, who on earth *could* they get to sing the part? These female singers were all so big-bosomed, so

41

earthly—Ashley reflected—the very reverse of the spiritual maiden of his imagination.

With arms crossed on his chest, Ashley thrust his long legs out still farther. His right foot came in contact with an object that immediately withdrew. He heard a sharp cry.

"Oh, my gracious," he exclaimed, and sat up, full of chagrin, for he realized that he had kicked his vis-à-vis on the ankle.

The girl gave a rueful smile and rubbed the injured ankle against the calf of her other leg.

"It's quite all right really," she said. "It didn't really hurt."

That timid rather touching little smile and the murmured words of forgiveness suddenly electrified Ashley. He stared at Rowan. The prim schoolgirl had turned into someone else before his very eyes; so slim, so youthful, with the fairest of fair hair tightly drawn back from a pure and rather intelligent forehead, and those huge eyes, velvety brown, looking at him with a quaint, half-friendly, half-frightened expression and the red blood staining cheeks and long, slender throat.

'Good lord!' he said to himself. 'Good lord! She's my "Snowbird". That's who she is!'

5

I T was a three hours' journey to Sierre.

By the time they reached Montreux it seemed to Rowan that the weather had changed completely. Far away over the distant mountains dark snow-clouds were still hanging with heavy gloom, but on either side of the railway line now a white world glittered in the sun, and the sky was the purest blue she had ever seen.

She stared out of the window, enchanted by the clean neat villages with their orderly little houses—all the roof-tops a foot deep in crisp snow. It was something she had never seen before except in pictures. She was so interested that she had little time for the young man who had been talking to her ever since they left Geneva. They had even shared some lunch together. He had bought a couple of those long crisp rolls with ham in them, and insisted on her taking one. Later on an official pushed a trolley down the corridor and served them with delicious coffee in papier mâché mugs, with transparent straws through which they drank the hot creamy liquid.

Rowan was quite entertained by Ashley Moore—somewhat impressed now that she knew he was a composer who had just leaped into fame. She was able to discuss music with him in a manner to command *his* respect. To him it was obvious that she was not lacking in knowledge of the subject. But *he* could not accuse her of trying to attract *him* (and Ashley, with his charm and vigour and artistic qualities, was well used to being pursued by women). This shy young girl appeared much more intrigued by the country which she was visiting for the first time than by her travelling companion. She asked him questions about Switzerland, and he told her all that he knew. Now, at Montreux Station, folding his arms, he smoked a cigarette and watched her as she hung her head out of the window. She was drawing in deep breaths of the ice-cold air. It was delicious after the steam-heat in the carriage.

"It's like champagne," she said, using the time-worn phrase.

"Better," he said with a slight smile, remembering the stage party last night and how his head had felt this morning.

"Not that I ever drink it," Rowan added over her shoulder with that quaint touch of primness which he found something of a bore.

'She is really too chilly. I won't let *my* Snowbird act this way in my opera,' he mused. 'She's got to be flesh and blood. *This* one is just an immature icicle.'

He had never met anybody so lacking in sophistication for her age. It had amused him to ask Rowan questions about herself and learn some of her background. He was always interested in people; that was part of his art and trade. He gathered little except that her mother had died and Rowan was alone, and joining her Swiss relations.

He could not have dreamed what passionate flood of feeling turned Rowan's pale face to burning rose as she looked up and down Montreux Station. *'Mummy's birthplace,'* she kept repeating to herself. Mummy had rarely spoken about it, but it was where she had been born. If only she could come back! And if only she had shared her dramatic secret with *her*, Rowan reflected; feeling the whole thing as only extreme youth can feel; with exaggerated emotion. If only Rowan could talk to her now, about her early life, and Rowan's own grandparents, and *Vivien*. Sometimes she tried not to think at all about her real mother. What did it matter that Vivien had been beautiful; so fascinating that she had managed to extract a lifetime's heroic devotion from her nursery-governess? What did it matter that she had fallen in love with

43

someone beneath her in station and married him without consent? Those things Rowan could have understood and forgiven. But *never* for ejecting her tiny helpless baby from her life, and from her thoughts. That was utterly heartless.

The train moved slowly on. Ashley rose and wound up the window for the girl who sat back in her corner again with a deep sigh.

"Have a cigarette?" said Ashley, offering his case.

"No thank you, I don't smoke."

"What *do* you do?" he asked.

"What do you mean?"

"Just that. You would not share my bottle of wine. You don't smoke and you don't talk much, do you? I was just wondering what does go on behind that clear unclouded brow."

"You're making fun of me," said Rowan in a mortified voice.

He laughed and lit another cigarette for himself.

"Not really. But you *have* a clear unclouded brow all the same."

"If you want to know the truth—it's full of cloud," she volunteered.

It was, he thought, her first effort at being even in the smallest degree confidential.

"Oh, you mustn't worry about anything—at your age there's no need," he said loftily. "You're just beginning, you know."

"Maybe," she said and her lids drooped. He could not help remarking on the extraordinary length and thickness of her silky lashes. If she wasn't so *frozen* she might be quite beautiful at moments.

He went on talking to her. She answered some of his questions as best she could but she was not used to the company of such a man of the world as Ashley Moore. As the journey wore on, she had to confess that he was *rather* an attractive man and obviously clever. She knew now that he was going up to Crans, which was another 2,000 feet above Sierre. He had ski'd, up there, before. One could go by road, he said, but the majority of people ascended the heights by funicular, that amazing little railway propelled by electric power—up, up to the shining heights.

She knew, too, that this winter he had been loaned a chalet with a piano in it and there he was going to start composing the music for his new operetta.

"You must come up some time and give me your opinion," he said.

44

"I'd like to," she said. "Thank you very much for asking me."

'I bet she doesn't come,' he thought. 'She'd be too scared. She probably thinks all men are wolves.' "Do you sing?" he added aloud.

"No," she shook her head.

"Have you any hobbies?"

'Oh, dear,' she reflected. 'How he does probe! It's frightfully embarrassing.'

She stammered that she only left school eighteen months ago since when she had been training in a secretarial college, and that apart from gardening, which she used to do with her mother, she liked music more than anything else, and reading—especially history.

This seemed to amaze Ashley.

"No sports?"

She had played tennis at her local club, she said, but hadn't had much time for it. She hoped to learn to ski now, of course, that she was in Switzerland.

"Well, you're bound to go up to Crans, so you can fall down outside my chalet and I'll pick you up and we'll play duets," he said with his slightly mocking smile.

By the time the train ran into Sierre, Ashley fancied that Rowan was beginning to thaw—to unwind a bit; and when she laughed and talked, she was really rather a sweet little thing. He was vaguely sorry to say good-bye to her. It struck him that she wasn't very happy about something, and she seemed so young and unfledged to be alone in the world.

"Now do drop in on me when you are up at Crans," he reminded her as he took her suitcases down from the rack for her and handed them out to a porter. "The chalet is called l'Étoile; it belongs to some Swiss people called Buet. I dare say your relations will know them."

Rowan thanked him. Standing on the platform she felt very small beside him. He seemed to tower above her. The warmth in those grey and intelligent eyes of his, seemed to her genuine. He had really been awfully nice, she thought. Mummy's theories about men were, perhaps, not altogether correct. Mummy used occasionally to talk with Rowan of sex and marriage and, when she left school, propounded some rather old-fashioned views, such as—*never talk to strange men*, etc. The average man, in Mrs. Gray's opinion, had seemed to be a danger to young girls. It would be 'nice' to meet a 'nice' boy and make a 'nice' marriage, she had said. But it all had to be 'nice' (which philosophy has been largely responsible for many a young girl believing that a man's innocent attentions were to be regarded, always, with suspicion). However, the intensive reading done by Rowan so far in her short life, had opened her eyes to other, less prudish ideas. And there were depths in her own nature, which, although unplumbed, *she knew to be there*; and which she felt were entirely natural. She had always believed there was something splendid about the attraction between men and women—that romantic as well as passionate love existed. In her reckoning, she was sure the two things must run parallel. For instance, she had seen for herself how deeply Bill and Ann Jenkins were in love even after eleven years of married life; that was an ideal of love to be followed, like a star.

She had, even during the last few weeks, while thinking things over, begun to feel that some of poor Mummy's beliefs had sprung from the fact that she was an old maid, a woman who had never actually been married—or known passionate love. (*Oh, poor, frustrated Mummy!*)

Anyhow, even Mummy could not have found the young composer of the train journey anything but charming and correct in his conduct. And if he had poked fun at Rowan perhaps it was what she needed, she thought. It stimulated her. She had felt a sudden desire to show Mr. Ashley Moore that she was not quite the silly schoolgirl that he imagined.

Then Ashley Moore was forgotten. A short man wearing a thick overcoat, woollen muffler and Cossack-shaped woollen cap came towards her. She knew at once that it was Mummy's brother; Rowan had remarked the likeness when she received the snapshot. She had sent him her own photograph, so he, apparently, recognized her.

"You are my adopted niece—Rowan," he said, holding out both hands. Like so many Swiss he spoke impeccable English.

She took the hands and squeezed them, tears filming her eyes.

"Uncle Jean!" she exclaimed.

Now he kissed her on both cheeks.

"Welcome to Switzerland, *chère petite.*"

She was too moved to answer. Vaguely she saw Ashley Moore disappearing in front of her among a crowd of skiers. Uncle Jean gave orders to a porter. He had a car waiting outside the station. His wife, whom Rowan must call Tante Elise, he said, was busy at the hotel. This was their very busy season. Sierre was such a healthy place; especially dry; many people stayed there rather than go up higher where the altitude affected those with a 'heart' condition.

"It is very good of you indeed to let me come, Uncle Jean," said Rowan.

He settled her in the car and they drove slowly down the main street. The Hôtel de Montagne was a little higher up out of the town, on the road to Crans.

"Your mother—for that is how I presume you always think of her—knew Sierre very well," he told her. "We had grandparents here whom we visited until they died. Marie and I used to come here for winter sports, too, and go up higher in the funicular at week-ends."

Rowan nodded.

"She must have told you of all these things," added M. Garnier.

Rowan stole a look at his fine-cut profile. He was tanned and a little wrinkled from much sun. She felt immensely comforted to be with him and knew that she had been right to make this move and come here. It *did* bring Mummy closer again.

She began to try and explain that she knew little about her 'mother's' early life; that she had become completely anglicized over a period of years.

M. Garnier shook his head a trifle sadly.

"I shall never understand why our Marie broke so completely away from me. You say she did not marry, but merely called herself *Mrs. Gray*? That was when she adopted you; but *why*? And why did she never come back to Switzerland?"

Rowan was silent a moment. She felt very uncomfortable. She had given this matter a lot of thought and decided that she could not tell Mummy's brother the truth. It was not her story to tell. So she merely informed him that when Mummy adopted her, she had decided to sever all connections with her old life and settle down as an English widow with a child.

M. Garnier shrugged. He could not understand it. The last time he had seen Marie—at the funeral of their parents—she had seemed her old affectionate self; but when for a year she had not answered his letters, he had written to her no more. He had, in fact, been so worried that he sent one letter to Lady Laker, for he knew that it was with the Laker family that Marie had made her life. He had asked if Marie was ill, or perhaps dead, and he did not know it. But her ladyship had replied that Marie was well and living in the country, but that for reasons of her own, she had no further wish to communicate with her family.

"I had hoped," M. Garnier ended, "that *you*, who have lived with her so long, could explain the mystery."

Rowan shook her head silently. The kindly Swiss man patted her hand.

"*Alors*, we will not trouble about the past. You are my Marie's little daughter. You will tell us much about her. Elise, my wife, and I, deeply regret that you are alone in the world. We would like you to feel that you have a home with us for as long as you want it."

"I'm terribly grateful," said Rowan.

He stole a look at her, saw the tears on her lashes and at once became cheerful and talkative. She had written such a good letter, she must talk in French with him, he said. When she did, he congratulated her. He could see that her dear mother had been her teacher, for she spoke with a Swiss–French accent. The average English who came out here spoke so appallingly.

"We have a son, Marc, who is just your age," he told her. "He helps us in our hotel but is a lot up at Crans where I have a cousin whom you've probably never heard of—Paul Garnier. He runs a big hotel, The Valdana, in Crans, for the winter sports, and in the summer, for those who play golf. Crans is famous for its golf course. Marc is usually up at The Valdana from Friday to Monday."

"It all sounds most interesting," said Rowan.

"We are, as you English say, a nation of *hôteliers*!" smiled Jean, "and when I retire, Marc will take over my business."

Rowan suddenly remembered Ashley Moore. She told M. Garnier about him.

"Ah—the Buets—yes I know them," he nodded, "they have a house in Geneva, and l'Étoile is one of the finest chalets in Crans. M. Buet is an architect, famous in our country. Your friend will enjoy being there. The Buet housekeeper, old Hortense, is also one of the best cooks in Switzerland."

"Oh, I can't really say Mr. Moore is a *friend* of mine," said Rowan hastily, "we only met on the train, but he did ask me to call and see the chalet and hear him play his piano, when I go to Crans."

"I must speak further to you about Crans," said M. Garnier. "You mentioned in your letter that it is a job you want."

"Oh, more than anything," said Rowan eagerly. "Is there a chance of one?"

"We must discuss it all with your Tante Elise. We did not know whether or not you need a holiday——"

"No—I've done nothing for weeks and weeks and I need a job. I want to take my mind off—off everything," said Rowan stammering a little.

"Exactly, so you may wish to help out at my Cousin Paul's hotel. It is right in the middle of his busy season—he is packed with those making the winter sports. His receptionist has been taken suddenly ill and gone into a clinic. They need a girl who can speak English and French and can write letters in both those languages."

"Oh!" said Rowan breathlessly, "would I really qualify? Oh, *I'm thrilled!*"

He smiled at her. He was pulling into the drive of a tall, square, solid-looking house with the words 'Hôtel de Montagne' written on it. They had already climbed a few hundred feet. The hotel looked down on the roof-tops of Sierre, and stood in its own grounds. The gardens were at the moment hidden in the snow.

"We must talk it all over," he said in his kindly way. "First you must meet my wife and rest from your journey."

But Rowan was too excited to rest. She was beginning to feel that Jordans, Buckinghamshire, *England*, were at the other side of the world. This was another life. She was surrounded by the mighty shining Alps, breathing in the pure cold air, feeling the warmth of the sun against her face. There was a chance of a job that she could do, and the whole idea was as exhilarating as the Swiss atmosphere.

Tante Elise proved to be a stout, neatly clad little woman with shrewd black eyes and grey hair drawn into a neat bun. She made Rowan welcome and was very friendly, if obviously less emotionally stirred by Rowan's arrival than Uncle Jean had been. But after all, Elise was no blood relation of Mummy's, Rowan reflected, and Uncle Jean felt as she did—that somehow the dead woman had returned mysteriously with *her* arrival here; Marie was near to them both again.

Rowan now discovered that Uncle Jean was an easy-going man, and that Tante Elise was the firebrand who ran the hotel magnificently—managed the staff—bustled about, tirelessly, and was anxious to satisfy her clients as only a Swiss *hôtelier* can do.

There was so much that was new and fascinating for Rowan to see and learn. The place seemed to smell of polished pine; all the floors had bare shining boards, with gay rugs on them. The double windows were curtained in spotless striped linen. The steam-heating was so hot as to be overpowering for Rowan who was not used to it, and there seemed to be a prevailing odour of freshly-baked loaves and fragrant coffee. Plants everywhere—of every kind. Huge cyclamens (never had Rowan seen so many buds to one plant. They seemed to like the Swiss air). Green plants with long glossy leaves, or tall spikes. Rows of gay plants in front of all the windows.

It was much quieter down here in Sierre than it would be in a proper sports hotel during the winter, Monsieur Garnier told his niece-by-adoption. His *clientèle* at the Hôtel de Montagne was mainly composed of middle-aged people—French, Swiss or Italian. (A lot of Italians came to Sierre.) Just a sprinkling of young folk, all in their gay ski-clothes and heavy boots to which Rowan was rapidly becoming accustomed. She even began to feel the urge to get into her own sports outfit and go up to the mountain-tops. She overheard such exciting discussions. How wonderful it was ski-ing today at Bella Lui, or Cry d'Err or Mont La Chaux; all of which were reached on the ski-lift—the famous *téléférique*—the air cable with its little compartments like miniature railway carriages hanging downwards, sliding over the heads of the pine trees. From these various stations the skiers could skim down to Crans again.

What a lot she would have to write to Ann and Bill about, reflected Rowan. Yet again she felt she had done the best thing in coming out here. So much of the gloom and the misery that had oppressed her spirit was lifting. Already she felt refreshed. There seemed something at last to look forward to. For the moment she intended to put the memory of that revealing diary out of her mind.

Over supper in their private sitting-room, the Garniers discussed her future.

Rowan had her first taste of fresh-water trout caught in the Lake of Geneva, beautifully grilled by the Garnier chef; the veal which was so plentiful in Switzerland; the rich pastries which were famous.

"I shall grow fat here!" she laughed.

"You need to put on weight—you're much too thin," said Tante Elise with a critical glance at the English girl. A dear little thing, she thought, and *très amiable*, but Madame Garnier could not begin to understand all this fuss about her dead sister-in-law's adopted daughter. Not that Elise minded Rowan coming, if

50

it pleased Jean; but personally, she felt that Marie had behaved very badly to her Swiss relations. There could be no good reason for her having neglected them, and for severing all connections.

But Elise was ready and willing to sponsor Rowan's job at Cousin Paul's place. Certainly, her French was excellent and she was well educated and had a good appearance. She might very well take the place temporarily of poor Suzanne Léfèvre who had appendicitis. Elise said that she would telephone Paul tonight and tell him that Rowan had arrived, then perhaps Marc could take her up to Crans in the morning for an interview. The sooner she could start work the better because they were very inconvenienced without a receptionist. Elise—who spoke only French to Rowan —explained that there were so many rules and regulations about foreigners taking jobs—it could not be official work. She would be just 'a relation helping M. Paul'. He would, of course, privately reimburse her. To this Rowan replied that she was not so interested in the money as the work as she would have no personal expenses.

"I am not extravagant, anyhow. I do not need a lot of pocket-money. I'm used to living economically with Mummy."

'*Pauvre Marie—je ne comprends pas!*' M. Garnier muttered to himself, shrugging his shoulders sadly. Mme Garnier looked down her nose. Then her expression changed to one of beatific adoration. The idol of her life—her son, Marc—had just come in. He had been up in his car to Montana to see a friend who was in one of the big sanatoriums there.

He was a big fair Swiss boy with a ruddy complexion and bright blue eyes (he resembled the Garniers who were all fair). He was an expert skier and made no bones about the fact that he was more interested in his sport than the hotel business which he was to inherit. He spoke a little English and German but showed a preference for conversing in his native language. He was relieved that his 'cousin by adoption' spoke French so well. He had a hearty laugh and manner and was full of good humour. Rowan could not help liking him.

"I am amused," he grinned at her, showing very white teeth, "to have a *petite cousine* from London. Not that I ever remember seeing my Aunt Marie."

"I'll show you lots of photographs of her—she was wonderful," said Rowan.

He regarded her with interest and open admiration. Rowan had changed from her travelling suit into a grey woolly dress with a

51

scarlet leather belt, emphasizing the extreme smallness of her waist. Her eyes were big and shining with excitement. He thought her very pretty.

He was already eager to teach Rowan to ski.

"We'll turn you into a little Swiss Miss yet," he said, looking at her out of the corners of his eyes.

6

ROWAN was a born letter-writer. In her remote, restricted life with the woman she had thought to be her mother, she had had small opportunity to indulge in this aptitude for writing because she had never been away from home for more than a day and only corresponded at length with two people in her life—a school-friend who later emigrated with her parents to South Africa and went out of Rowan's life, and the English mistress at the same school, to whom she still wrote at times. Now she could sit down and compose a really long epistle to the Jenkins—her sole remaining link with England and home.

Twenty-four hours after her arrival in Switzerland, Rowan covered sheets of thin paper in her small neat handwriting, giving Ann and Bill a vivid description of the journey, of Ashley Moore, of Sierre and her newly-found adopted 'relations'. And then—most exciting news of all: her day up in Crans and interview with M. Paul Garnier at The Valdana Hotel. She had been given the job.

For a month anyhow, until Mademoiselle Léfèvre comes back from the clinic, I shall work at The Valdana. I am starting tomorrow. There was a little hesitation because I didn't speak German but the concierge, Henri, who is an awfully nice man, seems to be able to tackle that side for me and 'Monsieur Paul', as they call him, was very pleased with my French. I took down his dictation as fast, he said, as his Mademoiselle Suzanne.

It was a thrill going up in the funicular for the first time with the Garnier son who calls himself my cousin Marc. (A cousin very far removed!) He's an amusing boy, if a trifle exhausting—such terrific vitality. He wants to teach me to ski, to luge, to skate, everything.

Paul Garnier isn't a bit like Uncle Jean. He is middle-aged, with merry eyes and a mop of grey curly hair and has a young and pretty

52

Italian wife whose name is Vittoria. He calls her Toria. Like all these women out here she seems, despite her youth, to be absolutely on the spot in the way she helps run the hotel. I've never seen anything run so smoothly as The Valdana. M. Paul has a wonderful staff.

We didn't go up to Crans in Marc's car because I was so anxious to try the funicular. It's a quite paralysing experience sliding up that cable on one's own power—a sheer ascent at times. Up, up, where the snows get thicker and the pine trees are so deeply embedded in snow you can hardly see the green needles. And with that piercing blue sky and the sun shining down on you, the effect is dazzling.

From Montana Station we took a bus into Crans which is about a mile and three-quarters away.

It is fascinating to see all the chalets built on the slopes of the mountains. They are pale, golden wood, beautifully carved, with coloured paintwork and gay sun-blinds. Lots of little shops all full of exciting, colourful ski-clothes. Marc, of course, says prices are exorbitant in Crans—put on for the tourists—and if I want to buy anything, he can take me to his places in Sierre, where they'll be much cheaper. He laughed about Crans.

"At our winter sports resorts we have to make what money we can in the season, and live on it for the rest of the year, so we must be forgiven," he said, and pointed out quite rightly that it's also this question of currency—so few Swiss francs to our English pound—that makes things seem so expensive. Nobody likes it, Swiss or English.

There are lots of hotels in Crans but I think the biggest and the best is The Valdana. It has such a wonderful position, high up overlooking Crans, which lies on a plateau right above the Rhône valley. Marc says in the summer the meadows and parks and lakes are superb and everyone plays golf. It isn't shut in like lots of ski resorts. You get such lovely fresh air.

From the pillared terrace and balconies of The Valdana you can look out at the most wonderful range of the Valais Alps, diamond-crusted with snow. You can see the 'nursery slopes' where all the initiates learn to ski—the children tumbling about on their fascinating little skis (there's an école de ski for them, too). It made me long for Jeremy and Scrap to be out here. There's a curling rink and there's skating, and you hear music drifting across the rink from a loudspeaker. It's all so jolly. And I've had a drink at what they call the Sporting Club, where they have thé dansants, and dance at night, and at midday everybody sits on the terrace and drinks aperitifs or coffee.

There was an earthquake in Crans in 1947, Marc says all the windows of the hotel were broken. The Valdana was rebuilt soon after that. It's a mixture of beautifully old carved wood, and modern luxury.

M. Paul interviewed me in his sunny little office in which I'll work and showed me the reception desk at which I'll also spend a lot of my time. I have to arrange bedrooms, welcome new guests and keep everyone happy when M. and Mme Paul are not in, and answer all the correspondence. Quite a job! But M. Paul said Henri, who has been with him for years, will keep an eye on me.

I'm to be the 'unofficial' receptionist without wages, but M. Paul seems very generous and said I need never want for a few francs in my purse and I'm to have two hours off every afternoon, and a Sunday whenever I want. I won't be needed on duty in the evenings after dinner, either.

Mme Paul showed me a dear little room at the top of the hotel which was Mlle Suzanne's own room. Tiny but with a balcony which luckily faces south and oh, the blessed sun pouring in, and that view of the incomparable Alps! I know I am going to be happy in that room. Thank you both, my dear kind friends, for encouraging me to come out here. You don't know what you've done for me. I really begin to feel I can forget Mummy's diary, and make believe that I really am half Swiss and have come back to my own mother's beautiful sparkling country.

The long letter ended with a description of the interior of The Valdana—the beautiful long, well-heated lounge with its dark blue-green walls hung with charming original sketches. Gay scarlet sofas and chairs. Small, intimate bar with carved woodwork, and tall windows looking as they all did across Crans, over the valley, to the mountain peaks.

"Mind you, you're lucky," Marc had said when Rowan enthused about the weather, "we have a high percentage of sunlight in Crans but it does snow and rain at times, I assure you."

"But even then it must be lovely," Rowan declared.

She had an excellent lunch with the Garniers and Marc, before the guests came in. The *salle-à-manger* was another wonderful room to describe for Ann and Bill. It had the latest form of concealed lighting, and long pullman-like windows shaded from the strong sun by a striped awning, beside which one could sit, and while eating gaze out at the view that never palled.

For the rest of that afternoon Rowan was treated as a guest rather than a future employee. Marc, who was interested in the accountancy side of the hotel on which he worked at week-ends, apparently didn't work very hard. He was too great an enthusiast for ski-ing and he was determined to turn Rowan into one. After lunch, he took her down the road to the village, where Rowan bought postcards for the children at Blackthorn Farm, and then up to the *téléférique* station. This was where the ski-lift up to the mountains began.

"It won't be long before you are able to go with the others and ski down," Marc told Rowan.

Dazzled, she stood looking up at the heights; watched a few skiers flying as though impelled by the wind, down those shining slopes, bodies slightly bent, hands clutching their ski-sticks—down, down—then as they reached the bottom curving, describing an arc—'stemming' as they called it; then coming to a full stop, still maintaining perfect balance.

"I'll never be able to do that!" gasped Rowan.

"You will, if I am to be your teacher," said Marc. "We shall have a fine time. I'm so happy you have come here, *petite cousine.*"

He pressed her arm against his. She could not take offence at the big boy who was only her own age, and seemed so full of good humour. But she was not sure that she liked his swift familiarity. She warned herself that things might be a little awkward with Marc; she must use tact and discretion if he was going to be in Crans for three days a week.

It was when they were walking back to the square outside *la poste*, where they would catch the bus back to Montana Station, that they ran into Ashley Moore.

He was just coming out of a photographer's shop. He carried his skis over one shoulder, and was wearing the same black outfit in which Rowan had first seen him. As he recognized her, he took off his dark glasses and came, smiling, across the road towards her. She felt an unaccountable pleasure. She knew that she was glad to see him.

"Oh, *hullo!*" she said with her shy smile.

"Hullo," he said, "so you've come up to Crans already."

She introduced him to Marc.

"*Mon—mon cousin,*" she stammered—"that is, a sort of cousin on my—my mother's side."

(Strange how upsetting it was to her to feel that she had no right to make the introduction, using such terms.) All pleasure, all delight in this beautiful village in the snows, seemed to crumple up before the swift recollection of all things connected with her birth.

55

But Ashley Moore saw only the sparkle which had gleamed in the big dark eyes of the young girl when she first greeted him. He and Marc shook hands, French fashion (on every occasion the French shake hands, he thought). Then he turned his attention to Rowan again.

"Not on skis yet?"

"No—I've only just drawn breath, so to speak," she laughed. "And anyhow I've taken a job."

He questioned her about The Valdana. Marc stood by, hands in his pockets, looking restless and eyeing the tall Englishman under lowered brows.

"You don't say!" exclaimed Ashley. "Why good gracious me, what a surprise. A darned nice job too. I love The Valdana—I used in the past, to stay at a cheap little hotel and spend my evenings in The Valdana Bar. Paul and Toria are great friends of mine. You'll probably find me there most evenings."

He added to Marc: "Haven't I seen you there?"

"Yes—I'm M. Garnier's nephew," Marc said a trifle stiffly.

"Ah, yes," said Ashley. He looked at Rowan again. She was wearing the Jaegar coat in which she had travelled but had on thick slacks, socks and boots. She looked a trifle more animated, he thought. He said:

"I'm just going up to Bella Lui. The snow's perfect for ski-ing today. I thought I'd have a holiday and start my work tomorrow."

Rowan politely tried to pull Marc into the conversation.

"You remember, Marc," she said, "I told you and your parents, I travelled to Sierre with Mr. Ashley. He is a well-known English composer and he is staying in l'Étoile."

"*C'est bien, là*," said Marc. "I know André Buet—he won the ski-jumping championship in Zermatt last year."

The two men discussed ski-jumping for a moment. Rowan listened with respect to the various terms with which she was soon to become familiar. All the ski-experts' jargon. Ashley produced his skis for Marc's inspection. Paul Garnier, last winter, had advised him to buy this kind—new light metal, faster than the old wooden ones, but the poor composer hadn't been able to afford them until this year, he laughed. He had been down to Ginetta's, the sports shop, this morning to buy a pair.

Once more he turned to Rowan.

"You're going to come and try my piano at l'Étoile aren't you?"

"Yes, of course," she nodded.

"I might even offer you a meal. The Buets have left me in charge of a superb cook. There's my chalet"—he pointed with one ski-stick over the roof-top of the photographer's shop to a little wooden building high up on the hill, flanked by snow-powdered pines. Then he moved off, and Rowan and Marc went their way.

On the way back to Sierre in the funicular Marc really annoyed Rowan by making an attempt to intrude on her personal and private life. If she went to visit the English composer, he would go with her, he declared. Whereupon Rowan who, despite her youth and inexperience could show determination when necessary, spoke up:

"I'm quite capable of paying my calls alone, thank you, Marc."

His good humour vanished behind a fit of sulks.

"Is he what is called by the English, the 'boy-friend'?"

"Don't be so silly! I hardly know him."

"Well, he looked at you as though he knew *you* very well."

"Really, Marc!" Rowan began to laugh.

Quite surprisingly, Marc remained sulky and did not speak to her again until they reached home.

But Rowan had been awfully glad to see Ashley again and apart from the excitement of this job in the beautiful Sports Hotel, she looked forward to going to l'Étoile to try that piano.

7

ABOUT a fortnight later, Ashley returned from a morning's ski-ing—still taking advantage of the dazzling weather—had a hot bath, changed into grey flannel slacks and a yellow polo-necked jersey and enjoyed a light lunch, served on the sun-warmed balcony by old Hortense.

Then, feeling refreshed, his face already burnt brown after so many days of this outdoor healthy life, he settled down to his piano.

He was well aware that he was not getting on very fast with *The Snowbird*. He had achieved some kind of opening, but what he wanted was an idea for a really haunting theme for The Snowbird, herself. Sometimes in the night, he got up, and came in here and ran his fingers over the piano-keys, thinking that he had found a melody—but he hadn't. It eluded him. Yet here in Crans he had all the peace and opportunity that he could desire for his work. The chalet was charming. André's piano was only an upright— but it was a Bechstein with a superb tone. The Buets had plenty of money. Everything in the house was modern and luxurious. This lounge was furnished with taste and elegance. It had the usual polished pine-floor and doors, and lemon and white linen draperies that pleased Ashley's eye. The view of the Alps from all sides was so splendid that it frequently lured him from his work. There were plants and flowers everywhere; all the wonderful spring flowers that one could buy at this time of year in Switzerland. It made an inspiring, lovely studio.

With a virgin sheet of music on the table beside him, pen in one hand, the other wandering over the keys, Ashley tried hard to concentrate. But his mind remained as blank as that piece of lined paper. He frowned, flung down his pen and walked to the balcony windows, hands in his pockets. If things didn't go better he would have to give up his ski-ing and start work in the early morning which was really his best time. This would never do.

Tom Wagner, his manager, had been on the phone to him last night, repeating what Ashley already knew from English papers bought out here, and press cuttings received (to say nothing of a heavy fan mail): *Summer Song* was a smash-hit. It was playing to packed houses. They wanted him on television, they wanted him to broadcast, they wanted photographs—life-stories—lord knew what else. But he wasn't going back. He had never craved for that sort of limelight. He had only wanted recognition of his own talents as a composer. His work was not in classical vein but, as Tom said, it was a cut above ordinary musical comedy. And of course he must follow up *Summer Song* with something as good if not better.

He wished Simon Cottar, his lyric writer and friend, could have joined him here; perhaps with him to co-operate he, Ashley, might have done a bit more. But Simon couldn't come. He had a wife who hadn't been well and as far as Ashley knew, the Cottars were on their way to Jamaica.

Yes, it had been a bad week for work. He had also been staying up too late; spending too much time up at The Valdana; sitting at the bar where pretty Toria and M. Paul helped to dispense drinks—and hospitality. The hotel was packed with rich clients from all parts of the world. There were plenty of exquisitely dressed, attractive women—both young and middle aged—some unattached—ready to go out ski-ing with Ashley; to dance with him in the evenings when the lights in the bar were lowered, while Maria, a blonde pianist from Zurich, played for them.

Ashley had always attracted women and he was by no means immune against the fascination of a pair of beautiful eloquent eyes and a tempting mouth. But he had not come out here for 'that sort of thing'. He had come to work.

His thoughts suddenly strayed to the little English girl, Rowan Gray. She was now firmly installed at The Valdana and already quite a favourite. The Swiss and French called her *'mignonne'* and *'sympathique'*. Paul's young Italian wife who was not much older than Rowan seemed to get on splendidly with her and, as Ashley had already seen for himself, Rowan did not appear to be without attraction for the male sex. That young fellow, Marc Garnier, was always hanging around the reception desk at weekends. And now there was a good-looking bachelor Norwegian skier, constantly pressing her to let him take her up to Cry d'Err in the *téléférique*. And that tall grey-haired Englishman who seemed to think Miss Gray 'quite a pet' (that was what he had called her when talking to Ashley in the bar one night).

Ashley had been quite surprised. He still thought of Rowan as a rather timid child without much in her. Admittedly she had gained in poise, and looks—even during her first week at The Valdana. Knowing a bit about the solitary life she had led with her mother in an English village, Ashley could see that life out here would be quite instructive to the young girl.

Last night, when he had run across her in the vestibule as she was coming off duty, he had remarked how the sun had 'caught her'.

"It suits you to be brown," he had said casually.

A chap could murmur a thing like that to any woman in a sports hotel and expect a smile and a casual reply; but Rowan's small brown face had flushed as crimson as though he had said something of unbelievable importance.

Amused—he had passed on, first reminding her that she hadn't yet paid her call at l'Étoile.

At this moment, Ashley remembered something else about Rowan: he had seen her on skis for the first time yesterday, Sunday, as he walked past the nursery slopes. She was with Marc Garnier who had constituted himself her instructor. Of course she had wobbled at first and fallen and looked scared to death, but after a few moments she had seemed well able to stand up and even propel herself down a gentle slope without losing balance. It was then that he had noted again the *Snowbird* quality of the young English girl. She was extraordinarily graceful; undeniably attractive in the long pale blue ski-trousers which fitted tightly, accentuating the extreme slimness of her hips; the short white waterproof tunic; the close-fitting hood. She looked fragile; yet strong, at the same time. When she fell again, Marc picked her up and they laughed together. Ashley had moved on. A couple of kids . . . a waste of time watching them.

But there might come a day, he decided, after Rowan had had more practice, when it would be well worth watching that slender beautifully poised figure skim confidently and swiftly down one of the steeper runs.

Impatiently now he turned from the window. He was wasting his time on such thoughts. He returned to the piano, struck one chord, then another. After a moment his pen began to move over the foolscap. Ideas were beginning to come. At half past four, when old Hortense came in with a cup of tea for the English *monsieur*, whom she found very charming and easy to work for, he did not even notice her; neither did he drink the tea which got cold.

When he stopped writing, he put the music in front of him and played over what he had written.

"Not bad," he muttered, "not bad; but not quite right—just yet——"

He did not hear the front door-bell ring nor see Hortense put in her head—nor hear a conversation that took place between her and a visitor.

Then, suddenly, as though some sixth sense warned him that he was no longer alone, but that he was being watched, he swung round.

Standing in the middle of the room was a tall young woman wearing black slacks and a short fur jacket over a black sweater, into which was tucked a silk scarf of brilliant pink. She was hatless. With positive dismay he stared at a face all too familiar to him; a face that might have been beautiful but for its expression which was one of brooding discontent that pulled down the corners of a large sensual mouth, and had etched little lines at the corner of long heavy-lidded eyes which were almost green in colour. Nobody, having looked into those eyes, could ever forget their strange colour. Certainly Ashley had not forgotten, much as he wanted to.

"Well," she said in a low drawling voice. "Surprised?"

He stood up, silent, the pen clenched between his fingers. It wasn't often that Ashley Moore was at a loss for words—he prided himself that he could tackle most problems. But this one defeated him.

Only a short while ago he had been thinking that Simon and his wife were on their way to Jamaica. He was flabbergasted.

"What in the name of fortune are you doing here, Fran?" he asked.

Frances Cottar slipped out of her jacket. She did so with a studied grace. Ashley, who knew her so well, was aware that everything that Frances—they all called her Fran—did or said, was for effect. She was a born *poseuse*. Perhaps it was her up-bringing—her stock in trade. She had been a mannequin until she was thirty, after which she helped run a hat-shop. Soon after that, at a cocktail party, Simon had met and fallen in love with her. (Poor old Simon! how Ashley had pitied him at the time.) He used to be even more of a confirmed bachelor than Ashley; more timid, afraid of woman's wiles. But he had gone crazy about Fran with her five-foot-nine of languid slimness, her green eyes, her voluptuousness. She was six or seven years older than he. Ashley knew that her figure was a miracle of preservation—that she endured a perpetual, self-inflicted misery of diet. She never seemed to eat—she was a slave to fashion; to beauty specialists and hairdressers. Perhaps only *she* knew that her hair was natur-ally a pale brown. She often tried new 'rinses'. Just now it was an ash-blonde, a pale blue, which was very effective with her deli-cate skin; a skin that never saw the sun—she wouldn't allow it to.

Fundamentally, Ashley did not like Frances or anything that she stood for, yet he had learned to his cost, the insidious charm that she could exert—the power she could wield, especially over rather simple trusting nice fellows like Simon.

Ashley had never thought of himself as being 'simple'; or un-suspecting. He liked to believe he was a cynic and that he had *known* what Fran was. He had been sure that her supposed 'deli-cacy' was, in truth, only supposition. He believed that she was as strong as a horse, but she could produce a 'migraine' or a pain of some kind, when she didn't want to do something that *Simon* wanted her to do. It was part of her pose to appear 'delicate', and 'brave' in the face of suffering.

Ashley despised her. But a year ago when Simon was away in the Highlands, visiting an old ailing mother, Ashley had been fool enough to take Frances out. It was the memory of that evening (and other evenings) which made him feel a trifle sick now in this moment when he saw her again.

"Why are you here?" he asked again.

She made a moue with her lips as she sauntered towards him.

"I've flown all the way from London to be near you: is that all you've got to say to me?"

"Where's Simon?"

"In London as far as I know."

"But he was going to Jamaica, to take you out there because you had been ill——"

"Ash, darling, do ask me to sit down and have a drink. You *can't* be so inhospitable." And she gave a little laugh and sank on to the lemon-coloured settee, knowing that it made a wonderful background for her black-clad figure. She stretched forward and took a cigarette from a box on the table. He stared at her wholly dismayed and watched her light the cigarette with a small jewelled lighter—looking at the length of her rose-pink nails—remembering how their long points used to fascinate him even while they repelled.

That was the trouble with Frances—all the time, with her, one hovered between fascination and repugnance.

"Why didn't you go to Jamaica?" he demanded.

"Because I had a row with Simon," she answered coolly, "and I decided to come out to Switzerland, which will be just as good for my health, if not better, than Jamaica."

"Why didn't Simon come?"

"After the first night of *Summer Song* he was kept so busy— there was so much publicity and as you'd buzzed off, he decided to cancel his own holiday. I told him I was perfectly well able to look after myself and that the mountain air should work wonders for me."

"You mean you're all alone?"

"Quite alone," she smiled up at him, with that coolness which he found exasperating under the circumstances, while he felt the sweat breaking out on his forehead at the mere sight of her.

"And Simon knows that you're in Crans, where I am?"

"Certainly. It's always safer to tell the truth than lie. I rang The Valdana from Town. They haven't a room at the moment so I am at the Hôtel de la Poste, but they said they could give me a bed at The Valdana the day after tomorrow. Of course Simon knows you're in this chalet. He told me to ask you to look after me until he comes to fetch me, which may be next week."

"You had no right to do this—no right at all."

"Oh, darling, I *know* you're working, and Simon said you wouldn't be very pleased if I interrupted you, but he was rather pleased I wanted to see you."

Ashley winced.

"What did you have the row about?"

"You."

"Me!" he said in horror.

She laughed, evidently enjoying his dismay.

"Oh, don't get worked up—I didn't tell him the *facts*. On the contrary, the row started about something quite different and Simon had had a little too much to drink, and was rather rude to me. He accused me of being cold to him, then of being unkind to his friends—and you were among them. He was upset because he said I so rarely asked you to our house; that you were his best friend, and so on. Well—in the end, when I said I would come out to Crans to get well and make my peace with you, he seemed quite pleased, so happy to cancel Jamaica."

A moment's silence. Then Ashley said in a low furious voice: "I wouldn't like to tell you what I think of you."

She gave that low laugh at the back of her throat which once he had found exciting. Now nothing about Fran excited him. She filled him with a sense of anger—of remorse where Simon was concerned, of infinite pity for him. What a mistake Simon had made! He knew it, too, perhaps, but was too loyal to let anybody, even Ashley see it.

During the last two or three years of their friendship, Ashley had been a constant visitor to the Cottars' small attractive house in Chelsea and little had remained hidden from him. He had watched the rot set in—the slow deterioration of that marriage—the slow painful death of Simon's belief in the woman he had married. He could no longer be blindly infatuated; of that Ashley was sure. The beautiful Fran was an utter egotist without heart, without pity. *He* knew it, now.

"Darling," came Fran's drawling voice, "isn't it time you realized that I am sincerely in love for the first time in my life—and with you?"

He turned from her speechlessly and stared out of the window.

On that night when he had taken Fran out to the opera, he had been foolishly proud to be seen with her. She had been wearing white Icelandic foxes over a silver sheath of a dress. Her hair (blonde then, without the blue) was cut short, waving softly over

her classic head. She had looked like 'a million dollars'. He had
laughed over the fact that *he* had had to go to Moss Bros. for his
own 'tails'; and be thankful that a musician friend had sent him
the tickets. He had given Fran an expensive supper at the Café de
Paris afterwards, knowing that he would have to go easy on the
drinks and cigarettes for himself for the next week. But he hadn't
felt he could take her to a lesser place. Simon had private means
and Fran was not the type to do anything on the cheap. She had
been so utterly charming to Ashley that night, but it had come as
a slight shock when she had openly admitted that 'Simon wasn't
right for her'.

"I don't think I've ever really loved any man," she had murmured as they danced, and then whispered the last four words:
"Until I met you."

Even now he could hardly bear to remember the rest of that
evening; what a damn fool he had been to feel flattered because so
beautiful a woman, older than himself in years and experience,
had said such a thing, then proceeded to prove it. He wanted to
forget how he had driven her back to her house—and gone in with
her to have 'one for the road'; then found her in his arms.

The hot passion of that next half-hour had amazed him.
Hitherto he had only had one or two light affairs with girls—
innocent enough—but he knew if he was not careful, the affair
with Fran would be far from innocent. Because Simon was his
friend, and Ashley had a strong sense of honour and decency, he
had torn himself away—before irreparable havoc had been done.

He had meant to stay away, but that was the difficult part, with
Simon his best friend, writing his lyrics, and always round at his
place; always begging him to join Fran and himself at some dinner
or party.

It had been a devilish year, Frances continuing to show herself
in a new fantastic light as the woman who loved for the first time,
Frances in remorseless pursuit of him. He had to admit that at
least it was not for his money then. Drawing his deductions—
those of a man interested in human beings, in character—he could
only suppose it was because he would have none of her that she
developed such a passion for him. On the few occasions when she
manœuvred to see him alone, she was so alluring, so tender, so
appealing with that air of suffering and sadness around her—he
had felt sorry for her. Once more he had gone so far as to take her
in his arms and kiss her, only to go away hating himself—and her.

Finally she began to make no further effort to see him. It was because she refused to invite him to the house that Simon, poor ignorant fellow, had quarrelled with her. But all the time, Ashley reflected, that he, himself, had been imagining that Fran had given up the contest and that her temporary infatuation had petered out—she must have been like a smouldering fire waiting to break into flame again. But this—this following him to Crans and preparing to stay here for the next week or two without Simon—he would not tolerate. He swung round.

"Fran, this can't go on. I've told you till I'm sick of it, that I do not love you, and I do not want you, and that even if I *did*, Simon is my friend."

Her long eyes narrowed and glittered at him. She drew a breath of her cigarette.

"Ash, darling, really, that old-fashioned '*nobler than thou*' attitude is awfully boring."

"It's not an attitude my dear girl, it's a fact."

"Darling, you've had a wonderful success—the papers are raving about you."

"That's irrelevant—I want you to know——"

"That you don't love me and that *Simon's your friend*," she finished for him.

"Haven't you any *pride?*" he asked incredulously.

She shrugged. "I suppose I used to have when I was terribly young. It's easy to be proud in your first youth. But I'm on my way to being forty, and you're the only man I've ever really wanted."

"I'm sorry," he said, "that doesn't move me."

He came and stood nearer her. She looked up into the coldness of his grey, frowning eyes. She sighed. She had tried so often in vain to explain to Ashley that it was his very hardness that attracted her—that granite touch, that cynicism, which set him apart from other men in her sight. Simon was such a soft-hearted fool; she could twist him round her finger and had always been able to. Many men had been at her feet. But not Ashley; and she wanted him more than anything in the world.

He said:

"Look here, Fran, I'm not going to waste time repeating what you already know—about being sorry that I ever held you in my arms or told you how much you attracted me—but that's all over. You don't attract me any more, and I want you to go away and stay away."

"So brutal," she murmured, "and I have come so far to see you, and Simon is hundreds of miles away. We're all alone on this lovely mountain top. At least it *could* be lovely if you were kinder. Dear, *dear* Ashley!"

"Fran, you've got to pack up and go back to London," he said through his teeth, "I want to work and this will wreck everything."

"But I shall inspire you."

"I want you to go," he said again, harshly.

Now she put up a long slender hand and drew it across her forehead.

"My head aches terribly—I can't bear your unkindness———"

"And I'm not going to be taken in by your headaches, Fran, or your nonsense about being in love with me."

"I am—I am," she whispered, and real tears came into her eyes, tears of frustration. She was blind to honour, to pride and to everything except her need for this man. As an unknown composer she had wanted him. Now as the great success, he was even more desirable.

She got up, extinguished her cigarette, made a quick movement towards him and linked her arms about his neck.

"Darling Ashley—even if I do go away in a few days—you could be nice to me for a little while———" she began.

At the other end of the room the lounge door opened, softly. Hortense, thinking this *monsieur* had arranged a small cocktail party, was ushering in another guest, without preamble. But it was only Rowan who had come to pay her first call at l'Étoile.

8

IF it hadn't been for Henri, the *concierge*, Rowan wouldn't have come to see Ashley at this hour. But Henri wanted to go down to Sierre to see his old mother tomorrow afternoon, and Rowan had willingly agreed to take his place in the Reception if he took hers this evening. As long as somebody was there at this time the Garniers didn't mind.

Rowan had just had a slight '*histoire*' as the French call it, with Marc. All this week she had dreaded him coming up for the weekend because he had pursued her so relentlessly last week-end, and phoned her daily from Sierre. He made it quite evident that he was what he called '*épris*' with his *cousine*-by-adoption. Last night, as soon as he had arrived at The Valdana he had hung around the office attempting to flirt outrageously. Even Mme Garnier had remarked on it. She whispered a word in Rowan's ear: her husband's nephew, she informed Rowan, was not like most stolid, level-headed Swiss boys. He had always been *amoureux* with some young girl in the district. Rowan must take care.

Rowan had laughed. She could certainly 'take care', she had answered with the new self-confidence that she was fast achieving. And she felt like that. The full busy life in this Swiss hotel in a position of some authority, constantly meeting strangers, had done her all the good in the world. She did not think the Jenkins would recognize her as 'the shy child' as they used to call her, and poor Mummy wouldn't have known her, either.

But Marc Garnier was persistent and tactless. He didn't seem to care that she did not want his attentions. The little scene had been about going to the Sporting Club to dine and dance tonight. When she had turned him down he had behaved quite ridiculously.

"You're going out with someone else?" he had accused her, and persisted in saying so; then asserted furiously that if he saw her dancing with another boy he'd break in on it and snatch her away.

That sort of thing had only one effect on Rowan; it fired her blood and she answered him with spirit:

"I don't mind whether you are Uncle Jean's son or not—you just haven't got control of *me*, and I shall do as I like!" she had flared.

Still smarting after this she had made her way up to Ashley's chalet. It would be nice to see the cool, intelligent young Englishman in his own *milieu* and she very definitely wanted to hear him play some of his own music.

Whenever Ashley dropped in at The Valdana Bar and stopped at the bureau to say good evening to her, Rowan was always pleased. She had begun to find that strong unusual face of his curiously attractive; and he was so full of character. He was a fascinating mixture. The artistically minded musician with the creative spirit; that indefinable quality of the dreamer and visionary—*and*—the man-of-the-world. There was something, too, of a boy—in him—the healthy lover of outdoor sports. Rowan had gone up to Cry d'Err last Sunday and watched him ski down; thought how well he looked on his skis. She also thought him almost handsome these days with his warm tan which made the grey searching eyes even more brilliant and strikingly light. She would like one day to have a long talk with him—about everything in life. She even toyed with the thought of telling him all that she had discovered about her true identity and see what he thought about it all. But somehow she did not think she would ever do so —or even tell anyone on earth.

When she walked into the lounge of the chalet and found Ashley standing by the piano with a woman's arms clasped round his neck, she had never felt more embarrassed.

She was miserably conscious that she had made a *faux pas* by coming here without warning him (not that it was her fault, for he had asked her to drop in any time she could manage—and old Hortense had shown her in). But as the couple, whom she fully imagined must have been locked in a close embrace, sprang apart and turned to her, she wished the earth would open and swallow her up.

She tried to blurt out a greeting. No words came. She wanted to turn and rush away but remained rooted to the spot.

Then Ashley came forward. She could not know how relieved he felt at the sight of her. She thought he was only trying to put her at her ease when he said:

"My dear, what a delightful surprise—come right in."

"Oh—I—really——" she began to stutter.

"Come in," repeated Ashley, and took her arm and pulled her towards the fireplace in which the pine logs were shooting bright sparks up the chimney on this frosty night.

"Fran," he said, turning to Simon's wife, "this is Rowan Gray— Rowan—this is Mrs. Simon Cottar, the wife of the man who writes the lyrics for my operas. You remember I told you about him."

The eyes of the two women met. Rowan was still very confused but she recognized the tall ash-blonde woman who tried to get rooms at The Valdana. She had thought then that Mrs. Cottar was beautiful and frightfully smart but not what she called 'friendly', like many of the clients.

Frances Cottar stared coldly at the young girl resenting her intrusion at this precise moment and wondering how such a girl came to be *persona grata* at Ashley's chalet.

Murmuring a scarcely audible *"How do you do,"* Frances walked to the sofa and picked up her fur jacket.

"I'll come and see you again when you're not busy, Ash," she said in a somewhat acid voice.

"By all means," said Ashley.

"Oh—if I've come at an inconvenient moment—I can go— don't let me interrupt——" began Rowan, pink and hot with confusion. But once again Ashley took her arm and held on to it as though to an anchor.

"Delighted to see you, my dear child. I asked you to come when you could. I want to hear you play. Mrs. Cottar is staying at Crans—and you haven't interrupted anything," he added with a significant look at Frances who returned it, her long green eyes smouldering malevolently like a cat's.

He insisted on taking Rowan's coat and telling her to unwrap her hood and scarf and make herself at home.

Perforce, Frances moved to the door. She knew perfectly well that she was not wanted. In any case, she had no interest in staying here with a third person in the room. She would come back and see Ashley tomorrow. She was going to make him realize that she would not accept her *congé* without a battle. There certainly, she reflected, could be nothing between him and the insignificant little receptionist from The Valdana. Miss Gray wasn't particularly smart. In Frances's estimate she could not begin to be a rival to a sophisticated and elegant woman. Just a nonentity, decided Frances, brushing Rowan, like an insect, off the earth. Ashley was behaving this way not because he wanted Rowan Gray's company but just to annoy *her*, Fran. She as good as told Ashley so at the front door as he opened it for her.

"Why did you ask that girl to stay—you *knew* what a lot we had to say to each other?" she whispered angrily. "You can't be interested in *her*."

Ashley gave a hollow laugh and whispered back:

"Oh, you're quite wrong, my dear Fran. She's my new girl-friend. I find her irresistible," he said mockingly.

Frances clenched her teeth.

"I won't let you do this to me——"

"I don't want to be rude, Fran," he cut in, "but there's a devil of a draught here and I haven't got my coat on. '*See you later, Madame Alligator,*'" he added with a devilish grin. "And take my advice and phone Simon and tell him you're going home, and *staying home.*"

Before Frances could reply, Ashley had gently closed the front door, knowing that he was being more discourteous to Fran than he had ever been to any woman in his life before, but not caring. He wasn't going to let Fran get away with her project, nor was he going to be blackmailed by her, because of his former passing weakness. It was all over and he was going to keep it that way.

He returned to the warmth of the lounge and spoke cheerfully to the young girl who was kneeling in front of the fireplace, spreading her fingers to the blaze. He said:

"You came at exactly the right moment, Rowan." He narrowed his eyes as he looked down at her, and gave a short ironic laugh.

The ready colour came to her cheeks. She stood up and said, without looking at him:

"On the contrary, I think I've intruded——"

Silence. Then with a frown Ashley pulled a cigarette out of the box.

"You don't, do you?" he muttered and struck a match.

Rowan was thinking of the strikingly beautiful woman, so chic, so slender, so haughty, whom she had just seen with Ashley in what she imagined to be a lover's embrace. Yet romantic though she was in the depths of her heart, she was ultra-sensitive and had a psychic feeling that it had not been a really romantic interlude. How could it . . . when that woman was the wife of Mr. Moore's lyric writer and friend? The memory of Mrs. Cottar's tall lissom body straining so close to Ashley, her arms around his neck, had somehow left an unpleasant taste which Rowan did not relish. But she thought:

'I suppose he's in love with her . . .'

She felt strangely disappointed—in Ashley Moore.

He made no reference to Frances. He moved to the piano and taking Rowan's hand, pulled her towards him.

"Come on—try the Bechstein."

"Oh, I couldn't——" she began with a childish timidity that half annoyed and half charmed him. Really, he had never met anyone so young for her age.

"Don't be silly—you know you play—and I want you to play for me."

"But I'm a rank amateur and you're a professional——" she began in an agony.

"Oh, sit down and play," he said crossly. "Otherwise I'll turn you out into the cold cold snow without a drink."

Now she laughed, her confidence returning to her. She had come up to l'Étoile full of eagerness to see Ashley Moore again. How strong he was! She was a little shocked at herself, but she could not help wondering what it would be like to have a man like this for a lover. She wondered if he was very very much in love with Mrs. Cottar. It was a pity he loved her, as she was already married. It must be awful for them both. Awful but rather mean with the husband so far away. She wished she hadn't come in and found them like that. The impression she had had of the two had been so fleeting that it had escaped her that all the wooing had been on the woman's side; that Ashley's arms had been held stiffly at his sides, and that he had not been kissing those hungry lips upturned to him.

Meekly, Rowan sat on the tapestry-covered stool and ran a hand over the keys. The piano had a fine tone—which not even the climate up at this altitude had destroyed. Far better than the Jenkins's old instrument, she thought—which was beaten upon at regular intervals by Jeremy, who thought (even if the rest of the family did not) that he was a born musician.

Thinking of Jeremy, and of Scrap's jammy little fingers also striving for mastery of the piano at Blackthorn Farm, Rowan felt relaxed. Her tension passed. She began to play a Chopin Nocturne which had been Mummy's favourite. At first she played badly, keeping her eyes downcast, not daring to look at Ashley. He, with a cigarette between his lips and hands in his pockets, stood in front of the fire listening. She was conscious that his gaze was on her. That alone made her nervous.

Benevolently, as though he were listening to a little girl playing he listened to Rowan. She was a funny child he thought; made a fellow feel rather protective and gentle about her. She herself, was so very gentle. She could be so easily hurt. He could not help contrasting her with that other woman who had just been here. How utterly dissimilar they were, those two blondes! Rowan, absolutely natural with her pale, straight hair, her shy dark eyes, her immature grace, not yet twenty. And the other—artificial from the top of her 'blued' head, to the soles of her feet; an experienced, greedy, exacting woman, nearing forty. She had come here to spoil Crans for him. Inwardly he raged, wondering how he could force her back to Simon.

Rowan stopped playing and turned to Ashley, hands folded loosely in her lap.

"I made an awful lot of mistakes," she said.

"You played beautifully," he said with an enthusiasm he did not really feel.

She got up.

"Now you must play to me."

"My dear, I'm not a pianist and I never play to anyone. I'm a composer."

"That's not fair!" exclaimed Rowan.

"Oh, you baby!" he said, and burst suddenly out laughing.

The atmosphere was clearing. The memory of Fran Cottar faded. Rowan seemed to bring the fragrance of spring into the studio. It was more palatable, thought Ashley, than Fran's heavy intoxicating French perfumes.

He seated himself at the piano and played for Rowan the melody on which he had been working for the last few hours. It might be interesting to see what impression it had on Rowan. She obviously knew *something* about music.

"I think it's a perfectly beautiful song," she said when he had finished.

"Don't flatter me. It's the theme which I want the Snowbird to sing and which will drift right through the opera, whenever she appears."

"Please tell me more about it," begged Rowan.

"You see—she's to be a strange elemental creature—child of the mountains—born and bred in a much more remote village than Crans. Been on skis all her life. I picture her as a sort of sprite—the way for instance she skims down the slopes with that bird-like quality; and when she sings she must suggest that quality. The part will have to be played by a girl with exceptional purity of voice—no passion—until she meets this man who wakens her first love, and finally shoots and deserts her. She comes down from the mountain tops to the sports hotel to look for him. There's a scene when he's drinking—he and his friend will laugh at her—it will be a brutal sort of scene; my tenor will have a wonderful song. The whole opera will have something of the Swan Lake atmosphere about it."

He continued—warming to his subject:

"There'll be a sort of symbolism between the cruelty of the man and the defencelessness of the wild bird. And throughout, the feeling of *snow*—of ice—I want the music to have a clearness—an intense coldness, with the contrast of the man's passions reaching crescendo—sung by a fine powerful voice," Ashley broke off.

He had been walking up and down the studio while he talked to Rowan. She stood by the piano, her hands behind her back, her gaze never leaving his face. That powerful face with the blunt nose and the grey black-lashed eyes which, to her, were incomprehensible. She didn't think she would ever understand Ashley Moore. He was something so new to her; vibrant and compelling; yet in a way he frightened her. She didn't know what to say to such a man. He made Marc Garnier seem like a gauche college boy, stubbornly trying to organize a petting party. But Ashley

Moore was remote—egotistical, in his way; an enigma, but a craftsman—she had seen his newspaper-cuttings, she knew that he was already famous and soon everybody would hail him as the composer of *Summer Song*. She felt elated and proud because he had told her all about his new work. The story had captured her imagination.

"I think it sounds absolutely fascinating!" she exclaimed. "Something new and appealing. There's never been an opera about a girl who's a sort of symbolic snowbird on the wing, and who will be the victim of man's heartlessness."

"You don't think it sounds too corny?"

"Corny——" she repeated the word, stammering. "No, I don't think so. It will be lovely and delicate and that theme you played to me is so right, except——"

"Except what?" he caught on to her last word.

Rowan bit her lip, her agonizing shyness convulsing her again. "Oh, I mustn't criticize *you*—your work——"

"For heaven's sake, I've *asked* for your criticism," he broke in angrily.

She could see that she had irritated him, which fact made her even more nervous. Then, as she kept silent, Ashley softened his manner.

"Come along, Rowan—no nonsense. We're friends—aren't we? And I've asked you to criticize. *You're* very musical, and I've written a song. Why did you say that you liked it all *except*—except what?"

Rowan summoned up her courage, went back to the piano and rather surprisingly, he thought, picked out the tune he had just played for her. When she came to the last phrase, she said:

"I thought *that* rather spoilt it. I wanted it to go on and on, not end so abruptly."

"On and on," he repeated. "Y-e-es! You'd like a repetition of that phrase, where the Snowbird sings:

> *"Like a wounded bird in pain*
> *I fall, I fall, I shall not fly again. . . ."*

He sat down on the long stool at Rowan's side. His strong fingers beat out the repeated rhythm, while he hummed the line:

> *"Not fly again, not fly again, not fly again."*

It ended on a soft melancholy note—like a dying cry. Then he turned to Rowan his eyes positively shining.

73

"By jiminy, you're right, *absolutely right*. It repeats the tragedy of rejected love. It *must* be repetitive—it will sound like the fading beat of a heart, struggling against death. You were right, Rowan, my child!"

"Oh!" she said breathlessly, her spirits lifting to his praise.

"It is one of Simon's most attractive lyrics, and although it only comes at the end of the second act, I've started on it," he said. "*Listen.*"

He played the song through again. When he came to the last stanza, she shyly sang it, leaning over his shoulder to peep at the writing on the foolscap.

> *"I fall, I fall, I shall not fly again."*

She had a very small but sweet, high voice. She had never sung except in school concerts, and for Mrs. Gray and their friends. It was nothing of a voice in Ashley's estimation, yet he received the impression, the illustration that he needed to inspire him in this moment, to help him manœuvre the composition. He was delighted. And somehow that very small childish voice reiterating the tragic stanza, "*I fall, I fall, I shall not fly again*," was infinitely pathetic.

"You were dead right!" he said yet again, and swung round to face her. There was no room in his mind for any memory of Frances now. He was exhilarated by the discovery that Rowan had helped him make, and which he had needed to perfect his day's work.

"Just a little thing, an outsider's impression, and it all falls into position. It's absolutely splendid. There won't be a dry eye in the house, if I work on those lines," he said exultingly.

His enthusiasm fired her. Her eyes began to glow.

"Oh, I'm so glad I helped."

"Of *course* you did."

"I think it will be lovely, but terribly sad."

"Many operas are sad. Some of the most famous. Some are almost unbearably tragic—like *The Consul.*"

"I like the whole idea of your Snowbird," said Rowan. "Only I know I'm going to wish she didn't have to be wounded. You *will* make her fly again, won't you?"

Ashley laughed and lit another cigarette from the stub of his old one.

"It'll be too like honey and treacle if I do. No, my dear, I want *this* to be my tragic opera. Besides, in Simon's libretto, she finally dies of her wounds."

"Oh!"

The cry came from Rowan as though she, herself, had been suddenly wounded.

Looking at her through his narrowed lids, Ashley thought, as he had thought in the train, of the curious way in which at times this young girl incarnated the Snowbird for him. He was experienced with women—a man who had led his life hard since he was twenty—and he could not be unaware that Rowan Gray was, emotionally, surprisingly immature. There was nothing exciting about her; yet her extreme innocence and simplicity were in themselves touching, even charming attributes.

He could see how easily *she* could be wounded. Quite naturally then, sprang to his masculine mind the thought:

'It might be interesting to teach this child more about life—and love.'

But he immediately discarded such a thought as being unworthy. Women like Fran Cottar could take care of themselves; *not this one*. Gently he said:

"Well, Rowan, don't feel too unhappy about the fate of my Snowbird. The operetta isn't finished yet."

He walked to the window, and added in a dreamy voice:

"I think the shooting must take place on a night like this—the crystalline stars in the sky, the moon touching those mountain-tops, and my Snowbird lying in the snow, struggling to pick herself up while the sound of the music and singing and laughter comes through the window. There will be a chorus drowning her voice, until those words: '*I shall not fly again.*' "

Rowan felt a sudden and inexplicable pain in her heart, in her mind. She shivered.

"Don't," she whispered.

He laughed, came back and linked his arm in hers in a friendly way.

"Little Rowan wants it all treacle and honey, and let's live happily ever after, does she?"

Her cheeks grew fiery red. She pushed him away.

"I think you're horrid. Why must there be brutality and suffering and pain in this wonderful world?"

"My dear," he laughed. "That's how life is made up and those who haven't learned to suffer, cannot really enjoy it. Listen to your Uncle Ash," he added, laughing again.

"Well, I'm sure it will be a success," she said a trifle stuffily.

"It's hardly begun—at the moment it's just an *idea*—at least so far as the music is concerned. And Simon's got quite a bit more to put in on the libretto."

"Where did you both get the idea?" she asked suddenly.

Ashley shrugged his shoulders.

"When I was last in Switzerland—I seemed always to see the analogy between these young skiers flying as it were, through the air, down from the snow peaks, and the birds that fly down in much the same way. I was taken by the idea of the purity of the girl's intent; of her absolute love for this man, then of her inability to fly farther, because of his cruelty. It's all 'my-eye', of course—nothing realistic about it. Now *Summer Song* is realistic, but I found myself getting sick of portraying modern life—the modern girl—equality of the sexes—nothing hidden—and so on—the whole bag of tricks."

"Don't you *believe* in modern woman's purity of intent then?" she asked, disconcerting him somewhat by the question.

"Her intent towards man?" he counter-questioned.

"Yes. Don't you think there *is* such a thing as real and selfless love?"

"No," he said in a harsh voice which shocked her.

"Oh!" she stammered the word.

"The whole thing will be symbolic—poetic licence. In other words, an operetta based on a fantasy, just as the *Swan Lake* is pure fantasy," he said. "If I were going to write more realistic stuff, I'd make it that the poor *chap* was wounded by the faithless woman and left to die in the snow."

"How frightfully cynical you are," exclaimed Rowan.

He laughed.

"What about that drink I haven't offered you?"

"No thanks, I must get back. I've been here nearly an hour."

"How wicked!" said Ashley.

"You do like to tease me," she said.

"You're really rather teasable," he grinned at her. "Come on—stay awhile—play me some more Chopin and let's pretend that all women are angels and all men brutes."

She had to laugh but shook her head and reached for her coat. He helped her into it. As he did so his hand came in contact with her swinging tail of hair. It was as soft, as silky, he thought, as a baby's. She *was* a child; but he liked her and she had done much more for him than she would ever know by that suggestion she had made for the finale of the Snowbird's song.

"Will you come again soon and help me write more of my

operetta?" he asked gaily as she moved towards the door, pulling on her woolly gloves.

She felt her heart leap with a strange pleasure at the invitation, but she did not immediately accept it. It had been a wonderful hour of music and ideas shared with a clever, attractive man—the sort of hour she had never spent in her life before. Secretly she longed to repeat it; but there remained the spoiling memory of Mrs. Cottar. And now, suddenly, without answering his question, Rowan said:

"Is your friend who wrote the libretto coming out here?"

Ashley's face darkened. Rowan had unconsciously revived his own memories of Fran and extinguished for him the light of musical inspiration for today—anyhow.

"I wouldn't know," he said abruptly.

"Mrs. Cottar is staying a fortnight or more—she's booked at The Valdana, as you know."

"I think you'll find she won't stay so long," said Ashley in a dry tone.

"Good night and thank you for the music," said Rowan.

Her heart seemed to flutter when he took her hand and kissed it in Continental fashion. An overpowering dominant attraction emanated from him. She could not define it—but it was there, assailing her senses. His strong personality, his genius, his brown rugged face, his queer light grey eyes which were very handsome; at times so kindly and at others so sardonic. Her shyness returned and she hastily pulled her hand away and darted to the front door.

"See you at the hotel," he called after her, "and we'll make another date for you to come up here."

"All right," she called back. She caught her breath as the icy air cut across her face. The temperature was well below zero now that night had fallen. Her boots crunched in the snow. The lights from the chalet windows shed an orange glow on the whiteness, guiding her down the path leading on to the road.

His voice followed her:

"Mind how you go! It's damned slippery."

"Okay—good night!" she called back.

Then the door was shut. She went on alone, moving cautiously as he had advised, down to the main road towards The Valdana.

She did not know whether she was glad or sorry that she had paid that call at l'Étoile. In a way she had got to know Ashley quite well—and she had learnt quite a lot about him. He had behaved irreproachably towards her. There had been none of the

77

nonsense that Marc tried on so blatantly. She liked Ashley—she trusted him—yet he *frightened* her. He was too worldly, too cynical. She believed he had really meant it when he had said that he used poetic licence when he stressed the defencelessness of his heroine. He obviously thought women more cruel, more destructive than men. And now suddenly for the first time for a whole week she thought of her own mother. How cruel *she* had been! Yes—she had deserted her little baby. She had gone to her marriage with Edward Ripsdale, as a living lie. What would Ashley say if he knew *that* story?

She suddenly realized that she hadn't told Ashley anything about herself at all.

9

ROWAN was going through a pile of correspondence—for once with the electric light on in her office, because the morning was so dark—when Marc Garnier came through the double doors leading into the vestibule of The Valdana.

His ski-suit and boots were wet with the snow which he had just tried to brush off with a broom kept for that purpose. It was snowing heavily, and had been so for two whole days.

Gloomily, young Marc drew off his gloves as he walked towards Rowan.

"What weather!" he grumbled. "As you say in English, *filthee!*"

She gave him a nod and a faint smile. She was always afraid to encourage Marc, and she always dreaded Saturday mornings when he came up from Sierre. He was such a nuisance. He had been lately trying to manœuvre business affairs here with his Uncle Paul so that he went over the accounts in *her* office. She could scarcely get on with answering correspondence in French as well as in English, with Marc trying to make love to her all the time!

She glanced at his red round face and wondered what Mummy would have thought of such a nephew. He was irrepressible. Sometimes one could not help liking him—when he played the clown and was naïve and genial. But he could be too bold—and his apparently serious intentions towards Rowan were as big a worry to her as to his own mother.

"Now sit down and get on with your own work and leave me in peace," said Rowan.

Marc drew a sigh, running his fingers through his fair wet curls. She was infinitely desirable to him—this cool prim young English girl with her expressive eyes—sitting so demurely at her desk. He could not believe that he was really a failure with her. Even now, as he passed her chair, he touched the back of her neck with his hand; whereupon she turned on him so angrily that he had to apologize. He sat down at his own desk.

"My parents wish me to take you home to tea next Sunday," he muttered, reluctantly opening his ledger.

Rowan liked Mummy's brother enormously and she respected Aunt Elise. She enjoyed going to visit Uncle Jean and talking to him about Mummy. She had heard so much of the young Marie's sweetness and goodness. Jean seemed to have been really attached to her. Fortunately Rowan had managed so far to avoid discussion of Mummy's 'marriage' and the inexplicable desertion of her own people and country. She said that she 'knew nothing' about it and Uncle Jean, seeing that it distressed Rowan, refrained from further questioning.

But Rowan did not want to go down to Sierre on Sunday and have to put up with Marc. It was bad enough having to deal with him up here.

"I'll let Uncle Jean know if I can get off," she said coldly.

She gazed through the doorway at the reception bureau where Henri was attempting to console disappointed guests who could not get out to ski. Everybody seemed to be wandering about trying to amuse themselves, reading books and papers, or playing cards. Only the more intrepid put on their waterproofs and trudged to the village shops through the blizzard. Rowan could hear Henri saying:

"The barometer is rising, *madame*, yes—I am sure the sun will come out this afternoon—then you will see how lovely Crans will be."

It was always so gay and busy at The Valdana—Rowan had grown to love her work. It was now three weeks since she had come out here and she looked like retaining her agreeable job for yet a further month. The unfortunate Suzanne had developed complications and would not be allowed back at The Valdana until the end of February. The Garniers seemed pleased with their hard-working reliable 'temporary', so here she would stay. These last few days had not been as busy as usual. Those who had come for Christmas or the New Year had gone, but after this fresh fall of snow, many more would be coming.

The applications for rooms continued to roll in. Rowan had already fixed Mrs. Simon Cottar up with a single room and Frances had moved in. Mrs. Cottar paid little attention to the young Receptionist but Rowan, fascinated, used to watch her walk through the vestibule or into the lounge and dining-room and think how beautiful, how elegant, yet how curiously unattractive she was. She was such a supreme egotist. But she had already collected a few male admirers including the Herr Doktor—a tall, fair, handsome German who was staying at The Valdana alone. It amused Rowan to note all the little flirtations, here—'pairings off'. The Herr Doktor was a great one for women and a superb dancer. Every evening they danced in the Bar. Not that Mrs. Cottar seemed to be very amused by her German admirer. She had only one idea in her head and Rowan knew well what it was. Whenever Ashley Moore entered the hotel, Frances Cottar was waiting for him. Her penchant for him was almost blatantly obvious. What he felt about her was less obvious—to Rowan, anyhow. She only saw the pair from afar. She had certainly never seen them dance together, although Ashley occasionally danced with other women in the hotel. But Rowan had seen him sitting up at the Bar beside Frances. Of course he could not altogether avoid her as she was staying in the hotel, and he made a habit of coming up in the evenings. But Rowan often wondered how he really felt about his friend's glamorous wife. *Was* there a real love affair going on? Or had Rowan's eyes deceived her that evening a week ago when she had seen that intimate embrace? She found herself wondering, frequently—hoping, curiously enough, that she had made a mistake.

She had not been back to l'Étoile, although once or twice when Ashley had dropped in, he had asked her to do so.

"I've finished *the* song, with a few minor alterations and I'd like you to hear it," he had said the day before yesterday. He had come in just before the snow-storm blew up, following an afternoon's ski-ing with Paul and Vittoria who were good friends of his.

Whenever Ashley entered the hotel and smiled or waved at her, Rowan experienced the sharp sweet pangs of awakening love. She was beginning to think of little else, save the temptation to go up there to the chalet when he next invited her. She was thinking of him even now while Marc tried to attract her attention, in between attempts to work.

80

Ashley did not usually come up to The Valdana at this hour—eleven o'clock in the morning. It was a surprise to see him, wet from the snow, as he walked up to the reception desk, pulling off his water-proof cap. He said good morning to Henri and beckoned to Rowan. She walked to the desk, the faintest touch of colour rising in her cheeks.

"*Bon jour*," he greeted her. "Heck of a poor day for ski-ing. Incidentally have you had any correspondence from a chap of my name—Moore—Laurence Moore?"

"Mr. Laurence Moore—yes. A letter from the Bahamas—Mr. Garnier was just talking to me about it."

"He's my uncle," said Ashley. "My very young uncle, who sometimes looks younger than I do," he laughed, "and he's just got himself married. He and his bride want a few weeks' ski-ing in Crans. They know I'm here. They sent Laurence's letter on to me from my flat. Uncle didn't know I had been loaned a chalet. He presumed I was staying here, in The Valdana. Of course they can share the chalet with me—they must. I've plenty of room. I wondered if you'd answered his inquiry, as he said he had written to you by the same mail."

"Oh, I'm glad you can take them," said Rowan, relieved. "We're so full, we just couldn't give them the suite they asked for."

Ashley divested himself of his snow-wet jacket and pulled down the thick black sweater he wore under it. Rowan thought he looked depressed.

"I had to ask them to stay," he said gloomily, "but it means my work will go to pot. Laury's all right but with a woman in the house——"

Rowan's eyes suddenly sparkled at him with a hint of mischief.

"You're too popular, Mr. Moore. All your lady friends seem to be pursuing you."

He knew that Rowan was alluding to that *other* woman and grimaced. He had still not managed to persuade Fran to 'toddle home'. She was the devil—absolutely determined to re-open the affair between them—well it had hardly been an 'affair' he thought —merely an hour or two's stupidity. But it had far-reaching repercussions. He could have cheerfully wrung Fran's pretty neck at times, and he'd even gone so far as to telephone Simon and suggest that *he* came out and joined Fran (it would be much safer if he did). But Simon had said:

"I don't think I will, old boy. As a matter of fact, Fran and I have had a bit of a dust-up and it might do her good to have a break away from me. I'll try and fly over next week to fetch her. Meanwhile look after her for me."

Ashley had rolled his eyes heavenwards as he put down the receiver.

Simon might not know it, but looking after Fran was a dangerous business. In despair—and rather than be singled out as Fran's boy-friend—Ashley was making himself pleasant to any of the girls who had a drink with him in the bar. There were several unattached females whom he knew would willingly join him in one of the usual 'holiday friendships'. Most bachelors found girlfriends in such places. And Fran was by no means the only unattached attractive woman in The Valdana. There was one charming Parisienne who came to Crans every winter, and whom Ashley found delightful; only as a comrade. He had met her here before. Brown-haired, golden-eyed, intelligent, but he really did not want to form any kind of sentimental attachment. He had come here to *work*. As he lit a cigarette, he grinned at Rowan.

"Can't you start a story in the hotel that I've got a wife and six children tucked away and that I'm not eligible," he said.

"Certainly if you want me to," said Rowan. "Tell me your children's names and ages so that I can talk about them."

Ashley pulled his ear, and closed one eye thoughtfully.

"Well, the eldest has long fair hair and a fawn's eyes and is called Rowan. I chose it because it's a very unusual name, and she's rather a dear little thing."

Rowan's cheeks were scarlet but she had to laugh.

"If that's meant to be *me*—I'm not anxious to start calling you 'Papa'."

"Why not, wouldn't I make a nice Sugar Daddy? You could croon '*O mein papa*' to me."

"You *are* absurd!"

It amused Ashley to watch her blush so furiously. Somehow his spirit felt quite refreshed after a chat with little Rowan.

"Now, look," he said. "No refusals this time. Come up and hear my new composition this evening."

Her heart beat violently. His treatment of her was light, airy, innocuous and yet he had this power to cause an earthquake tremor in her young soul.

"I don't think I can," she said. "I'm too busy, honestly."

"Tomorrow's Sunday—you get off on Sunday afternoons and evenings. Come tomorrow, after tea."

She chewed her lower lip nervously and dug the point of her pen into the palm of her hand, making a silly blue stain. She knew perfectly well that she ought to go down to Sierre and have tea with *Oncle* Jean and *Tante* Elise; and that probably Marc was straining his ears to hear every word she was saying to Mr. Moore. It was all so difficult. But human nature being as it is, she succumbed to temptation.

"All right. I'll come up on Sunday," she said.

Ashley felt relieved. Not only did he want Rowan to hear the end of the song that she had inspired, but it would put paid to any hopes that Fran entertained of getting him up on the heights of Bella Lui where the snows were so splendid and the ski-ing would be so good if the weather changed for the better. One could certainly have delightful picnics up there, sitting outside the ski-hut in the sun, eating and drinking, before taking the downhill route.

"You *must* take me with you—you can't be so beastly to me," Fran said.

But now he could tell her that he had to do a special job with 'a collaborator'. He felt hard—hard as nails about Fran—and didn't mind admitting it. He wasn't very proud of the few kisses she had seduced him into taking from the wife of his best friend.

He took another look at his new 'collaborator'. He felt rather tenderly towards Rowan.

"I really think I will let you call me *Poppa*," he said.

"Mr. Moore—I've got a job to do," she said severely.

"Miss Gray, I will retire," he said with a bow. "My apologies. See you on Sunday, if not tonight and every night in the bar where I waste my youth drinking fabulously expensive whiskies."

She said:

"I'll cable to Mr. Moore then, because they're leaving Nassau tonight, aren't they? The letter said that Mr. Laurence was going to join you here, and that if there wasn't a room in The Valdana we were to get them one somewhere else."

"Yes, send a cable, and say you know they'll be staying with me. I doubt if they'll get to Crans before Monday, anyhow."

Ashley was about to move off, when he looked back at Rowan.

"You believe in romance, don't you? Well, you'll be seeing a real live one soon. My fond uncle has been a confirmed bachelor all his life (he is now only forty) and he's just fallen in love with this beautiful creature whom he met in Florida—an English widow with half a million. Clever Uncle Laury, always fond of money—and married to half a million."

"You are horrid," said Rowan, "how do you know he didn't really fall in love with *her*?"

"I don't know. I can only guess. I look forward to meeting the lady who got my hard-hearted uncle. One might almost say that *he* has been shot on the wing and 'will not *fly again*'."

He walked off, laughing. Rowan returned to her desk to send the cable to Mr. Laurence Moore. Really, she thought, she believed that a lot of this business from Ashley was a pose, that he wasn't nearly as harsh about life and love as he pretended to be. Nor as cynical about women. How could he be, when he was capable of writing such beautiful, stirring music, and of creating an operetta like *The Snowbird* which was the very opposite of his so-called outlook on life? It was full of deep emotion and the main theme was the tragedy of a girl deserted by her lover—yet still loving him.

Marc whispered to her in a fierce undertone:

"*Alors*—you have been making a *rendez-vous* with that Englishman. It is for *him* that you neglect me."

"Oh, get on with your work, Marc, and leave me alone," she snapped.

"He is no good," Marc continued to whisper. "Everybody in the hotel says that this Madame Cottar who is like a mannequin, is his *maîtresse*."

Rowan sprang to her feet. She looked at Marc with stormy eyes.

"They have absolutely no right to say such a thing and I detest scandal," she exclaimed.

And without listening any further to Marc, she called the page boy to take the cable to the *poste* and went up to her own room to fetch a handkerchief. She had a suspicion of a cold this morning. Colds and little fevers were not unusual out here where the changes in temperature were so sudden and drastic.

Once again she had a picture in her mind of Ashley and Fran together. The word '*maîtresse*' was horrible, thought Rowan, and somehow it was also horrible to her to have to reflect upon that piece of scandal as related by Marc. Possibly it was all jealousy on his part and there was not a word of truth in it, but she wished he hadn't said it.

"But it might be true," she said aloud. She stood at her window, looking across the balcony at the grey-black clouds that were rolling across the mountains so magnificently. The snow-flakes whirled against the panes obliterating the usually brilliant scene. She felt suddenly full of foreboding.

"I won't go to the chalet on Sunday," she said through her teeth. "I don't think I altogether trust Ashley."

But when Sunday came she knew that she *must* go. She could not keep away.

10

THE blizzard continued to rage for another twenty-four hours. Late on Saturday morning it stopped. The clouds suddenly rolled away revealing an infinity of heavenly blue sky. A brilliant sun poured down upon Crans like a benediction. Rowan had never seen anything so beautiful. The whole village was deep in snow except for the main roads on which men had been busy with their ploughs, working day and night to clear the thoroughfares between Crans and Montana. It looked to Rowan for all the world, like the picture-postcards which she had so often seen in England. Crans resembled a child's toy village, with its little chalets, so symmetrical, so neat, the deep snow like carved sugar on the roof-tops. Thousands and thousands of pine trees up the mountainside glittered in the sparkling light. It made her blink this morning, and reach for dark glasses.

Within an hour Crans had woken up. Crowds of young skiers poured out of the hotels, and with their skis over their shoulders moved towards the *téléférique* and queued for the ski-lift up to Bella Lui and Cry d'Err. There was much movement down at the Suisse École de Ski; children swarmed out with their toboggans, frustrated players hurried to the curling rink. Once again music filled the air. The barometer was high and it was going to be a wonderful day for *le sport*.

Everybody's spirits seemed to rise with the temperature. Rowan, too, felt happy when she woke up on that Sunday morning to yet another radiant golden day. She had had a long letter from Ann Jenkins, with all the home news. She had also managed to make some sort of peace with Marc by promising that she would go out with him today if he would behave as a *friend* and no more. He had arranged to take her on to the nursery slopes and give her another ski-lesson, after lunch. The outlook was altogether brighter.

As soon as Rowan got down to the office, Ashley telephoned to her:

"Hortense tells me that Mrs. Cottar has already phoned twice, trying to speak to me, and was told I was still asleep. I'm hard at work, Rowan, and I think I've found a superb theme for my hero. I *don't want* to be disturbed. If Mrs. Cottar asks to be put through to me again, and you or Henri take the call, for lord's sake say my line is down."

Rowan was only too pleased to say 'yes'. But later, after Mrs. Cottar had been told about the 'breakdown' she came down to the reception-bureau and spoke to Rowan with obvious annoyance and suspicion.

"*Why* can't you get through?" she demanded.

"The line is down," Rowan lied again for Ashley's benefit.

"How long do they take to mend wires in this country?"

"I'm afraid I don't know," said Rowan.

At this moment an unfortunate thing occurred. Little Mme Garnier, passing by the desk, called out to Rowan:

"You are going up to l'Étoile to have music with Mr. Moore after tea—didn't he tell me? Well, Paul has the special polish Mr. Moore wanted for his skis. Will you ask me for the tin before you go?"

"Certainly, *madame*," said Rowan.

She hardly dared look at Frances Cottar. When she did so, she saw that the older girl's face was a mask of rage. The green eyes sparkled with jealousy—*just* like a cat's, Rowan reflected. Oh, surely, Ashley Moore *could not* love this woman? If he did, he had a funny way of showing it; he seemed anxious to get away from her.

Then from Fran, in a voice as cold as Mont Blanc itself:

"So you have been invited to tea with Ashley?"

"A-after t-tea," stammered Rowan, wishing that her cheeks did not always turn such a tell-tale colour, and that she need not be made to feel so young and silly in front of the sophisticated Mrs. Cottar.

"I was asked, too," said Fran, "but I refused because, you know, Ashley is working desperately hard on the new operetta. Of course I am so used to his ways. My husband is just the same, and they hate being disturbed. Ash is very hospitable but I think one ought to leave him alone while he is in the mood to work—don't you?"

Rowan felt a swift resentment which she was too polite to show. She said:

86

"If Mr. Moore is in the middle of work, I'll naturally just leave the polish, and go."

"Shall *I* drop it in for you, this morning?" asked Frances.

For an instant Rowan was flummoxed. But she had a spirit that could assert itself very definitely at times, and she felt a sudden active hatred of Frances Cottar; a desire for once to be the victor instead of the vanquished. Looking down at some papers which she was gathering together on Henri's blotter, she said:

"I don't think *madame* has the tin ready yet, thank you, Mrs. Cottar. Anyhow I'll take it to Mr. Moore later; I said I would."

Frances, in her turn felt frustrated, and a seething bitter dislike of this insignificant young girl who was trying to appropriate Ashley. She turned away without a word. As she left the hotel, she stared through her dark glasses up in the direction of l'Étoile. She felt driven almost to madness. To make Ashley nice to her again—ready to 'play' if nothing more—was fast becoming an obsession, threatening to destroy her reason. She gave scarcely a thought to the husband who had for so long tried to please her and satisfy her every whim. *She wanted Ashley.* To be turned down by him—avoided—put aside in favour of a girl like Rowan Gray, roused all that was worst in her. She had no doubt whatsoever that Ashley was not seriously interested in Rowan, but he had invited her to his house, and he refused even to speak to *her*, Fran, over the phone. She knew perfectly well that his line was not out of order.

In blind anger, Frances contemplated doing something desperate—trying to force Ashley's hand. She would warn him that if he didn't change his tune she would write to Simon and say that Ashley was her lover. *That* would put the cat among the pigeons, she thought revengefully. As for Miss Rowan Gray—she would have another little talk with *her* quite soon, and make it clear that there was an intimate relationship between Ashley and herself. Whether true or not, Rowan would have to believe it.

Fran heard the hoot of a car-horn behind her. A big blue Mercédès-Benz with the Herr Doktor Ribbenfeldt, at the wheel, pulled up. The German stopped and opened the car door.

"Good morning. Isn't it *wunderschön*! Jump in and let us drink together a coffee in Montana," he said with an eager look at the tall chic English woman.

Fran did not want to go to Montana with him. On the other hand he fed her vanity and she had to admit that he was a better dancer than Ashley who had the usual preference Englishmen have for 'propping up the bar'. But her mind was smouldering, circling around l'Étoile as she drove with Ribbenfeldt into Montana.

It was a memorable Sunday for Rowan. The ski-ing with Marc went well. He behaved more reasonably and she was beginning to feel happier and more confident coming down the slopes. Very soon, Marc told her, she would be able to go higher up, and make a more difficult descent.

As the sun went down—casting a violent glow of orange-red colour upon the mountain peaks—Rowan bathed and changed for her visit to the chalet.

Somehow she had never felt more excited. She refused to dwell on the thought of Ashley's association with Mrs. Cottar. She only knew that she looked forward tremendously to spending an hour or two in Ashley's company and that she longed to hear his new composition.

She dressed more carefully than she had ever done in her life before; choosing a fine-pleated dark blue skirt with a tight-fitting jacket, and a white wool sports shirt with a collar which she fastened with a cameo brooch that had belonged to Mummy. She brushed her fair hair back smoothly and tied it loosely with a black ribbon, instead of pinning it into a bun as she did for the office.

Yesterday she had bought herself a pair of inexpensive white ear-rings, fashioned like edelweiss. She clipped these on, put on snow-boots, her camel's-hair coat and warm gloves, then slipped out of the hotel.

Hortense opened the door of Ashley's chalet cautiously, as though on the look-out for intruders, but she knew Mademoiselle Gray by sight now and at once let her in.

The next moment Rowan was there, where her heart told her she so much wanted to be. In the warmth of the big long room full of the fragrance of pine logs burning, of Ashley's cigarette smoke and the scent of white jonquils which were massed in a big china bowl on one of the tables. One standard lamp was already alight, close to the piano. Ashley sat poring over a sheet of music, a cigarette between his lips. He glanced up as Rowan came in and she would have sworn that he looked glad to see her.

"Hullo there! Come along in. Take off your coat and listen to this——" he said.

And that was all that he said, for the next moment he was playing to her; murmuring Simon Cottar's lyric. He had no particular

88

voice but could croon the words of the new song pleasantly enough.

Rowan, from the depths of an arm-chair, watched and listened. Ashley's hair was ruffled. He wore the old slacks and black sweater that she knew well. There was a half-filled glass of whisky and water and an ash-tray filled with cigarette stubs on top of the piano. Ashley at work! No graces, no nonsense, no thought for anything but his work; deep in it, with the supreme egotism of the real artist. Rowan had never come in contact with it before but she was beginning to know and, she believed, to understand him a little. And she could not help but be thrilled that he was playing for *her*. When he stopped and turned round to her, his grey brilliant eyes were half unsatisfied, half hopeful.

"Well—is it any good? Is it as good as '*I shall not fly again*'?"

"Better in some ways," she said shyly.

"You're dead right, my child. It *is* better. They won't hum it as they leave the theatre, which I hope they will do with the Snowbird theme, but it's a much more intellectual piece of work. The best I've written yet. I'm not sure I like *this* stanza. . . ." He turned to the piano and struck a few chords. "It wants altering, don't you think?"

"I think it's fine," said Rowan, "but I do wish Mr. Cottar's lyrics weren't so *upsetting*."

Ashley frowned at her.

"How—upsetting?"

"Well, I know the Snowbird is supposed to be a tragic figure but the man seems almost too brutal. He's so dominant—so pleased with himself because he has the Snowbird in the hollow of his hand!"

"Like me," said Ashley with his devil's grin. "I like women in the hollow of my hand."

"I don't believe you do at all."

He got up and took a sip of his whisky.

"But I *do*, and funnily enough it is poor old Simon—the one who writes the cruel words—who isn't like that. He's really the weak one with women—if you want to know the truth. Fran's got him in the hollow of *her* hand."

Rowan lowered her lashes, then handed a little parcel to Ashley.

"This is your special polish from Monsieur Paul. As a matter of fact Mrs. Cottar wanted to bring it to you this morning. She seemed to think I ought not to come up here and interrupt your work."

Ashley scowled.

"She can mind her own business and thank the lord you didn't let her come. Quite frankly I don't want to see her. We don't exactly get on—the beautiful Frances and I."

Rowan would not have believed it possible to feel such relief; her heart positively leapt.

"But Mrs. Cottar is so attractive——" she began.

"Don't let's talk of her," said Ashley abruptly. "Let's talk about *you*."

"No . . . about the Snowbird."

Now he smiled at her with that benevolence that he somehow felt towards Rowan.

"You're very sweet," he said. "And don't blush. You *are*—but I've been working on the Snowbird all day and I'm going to have a rest from it. I want to hear about you."

"There's nothing to hear."

"Now don't be too self-effacing." He flung himself into a chair opposite to her and ran his fingers through his untidy mop of hair, muttering: "It's time I got this cut. Do remind me to go to the barber's. I hate to look like a long-haired artist."

"It *is* a bit long," admitted Rowan, but she thought how strong and thick that hair was—how vital—like Ashley himself. He was tremendously strong, not only in physique but mentally. He gave her the impression that he would always be the master in any situation. She could almost believe that he had meant it when he said that he liked to have a woman in the hollow of his hand. Yet she hadn't cared much for that. She would not want Ashley to resemble the man in his operetta—the brute who could hurt women with callous disregard.

"I really *do* want to know more about you, Rowan," said Ashley suddenly. "I always seem to do all the talking, and you're such a reserved little thing. Someone told me in the hotel that you were half Swiss. Are you really a niece of Paul's cousin, Jean?"

Rowan's pulses jerked. She had been wondering when—if ever—Ashley would start inquiring into her family history. For a moment she did not answer but stared into the fire, chewing her lower lip. She felt nervous and hesitant. The tranquillity of mind which she had gained since her arrival in Crans vanished in a twinkling. The painful memories roused by Ashley's innocent question reduced her to the old Rowan—the unhappy girl who had read that all-revealing diary after the death of the woman she had thought her mother. While she struggled with her feelings,

Ashley looked at the bent young head. He was not an insensitive young man and he felt suddenly that he had intruded. He apologized.

"Don't think me idly inquisitive or impertinent—I only wanted to know about you, honey," he said.

His charm, which he could exert at will, warmed and recreated her in a strange way. The word 'honey' fell so pleasantly on her ears. And suddenly there rushed across her a great wave of longing to tell Ashley her story.

She said:

"You aren't at all impertinent. It's nice of you to be interested. And I'd like to tell you, because you're an artist with an inquiring mind. You understand nature, and humanity interests you, doesn't it?"

"Of course," he nodded.

"I'm not Swiss," she blurted out. "I'm no blood relation of the Garniers at all."

Ashley, who had been only mildly curious, now became interested. Had he misjudged the little mouse? Was there a real story behind that cool nun-like exterior?

She turned and raised the large eyes which he had likened in his mind to those of a gazelle—so deep, so timid, so tender, they were.

"Don't tell me if you don't want to," he said abruptly. "But we are friends, you know."

"Thank you—I feel we are——" she stammered.

"Have things not always been too easy for you?"

"Yes—up to a few months ago—much too easy. I lived a sort of hermit's existence, very much protected and loved—with my—with my adoptive mother."

"Adoptive? Don't tell me you are a Little Orphan Annie out of an Adoption Home?" he asked with a gay yet kindly laugh, trying in his man's way, to make light of her troubles and so put her at her ease. But there was no laughter in the young girl's large eyes as she continued:

"Yes, I was adopted, but not out of a Home. And I only found out the facts after my—after Mummy's funeral. You'll think it rather melodramatic—perhaps."

Ashley rose and poured himself out a weak whisky. He never drank strong ones. He was against heavy drinking—more because he wanted a cool clear brain for his work than on any moral grounds. Let other men do as they like, was his motto.

He returned with the glass and stood looking down at Rowan.

"You intrigue me," he said. "Carry on. You can be quite sure that what you say will be kept in strict confidence."

"Thank you," repeated Rowan. "Well, I *would* like to tell you about it. My friends, the Jenkins (our neighbours), who took me in after Mummy died are the the only people in the world who know. They think I ought to try and forget it all. And out here in the mountains I *have* found some sort of peace. I'm not nearly as nervy and unhappy as I was when I first found out, but it does haunt me. I just can't get over what my—my own mother did, and what she *was*."

Ashley sat down and said:

"Get it off your mind, sweetie. It'll do you good. And then Uncle Ash will give you his advice. I think things are better for not being locked up in a person's mind. Tell me your story. You needn't mention any names, or give anybody away."

"I won't," said Rowan. "I'd rather not."

So Ashley listened attentively while Rowan unfolded the history from start to finish, just as she had read it in 'Mary Gray's' diary. But she spoke of the Lakers only as Sir Charles and Lady X. And of 'Vivien' as 'my mother' (though finding it difficult to use that name in relation to the unknown woman who had given her birth). She gave Ashley an exalted picture of the saint-like, Swiss nursery-governess who had borne the brunt of the whole affair.

When the tale was ended Ashley saw that Rowan looked quite pale and drawn. Her fingers were shaking. He had been entranced by the drama, and was interested to see how strongly she reacted to the telling of it. Easy now to believe that Rowan, like the Snowbird of his operetta, had a deep capacity for suffering— and for loving, too.

"My dear," he said as she sat silent, "thank you for telling me. But really—you must not let it upset you quite so badly. It all happened a long time ago, you know, and you're a big girl now."

She tried to laugh with him.

"Oh yes—it all happened nineteen years ago, but it was such a shock to me."

"Naturally."

"I hated learning that I wasn't Mummy's daughter but had been brought into the world by such a hateful girl."

"Well, as I see it," said Ashley, "your mamma was only a youngster herself when it all took place. She was carried away by infatuation. Of course it's right and proper that you should have a strong sense of morality, and feel it was all wrong. And naturally if she'd had a good strong character, and a sense of honesty, it wouldn't have happened. What you really dislike is the fact that she cast *you* off so callously, isn't it?"

"Yes, I think it was terrible," said Rowan, her cheeks reddening, "it was so *callous.*"

"My dear child, don't be too hypercritical. No very great crime was committed. Thousands of young girls make runaway marriages of the kind that she did, and thousands get rid of their babies—and get divorced. It may all seem rather sordid to you, because you are an idealist, but I think you are inclined to over-dramatize the whole affair, and allow your feelings to run away with you—if I may say so!"

He grinned at her suddenly in that boyish way that made him look so much younger than his years and added:

"Now Uncle Ash is really delivering a homily. Just because *you* may have a strong will, dear Rowan, and a frank nature, you shouldn't be too hard on girls like your mamma who was of weaker fibre. You must learn to be tolerant. I don't advocate that *you* should shed your high principles, but try not to become too smug—or too censorious."

Her eyes flashed at him in dismay.

"Oh, I don't want to be *smug*. And it isn't that I don't understand that my—my mother fell in love with the chauffeur, or that she got married secretly, under age like that. I understood *that* part. It was romantic and rather sweet—even though it hurt her parents so much. *That* wasn't her crime. It was how she acted afterwards. My—my father must have been rather nice. The diary said that he was; that he had every wish to do the right thing and make amends. He was brave, too—he got decorated in the war—Mummy said nice things about him in the diary. But even she, who loved my mother so passionately, had to admit that my own mother acted with dreadful callousness. In a flash she got tired of both her lover and the whole affair. She had me against her will. *She never saw me*. She just wiped me off the face of the earth, then went and married some unfortunate man who thought she was an innocent young bride. I think it was hypocritical, and horrible."

Ashley shook his head. Dear life, he thought, how hard the very young and pure can be! How intolerant of human frailty. Yet there was something rather naïve and fresh about it, something very touching about the way Rowan felt. Her exaggerated emotions moved what Ashley called his cynic's heart. And he knew deep down that in some ways he, too, was still an idealist. He had started that way, until life and experience had knocked some of it out of him. But in the face of this young girl's attitude —indeed her whole personality—he could feel almost sorry that one could become so lax; regard such stories as Rowan had just told, as of little consequence. As for the 'farming out' of a child by the daughter of a titled couple in pre-war years—the mother's indifference—her willingness to deceive—all such things had happened many times before. They were unpleasant and regrettable. But it was rather refreshing to Ashley, who had met and talked with many women, young, middle-aged and old, to find *someone* left with these high principles—these shining standards. Involuntarily he leaned forward and put a hand on one of Rowan's slim drooping shoulders.

"You really are a poppet," he murmured.

She caught her breath.

"But Ashley—it *was* wrong of my mother—she couldn't have been a nice person, could she?"

"No—she was possibly a spoiled, selfish egotist, my dear, and there are heaps like her."

"Well, I don't want to feel that I am *her* daughter instead of Mummy's," said Rowan almost sullenly.

"I don't suppose you do. And learning the truth so suddenly after your adoptive mother's death was disagreeable and upsetting for you; but don't let it turn you into a 'psycho'."

Rowan really laughed now, some of the emotional weight lifting. She said:

"No, of course I won't. And thank you for all your help. But you can understand one *doesn't* much relish the thought of such a mother."

"No. I loved and respected my own mother very deeply. I was only a schoolboy when she died in an accident, and it hit me for six; young though I was."

"Oh, I'm so sorry, and I understand what *you* must have felt!" exclaimed Rowan with a swift deep look at him.

He caught that expression in her eyes and was slightly shaken by it. For the first time he felt the allure of her essential femininity. There was, he thought, a definite attraction in this shy, retiring young girl who was so emotionally 'tied up in knots'. He had the strangest longing to reach forward and take her in his arms and cradle her against his heart. She seemed to need love and understanding. Her very purity of soul, of mind, rendered her as lonely as those high mountain peaks out there covered perpetually by the untrodden snow.

She sighed:

"I don't want you to think me intolerant or priggish or anything, but I wish my mother had given some little thought to me."

"Perhaps she did," said Ashley, "who is to know?"

"Mummy knew. She never saw my mother again but she knew. My mother was heartless. I don't think she ever loved anybody in her life. My poor father was just a whim with her—then there was this nice man older than herself whom she married. He died and I expect by now she has married again. But I can't imagine it would ever be for real love. And *think*, Ashley, she never made the slightest attempt to see me. I stood between her and money and position and pleasure and oh—it's that side of the story that makes me feel so *ashamed* to belong to her."

"Honey, you don't belong to anybody but yourself," said Ashley, and slightly bored now, he got up, sat down again on the piano stool and began to play.

He thought Rowan had said enough. In a way he was an understanding young man. But it was no use for her to go on brooding. Without looking back at her, he added:

"I'm glad you've told me. Thanks, my dear, and I really feel I know you better now. You're a sweet thing and I'll never repeat a word to a living soul."

Rowan looked at the back of his rough bright chestnut head; at the hair that he said needed cutting. The studio was full of the sound of music. He was playing a tune which she did not recognize. He seemed to have drawn right away from her. She began to feel afraid that she had bored him by telling him about her mother and the past. She also felt an inexplicable longing for Ashley to be close to her again; to smile at her with those wise, grey, shining eyes of his. She didn't really understand half the things he said, yet he had grown to be the most important person in her life (if he but knew it, she thought). She sat mute, locking her fingers together in an agony of effort to regain her self-control.

After a few moments, Ashley swung round from the piano to speak to Rowan but the words died on his lips. He saw two huge tears glittering on Rowan's lashes, then slowly they rolled down her cheeks as though all the sorrows of the world had suddenly come upon her.

First he laughed. Then he grew serious. He leant forward, took both her hands and pulled her against him.

"Oh, my dear, my dear silly little sweet, what *are* you crying about?" he murmured, and the next moment, before he could restrain the impulse, he had gathered her right up in his arms and kissed her on the mouth.

11

Almost at once Ashley regretted that kiss for the response from Rowan's young, untried mouth was unexpectedly warm and sweet. Only for the fraction of an instant she hung back as though suspended between fear and rapture, then was all his—yielding, pliant in his arms, her eyes closed, her lips moving under the pressure of his.

He drew back gently. He was sorely tempted to repeat the kiss but knew that he must not do so. Already he had done too much. Little Rowan was as sensitive as those very piano keys when touched and it was he, the player who called the tune. It must not be. For one thing he did not want to become emotionally involved again, even though there was nothing really to keep him from making a little light and innocent love to Rowan Gray; they were both of them free agents. But he was not a marrying man— on that he had long since decided. He was only just beginning serious work. He did not want a wife or children to hamper him. One day, perhaps, but not now. Especially not now since he had seen the unhappiness of Simon—once the happiest of men—due to his marriage. And above all he did not intend to play around with a girl as immature as Rowan. She was much too nice. He felt really fond of her and for a moment he had felt a little more than that. But the moment passed.

He adopted a light bantering tone as he stood up and grinned down at her.

"All kissed and made better? No more tears?"

It was a hard task for Rowan to reply as lightly. It was the first kiss of passion any man had laid upon her lips. Utterly, utterly different from the innocuous attempts that boy, Alan, in Buckinghamshire, had made to kiss her good night. Different from anything in the world she had ever imagined. Yet *all* that she had imagined a kiss should be between a man and woman in love.

She was wholly in love with Ashley now—thrilled and enchanted, glowing from the first wild passion that he had evoked.

She could hardly breathe—or speak. But already Ashley had turned from the sight of her big shining eyes and resorted to the usual cigarette. He was chain-smoking and much too nervy these days, he thought, frowning. He had better take forty-eight hours off from this darned operetta, and stay on skis, out there in the snow This sort of thing—a firelit cosy interlude with a charming young girl who was a mere schoolgirl still—was a mistake.

"Sure you wouldn't like a drink, honey?" he asked.

She answered in a small voice, her hands clenched tightly so that her nails dug into her palms.

"No, thanks."

"Got any inspired ideas for me this evening?"

"No—I don't think I have."

He refused to look at her but sat again at his piano and began to play. He was not unaware that his kiss had disturbed Rowan. Damn it, he thought angrily, it had disturbed *him*, but there must be no more of it. He wanted to give Rowan a chance to put a rein on her too eagerly roused emotions. That was the worst of very reserved people—he reflected; summon a woman's deepest ego into the open and there was no knowing what might not come out of the depths. There was no doubt about it, Rowan was not a shallow person; on the contrary.

She was grateful for the back he turned to her. With trembling fingers she took a handkerchief out of her bag and glanced at the mirror in her compact. She saw a smear of pale rose rouge on one corner of her cheek and chin; that was where his lips had strayed from hers; lips still tingling—burning—hungry for another kiss. It was as though he had roused a torrent that must be stemmed at the source. She knew perfectly well that he did not want to kiss her again and that he did not love her. How ridiculous to think that he could; to suppose that he had kissed her for any other reason than to console her, as he would have done a weeping child.

But Rowan was child no longer. She was a woman, deeply and hopelessly in love with Ashley Moore. She had to summon all the pride in her nature to help her, to restrain her from going up and putting her arms about his neck, pressing her cheek against the warm bronze of his.

Oh, I love you—Ashley, I love you! That was what she wanted to say and did not.

He stopped playing, cigarette between his lips, and took a cursory glance at her. She spoke to him calmly.

"That was a nice tune, Ashley; what was it?"

"Not one of mine," he said. "Something I heard in a cabaret before I left London. 'Autumn Concerto'. Rather nostalgic."

"Very," she said.

Their eyes met. He scowled. When he got up he began to walk restlessly the length of the lounge, and back. 'Dammit,' he thought, 'I should never have kissed her, and I wish she would go away because I want to kiss her again, *and she wants me to*. It's the devil!'

Hadn't he learnt to keep his emotions leashed? Hadn't that episode with Fran been lesson enough?

Curiously enough it was of Frances Cottar that Rowan, too, was thinking that very moment. With a new bitterness, a sudden fierce jealousy, she remembered how she had come into this room and so obviously interrupted a passage of love between them. Remembered the awful scandal that Marc had repeated about Frances's relationship with Ashley. She ought not to allow herself to feel as she did, thought Rowan. She had obviously led far too sheltered a life with poor Mummy.

And now a new and rather dreadful thought struck Rowan. The blood of that sweet calm Swiss woman whom she had called 'Mummy' did not run in her veins. She was the child of Vivien Laker and of a hot-natured, wild young Cornishman. From him she had inherited her intense impulsive nature. She was only just beginning to *live*—to see what life could do to one—what passionate love could mean—and she was aghast by the impetus of it all.

"If you'll forgive me, I must get home——" she began.

Ashley stopped in front of her. She thought he looked flushed and cross. He said:

"My dear child, you've only just come."

"Have I?" she said helplessly, because she felt that she had been here a whole lifetime from which she had emerged a new being. She would never be the old Rowan again as long as she lived. She must not, *must not* love this man, she told herself in a frenzied way. She was bound to be hurt; she knew it. She must not try to see him alone again.

But now Ashley saw that the dark big eyes which had been all passion and promise and burning joy when she was in his arms, had grown blank and expressionless. He did not gauge, correctly, the full cyclonic force of the emotion he had awakened in her; nor realize that the kiss which had meant to comfort her so tenderly, had for ever destroyed her peace of mind. The kind streak that was never far below the surface with Ashley, rose again. He thought that she looked so forlorn and puzzled that he wanted to make her happy again. With a stupidity unusual for Ashley, he went up to her, put his arms around her and hugged her.

"Sweetie, you're angry because I kissed you just now? I'm sorry. You're such a darling. I'm really quite fond of you."

Once more she felt poised between heaven and earth and her heart leaped within her breast. But she stayed motionless, not speaking.

He said:

"Are we friends?"

Then her slight young body surrendered to his and she put up both her hands and touched his cheeks, and said in a strangled voice:

"Ashley—*Ashley!*"

The man was lost again for she was so singularly sweet. Again he kissed her, gently first and then with mounting passion. Now he heard her say the words that he dreaded even while they flattered and he would have given anything to undo the harm he had done, but knew it was too late. For she said:

"I love you. *I love you.*"

His arms dropped to his side. He ran his fingers through his hair and stepped back a pace.

"Darling, you don't at all. That's a lot of nonsense. And you just mustn't look so entrancingly at me if you don't want to be kissed. You're just very fond of Uncle Ash and he's going to go on being fond of you and giving you good advice. Now do sit down, honey, and relax and have a glass of sherry."

This time Rowan was flooded with shame for the words she had spoken and for her artless (shameless she called it) disclosure of the way she felt about this man. But her spirit gathered strength, and she had never been stronger than now when she put the back of her hand against her trembling lips and actually laughed.

"If that's the way uncles kiss their nieces, I'm shocked," she said. "Goodness! And how *dreadful* of me. I never thought I could behave so badly."

He turned from her, shutting his eyes. *He* was the one who had behaved badly, he thought, and the devil of it was that this child was beginning to get under his skin. But he wasn't going to let it go on. He was enormously grateful to her for her laughter and jesting.

"What about that sherry?" he began.

"Yes, all right," said Rowan defiantly. Still struggling with herself, and with the tears not far from her eyes, she took the glass he handed her and began to sip the first sherry she had ever drunk in her life. Again and again she used to refuse those poured out for her by Bill at Blackthorn Farm.

But she wanted to show Ashley that she didn't care—nothing would induce her again to let him see the effect his kisses had on her. She told herself that she must 'grow up'—she must not take a man like this one seriously. And above all she *must not* come here alone any more.

It was at this moment that they both heard the hoot of a car and sound of wheels with chains on scrunching over the snow.

"Someone's coming up the hill to l'Étoile," said Ashley.

Rowan reached for her coat.

"I'll go."

"Wait a minute," he said. He was half afraid that Fran had decided to drive up there and yet—surely not—on such a fine evening she would walk from The Valdana.

He went out of the room and left alone, Rowan dived into her bag for compact and comb; powdered her face, combed her hair back and once more attended to her lips. She could hardly recognize the face that looked back at her from that tiny mirror.

"You've put on ten years in ten minutes," she said with an hysterical little laugh.

Then she heard a car door slam and the sound of voices.

Ashley came back into the lounge, a cold current of the icy air blowing in from the front door. He said to Rowan:

"Stay a second, if you're not in a hurry. Meet my uncle. He and his wife have arrived—they got an earlier plane than they thought and landed from Paris at midday, so they caught that train we came by."

"Can I do anything? Shall I tell Hortense?"

"Yes, if you would, Rowan, tell the old girl to make it three for supper—she can give us one of her fabulous omelettes if she hasn't anything else. I don't suppose my new aunt-in-law will want to go out again tonight."

"Oh, yes, I will," said a high bell-like voice—a surprisingly young voice—from the doorway, "your new aunt is always ready to go out and have fun, as Laury will tell you."

Rowan was cornered. She had meant to escape. She felt in no mood to meet strangers. Deep in her heart all she wanted to do was to get away and be alone and think about *him*; remember all that had happened—all that must never happen again!

The Moores came in. Rowan saw a tall man wearing a tweed travelling coat and silk scarf—thin-faced, with grey eyes and bronze hair, not unlike Ashley but with more aquiline features, and a great many lines. A young-old face. He was impeccably dressed—very much a man of the world. With him was a woman whom Rowan would also describe as having a young-old face. She might be twenty—she might be forty. She was so beautifully made up that one could not tell what age she was. There did not seem to be a line on that small, heart-shaped face.

The first thing that struck Rowan was the size and colour of Mrs. Moore's eyes—violet blue with lashes heavily blackened. She wore a mink coat and a black velvet embroidered cap which all but hid a mass of auburn curls. (Later, Rowan was to know that that hair was naturally fair but had been tinted to this rose-gilt colour by a famous New York hairdresser.) She was breath-takingly pretty. Yet Rowan thought she looked a bit like Frances Cottar—too hard and artificial for real loveliness. And her lips were too thin. She was smiling gaily, first at her husband, then at Ashley and when she smiled she was dazzling, Rowan thought. Lucky Ashley, to have a new aunt who looked like that and *what* a mink! Then (as Mrs. Laurence Moore let her fabulous coat slide open) what a figure! She was tiny but perfectly in proportion, and exquisitely dressed.

Ashley came forward and made the introductions.

"Miss Rowan Gray—my Uncle Laurence—and my newly-made aunt," he said.

"How do you do, Miss Gray," said Laurence in a friendly way. He shook hands with Rowan.

Mrs. Laurence smiled and murmured something, with scarcely a look at Rowan. She was gazing through her long lashes at Ashley.

"My, *my*, what a handsome nephew I've acquired!" she said with a mock American accent. "But I'm not going to be called 'aunty'. . . . I don't look like an 'aunty' do I?"

"You certainly don't," he said admiringly, and thought with some amusement that old Laury had done well for himself, getting married to such a pretty woman, barely middled-aged, and with a fortune behind her. She looked entrancing. As she drew off her gloves, the huge solitaire diamond on her marriage finger sparkled like blue fire in the lights which Ashley had now turned full on.

Laurence said:

"Her real name doesn't suit her. I call her Petal."

"Charming," murmured Ashley, "but why?"

"My dear boy," said Laurence with a grin that made Rowan think he was very much like an older Ashley, "you've no imagination. Can't you see that she looks like a small rose and smells like one? She reminded me of rose petals as soon as I saw her, so Petal it has been ever since."

"Petal it shall remain," said Ashley, "and not mine aunt. After all *you* were never mine uncle, were you, Laury?"

Mrs. Moore took off her mink, threw it over the arm of the sofa, pulled off the velvet cap and patted her curls. She really was a picture, thought Rowan, and her skin had a rose-petal quality. She looked absurdly young to have been a widow. (Didn't Ashley say that the woman whom his uncle had married was thirty-eight?) She certainly didn't look anywhere near forty.

"Come and get warm, Petal," Ashley addressed himself to his uncle's wife, "and let me mix you a cocktail."

"I can't think of anything I'd like more," said Mrs. Moore in her high flute-like voice. "And I want to hear all about Laury's past. I know so little about this wonderful handsome husband of mine. He just arrived in Miami where we first met and we had a drink together at a party, and the next moment we were looking for what they call out there 'a preacher'—to marry us."

"I always thought Laury would fall with a *wham* from his high estate of confirmed bachelor, and rush for the matrimonial shackles," said Ashley, busy with glasses and bottles. "But I assure you he's never been serious about anybody else, as far as *I* know."

Little Mrs. Moore gave a huge sigh, seated herself on the arm of the sofa, showing slender girlish legs and the smallest feet Rowan had ever seen, in high-heeled shoes. She examined her face with a small gilt mirror that she had just taken from a big crocodile bag.

"Well, I'm going to tell *you* something, Ashley," she said. "Laury is *my* first real love, too. You know of course that I was married before, but it wasn't like this—I'm just *crazy* about Laury."

"Darling," murmured Laurence Moore, and came and stood beside her and put an arm around her, "you couldn't be more angelic!"

Rowan tried to cut in, feeling embarrassed and out of her depth.

"I—er—I really must go," she began.

'Petal' went on speaking as though she hadn't noticed that Rowan had made a remark.

"We've got so much to tell you, Ashley. Of course I've heard all about you and your successful operetta. We read about it in the English papers when we got over to France. Laury is terribly thrilled."

"Incidentally," put in Laurence Moore, taking two glasses from his nephew and handing one of them to his wife, "I was telling Petal when I first met her that I'm quite sure you and I once met her first husband. Do you remember that day we went to the Yacht Club at Cowes to lunch with that fellow Dick Esher who was at Eton with me? The year Eddy Ripsdale won the race?"

"Ripsdale," repeated Ashley, pushing a box of cigarettes towards Petal. "Oh, yes, Rip was a grand fellow. Yes, of course I remember. You were Mrs. Edward Ripsdale, weren't you, Petal?"

"M'mm," she nodded, sipping her cocktail. "That was me. But I want to forget about me as Vivien Ripsdale. In spite of Rip's fortune I wasn't really happy. I think he had lots and lots of love affairs and I've always longed for somebody just to love *me* only. . . ." She rolled her eyes theatrically and laughed. "I think that's how my Laury cares—just for little me; so I'm too divinely happy."

The pretty high-pitched voice that should have belonged to a little girl rather than to a woman nearly forty, stopped abruptly. For Ashley was no longer looking or listening. He had put down his glass and rushed to the doorway.

Petal turned. She was a little perturbed to see that the young girl to whom she had just been introduced stood swaying, a hand to her head.

As Ashley reached her, the girl clutched at him.

'Oh, dear,' thought Petal. 'How ghastly she looks! I hope she isn't going to faint. It would be horrid.'

But Rowan did not faint. Ashley pushed her into a chair and told her to put her head down on her lap.

"Maybe it's too hot in here for you. The Swiss central heating is terrific—plus the fire," he muttered.

Rowan made no answer. She was quite incapable of speech. For a moment, as she listened to the bell-like voice of Ashley's new aunt-by-marriage, she had felt the room revolving around her. She had been thunderstruck. Fascinated, she stared at Mrs. Moore's beautiful little face.

Before she became Laurence Moore's wife, this woman had been Mrs. Edward Ripsdale! *Vivien*.

The incredible truth hit Rowan like a physical blow, almost knocking her out.

'This is my mother,' she thought and kept thinking: *This is my mother*.

Ashley returned with a glass.

"Here—sip this—it's brandy."

She shook her head.

"No, thanks. I'm all right now."

Mr. Moore walked up to her. He had a pleasant, easy manner. He looked down at her with shrewd, kindly eyes. Until he had met and fallen in love with the extraordinarily beautiful, youthful widow of 'Rip' Ripsdale, Laurence had intended to remain unmarried. Not that he disliked women, but because he was something of an egotist, too busy getting what he wanted out of life to be anxious for matrimony. He found, frankly, that most women demanded more than they were prepared to give in return, and that the art treasures which he spent all his spare time in collecting, were more rewarding. But he had always liked children. He had a soft spot particularly for the small and helpless and it was that quality which redeemed his nature from coldness, and gave him an unexpected kindliness.

He was quite distressed to see how deathly white and ill young Miss Gray was looking.

"Are you all right now? Shall I take you out into the fresh air?"

She raised her eyes to his. She was trembling visibly.

"No, I am quite all right."

Vivien whispered to Ashley:

"What's the matter with her? Who is she?"

"Rather a sweet girl—great friend of mine," Ashley whispered back. "Just got a job behind the desk in The Valdana."

"Oh," said Vivien, and dismissed the thought of Rowan with supreme indifference.

Ashley walked up to Rowan again.

"If you're not feeling fit, I'll walk back to the hotel with you, my dear," he said.

But now the blood had rushed back to Rowan's head. Her cheeks were fiery. She got up and stood firmly on her feet, tying her scarf.

"Good gracious, no, I wouldn't dream of it. You must stay

with your family. I am as right as rain now. As you say—it was just the heat."

The woman who was now called 'Petal' volunteered to make herself gracious to 'the little girl from The Valdana'.

"You're not like me, Miss Gray. I shrivel up in the cold. I've lived for the last year in America and got used to real steam-heating. I *dread* England where so many houses one has to go to are so absolutely icy!"

Rowan tried to make some sort of reply to this but failed. With her hands clenched in her coat pockets she stared as though fascinated at the older woman. Stared with eyes that were full of a deep nameless emotion. *Her mother.* Oh, it couldn't be true, she thought; this small exquisite woman so obviously from the rarefied world of millionaires—*her mother*! Different, *so* different from Mummy. Dressed by the most expensive *couturière* . . . everything about her madly expensive, from her gorgeous mink coat to her fabulous diamond ring. And what of her fabulous face? The sort of face that artists have painted from all time, immortalizing the pure perfection of line; she had, in fact, the look of one of those angels in a Leonardo da Vinci; so classic was the outline. High cheekbones, large, lustrous eyes, pencilled brows, well-shaped head, with the shining halo of rose-tinted curls. She looked angelic enough, thought Rowan, in a high fever of excitement, for any man to want to pick her up and caress her—protect her from worry or trouble. Go on petting and spoiling her—at any cost.

That was what Edward Ripsdale had probably done. This childlike quality was what Laurence Moore had probably fallen for, too. *And what of my father?* Rather hysterically, Rowan asked herself the question. In this critical moment, every word of the diary seemed to flash through her mind. (Petal was so exactly like the Vivien that Mummy had described. The charmer, the heart-breaker whom one forgave all sins.) *She* had been forgiven hers. She had been sheltered and protected by her mother and governess when she was younger than Rowan was now (she must have been exquisite). And she had even been let off lightly by her discarded Cornish lover.

But what had she done to poor Harry Treloar? What had she not done to all these men whom she dazzled and misled with her Leonardo da Vinci beauty. The beauty which was a mask to hide a cold and ungenerous spirit—her vanity, her greed, her love of sensation, and for all the good things of life. She grabbed at them without ever paying an honest price for one of them.

'Dear me,' thought Petal Moore (one time Vivien Ripsdale—one time Vivien Laker), 'how this girl stares. She makes me feel quite uncomfortable!'

Ashley knew intuitively, that something had upset Rowan, but he did not know what. He, himself, was slightly put out by this sudden arrival of his uncle and the new wife. It was such an abrupt ending to his emotional hour with Rowan. But he thought now that it was time Rowan went home. It was all too awkward.

Petal continued to be 'nice' as she called it, to the young girl who was behaving so queerly.

"I expect I'll see you at The Valdana Hotel," she said, and gave Rowan her most dazzling smile.

To the young girl, it was as though she was being plunged into a fire. It consumed her. Fortunately, some latent sense of humour asserted itself and saved her from disaster.

'My own mother and she doesn't even know me,' she thought. 'In this case it certainly isn't "a wise Momma that knows her own child". It's just fantastic. There's no pull between us. No queer alchemy. No chord has been struck. Nineteen years ago she threw me out without ever having seen me, so why *should* she feel anything about me?'

And now, suddenly, the scorn in which Rowan had held her mother when she read that fatal diary, replaced the disturbing feelings that had naturally rent her when Mrs. Moore was first revealed to her. She despised Vivien for what she had done both to her young, unhappy lover and to her child. And for doing what she had done to Mummy. Brave, self-sacrificing Mummy who had taken *her* place and done *her* job in order that *she*, Rowan, should not suffer.

Of one thing, Rowan felt fiercely glad. Nobody could say that she resembled her mother; except perhaps in the small nose and the high cheek-bones. Other than that, Rowan was quite unlike the small, lovely creature who was now enjoying her *third* honeymoon. Pretending, thought Rowan, that Laurence was the only man she had ever loved. (She who was incapable of love!) Rowan preferred to believe herself like her father—she was so much taller than Vivien—and she had inherited the dark burning eyes of the Cornishman.

Maybe at one time her mother's hair had been Rowan's colour, but now with its fancy dye, it was quite different. Passionately, Rowan *wanted* to be different from 'Petal'.

She was in a daze as she walked out of the room—murmuring a vague good-bye, for politeness' sake, to the Laurence Moores.

In the hall, Ashley took one of her hands and gently kissed it.

"Thanks, my dear, for so much," he said in a low significant voice.

"There is nothing to thank me for," Rowan answered, lowering her head.

"You're still trembling. Are you ill, Rowan?"

For an instant she had a wild inclination to tell him the truth. But she refrained. She must never do that.

"I'm perfectly all right. Go back to your uncle and aunt," she whispered, and drew her cold hand away from his warm one.

"I'll be seeing you," he said. "We'll have some more music— Laury and his wife won't stay long. I think they want to go to Rome quite soon."

Rowan remained silent. Her heart-beats were fast and frantic. A short while ago she had been clasped in this man's arms and his lips had taught her all the meaning of love and life. But he did not love her, and now everything was spoilt. Spoilt not only by the fact that he did not love her but by this monstrous coincidence that had brought her own mother into focus; right into her life.

"Something *is* wrong—what on earth has hit you so suddenly?" she heard Ashley's voice.

"Nothing," she said in a strangled voice. "Please open the door for me."

He shrugged his shoulders. He could only suppose that this was a *crise de nerfs*. He really must be careful how he behaved in future with the girl. He tried for her sake to see her off on a more cheerful note. Giving her his schoolboy grin, he whispered:

"What do you think of Aunt Petal? Quite a heart-shaker, eh? Uncle Laury's got it badly. I must say she looks luscious—although she isn't my type. But she's rather like a beautiful jewel in a velvet box and I suppose Uncle Laury has added her to his collection. What do *you* think of her?"

Rowan moistened her dry lips with her tongue. Again, her sense of humour prevailed. She wondered what Ashley would have said if she had answered:

'*Your new aunt is my mother. You and I are* almost distant cousins. . . .'

Without answering his question she began to laugh hysterically.

Then when Ashley opened the front door to the night of frost and stars and a moon just coming up over the snow-covered peaks of the mountains—she slipped out. He heard her laughing as she walked away.

He could not really explain that laughter. But it disturbed him. Frowning, he shut the front door again, and shivering with sudden cold, returned to his guests.

12

ALL night in her little room on the top floor of the hotel, Rowan tried to sleep and found it almost impossible. She even began to wonder if her slight cold had developed into flu—she felt so feverish. First she was hot, then she was cold. Her mind went round in circles. She kept thinking about the amazing meeting with her mother. She could not have imagined that anything could be so disturbing. To the depths of her being she was upset.

"My mother," she kept murmuring the word, "*my own mother!*"

But she murmured it with resentment rather than love. All that was unforgiving and hard in her young puritan soul fought against any natural inclination to tell Mrs. Laurence Moore the truth and try to establish a relationship between them. She could not imagine that Petal would want the world to know that she had a nineteen-year-old daughter here in Crans, working as a receptionist. She could not picture herself being clasped in those slender girlish arms, nor imagine that flute-like voice calling her 'my darling child'. But the fact remained—Petal Moore *was* her mother. Nothing could wipe that out of Rowan's mind nor restore the balance of her emotions. She was right back where she had been when she first read the diary and learned the truth.

The early hours of the morning found her sitting in a dressing-gown, huddled on the edge of her bed. She had drawn back her curtains and pulled up the heavy shutters. She looked on that gorgeous vista of mountains and valley—a still white world, glittering in the moonlight, flanked by dark violet shadows that were sharply etched in contrast.

She thought of that beautiful chalet in which *they* were all sleeping. Beautiful Petal—*Vivien*—with the handsome charming husband whom she seemed to prefer to the others in her life. What did he think about her? Rowan wondered. No doubt that she looked much younger than she really was, for Petal could pass anywhere for a girl in her late twenties. No doubt he thought her as good and angelic as Edward Ripsdale had done. And Mummy had loved her, too, when she was a little girl, but Petal had not loved her own baby. She had never bothered whether it had lived or died.

"I don't know what to do," Rowan said aloud, hugged her breast with her crossed arms and shivered. Her face looked small and pale in the moonlight. "I suppose I ought to pack up and leave Crans."

Yet she did not want to go. There was Ashley up there in the chalet; Ashley, whose casual embrace, tender friendly attitude, had roused all the depths of passion in her. With her whole heart she wanted to stay, to be near *him*.

Since she had come to Switzerland, Rowan had changed much —learnt much. She felt a thousand years old, she told herself wryly. One thing was certain. She was a woman in love, and one who loved without hope.

She went back to her bed and tried in vain to sleep. When the dawn came, she was up again watching the first gold light suffuse the eastern sky. The stars faded. Soon the sun touched the mountain peaks with rose. It was incomparably beautiful. A scene Rowan had grown to love. But somehow this morning the thought of her mother's rose-gilt head and the very memory of Petal's beauty and seductive charm, filled the young girl with a kind of mingled horror and fascination.

She looked so ill when she went down to breakfast that the kindly Italian, Madame Garnier, remarked on it.

"You would like to go to bed? You are ill?" Vittoria asked with a sympathetic look at the English girl's wan face.

But Rowan shook her head. A passing chill. She preferred to do her work, she said.

So the new day began. Rowan tried to concentrate on her job but found her mind sadly distracted—all her thoughts circling around Ashley's chalet, and its new inmates. She began to feel haunted. She wondered what she could do to make things better —to restore her equilibrium.

She longed to share her fantastic secret with somebody, but knew that she must not. Above all, she must not tell Ashley who was now so very, very distantly related to her.

She dreaded the moment when the Moores would come down to The Valdana, which she knew they were sure to do before the day ended.

One by one the hotel guests came up to the bureau in their usual way to ask Henri or Rowan for papers and mail. The early birds went off to ski, taking their paper carrier-bags, containing a picnic lunch which they would enjoy up in the mountains. It was another day of dazzling sunshine. A gay note prevailed. When Henri wasn't there, Rowan had also to be bright, to say '*Bon jour*' to everybody, to remark gaily on the beauty of the day, to bid the skiers '*Bonne chance*' as they went off.

The Herr Doktor had found a new friend, Rowan noted—a glamorous brunette, an English actress newly arrived, recuperating from a nervous breakdown.

As he walked arm-in-arm with her through the lounge in his masterful rather arrogant way, Rowan watched the big blond German. She heard him say:

"We will go early to the *téléférique*, yes, my dear—and stay all day up at Cry d'Err with our lunch. We will see how many times down we can ski. *Wunderbar!*"

The brunette flicked long eyelashes and echoed the word: "*Wunderbar.*"

Rowan watched, and listened. She thought:

'They have no cares, no worries. They are lucky. But I feel as though I am wandering in a jungle; that at any moment something awful will happen to me.'

When Marc arrived she had no time for him. She was so irritable that he left her alone.

"You are certainly not agreeable with me, *ma petite cousine*," he grumbled.

She made no reply but the thought immediately sprang to her mind: *He is only a cousin by adoption—not as near to me really, as Ashley.*

She thought the morning would drive her mad. She decided to slip out after lunch, take her skis and go up in the *téléférique*, and try to come down alone; even if she fell repeatedly. She had learned the right way, she hoped, to fall without breaking a limb. She must get into the fresh air, have some exercise, make herself so physically tired that she would sleep later on. She must try to put things out of her mind.

Maybe, later, she would write and tell Ann and Bill what had happened. To them, alone, she could tell the truth. It would help her to share this heavy difficult secret with someone who already knew her history.

'Fate must be laughing,' she thought, 'to have arranged such an irony—to bring me and my mother face to face in Crans—the place to which I chose to come in order to get over my troubles!'

Inevitably, Frances Cottar walked in her languid way up to the desk, saw Rowan sitting in her office and beckoned to her.

"Good morning," Rowan said coldly, as she joined Frances.

"Well, did you go to the chalet after all? And interrupt the work?" Frances drawled, looking at Rowan through her cat's-eyes.

Rowan felt that she had enough on her mind without adding Frances and her spite and jealousy to the weight. She threw her fair young head back and answered with less timidity than usual:

"Yes, I did go and I *didn't* interrupt the work. Ashley says that I helped him. He played to me."

Frances did not see that this was merely bravado and that the young girl was, in fact, miserable and on edge. She glared at her.

"Good luck to you, my dear, but I know Ash so well—let me warn you. He flatters women because it amuses him, but it wouldn't do to take him seriously."

"It wouldn't do for me to take you seriously either, Mrs. Cottar," said the younger girl, trembling with a sudden anger mingled with despair.

Frances was taken aback. She had not expected the shy Miss Gray to stand up to her. She began to read more into Rowan's attitude than was there. Could it be possible, she wondered, that Ashley had gone mad and was starting an affair with Rowan?

'I shall never accept it if he does,' Frances told herself. 'I shall break up my marriage and accuse him to Simon. I shall hurt him. And I shall hurt this girl!'

She drew on her sheepskin-lined gloves. Her usually pale face was crimson with rage.

"I am just on my way to l'Étoile. Perhaps Ash will find *me* inspiring this morning."

"He has his uncle and aunt with him," Rowan said.

"Oh? When did they arrive?"

"Last night."

"That will be his uncle who has been living in America lately—I didn't know he had a wife."

"No—he has only recently been married," said Rowan. And her whole body seemed to shiver at the memory of Laurence Moore's wife.

Fran's brain worked busily. It was a blow to her to know that Ashley was no longer alone but sheltering in the bosom of his family. And to think that this young girl had been up there last night and met his relations, while she, Fran, had stayed alone—outside the circle. The idea infuriated Fran. She had come out here to make Ashley interested in her again—to force him to fulfil the promise of that night when he had lost his head over her. Her vanity was horribly injured by the failure of her mission. Now she felt she would do anything rather than allow a nondescript young woman like Miss Gray to succeed where she, Fran, had failed. (She who had so much more to offer a man.) What was there about this mouse of a girl with her big, dark, frightened-looking eyes that could possibly stir the heart of a man of the world like Ash?

Fran tore off her gloves again and pulled down the zipper of her snowproofed jacket. She had reached a decision. She was going to cause trouble, if nothing else. She was not going to let Ashley get away with his indifference to her.

Turning to the head-porter, she spoke to him in a loud voice that Rowan was forced to hear.

"Get me a call to London, Henri," she said. "Here it is, I'll write the number down for you. Make it a personal call to my husband, Mr. Simon Cottar."

'What is she up to now?' Rowan asked herself.

She wrote a jumble of words on her typewriter. She could not focus properly. She tore up the page.

Mrs. Cottar took the call in her own bedroom. What she said, nobody knew, but after it Henri informed Rowan that Mr. Cottar was flying out to The Valdana tomorrow. Rowan must ring through to the other hotels and find him a room.

Rowan found a room. But the news set her wondering. . . . What mischief was that handsome, catlike creature up to? Why was Ashley's friend and collaborator rushing out here at a moment's notice—and only for forty-eight hours? She had been told to book the room for two days.

Rowan was mystified, and still more so by the cold spiteful smile that Fran gave her as she passed by the reception and walked out of the hotel.

'She is up to no good, that is certain,' thought Rowan. Then she stopped thinking about Fran and her husband. She had enough on her own young mind without concerning herself too deeply with other people's problems.

But she found herself remembering Fran's sudden telephone call to London with uneasiness. Supposing it was true that there was an affair—or had been one—between Fran and Ashley? *Did the husband's coming out here mean trouble?*

Rowan began to feel that she had been flung out of her tranquil routine life at home when Mummy was alive, into an absolute maelstrom. In this peaceful place, surrounded by the dignity and silence of the mountains, a strange whirlpool seemed to be circling around her, threatening to suck her into its violence.

As she had dreaded—but anticipated—the three Moores came down from the chalet to lunch at The Valdana. Henri said that M. Moore had rung through to book a table, saying he would eat one meal out while his relations were with him, to give poor Hortense a rest.

Rowan wished agonizedly that she could run away and avoid seeing Petal—and Ashley, too. But Henri went off and she had to stay. She had her own lunch at midday but she returned on duty at half past twelve, just as the Moores entered the vestibule.

It was as though her heart turned over when Rowan saw that small exquisite figure of the woman who walked up to the bureau between the two tall men. She began to tremble and had to clutch the edge of the pinewood desk for support.

This is my mother, she thought, bemused.

Petal Moore looked her best this morning. She always slept well—the dreamless sleep of a child who has perfect health and no *souci*. She'd always been like that—once and once only in her early life, when she was Vivien Laker, had worry kept her awake.

She looked fresher and even younger than when Rowan had first seen her. She was wearing a smart pair of black slacks and a white jersey over which was buttoned a tight-fitting white waterproof coat with a little white hood framing that incomparable face; just two soft curls escaped over either ear. As she approached Rowan, she smiled in what seemed a really frank friendly way. Petal prided herself on charming everybody, not only personal friends but what she called 'underlings'. She liked to be popular —to tip generously; to be fawned over by waiters, porters, *femmes de chambre*—salesgirls in shops—anybody with whom she came in contact. She knew that they always said 'what a darling' she was, after she had gone.

Admiration was the breath of life to Petal. That and the existence of her own youth and beauty. The mere prospect of growing old made her shudder. She wanted to be twenty-five for ever.

Nobody really knew how old she was; except of course those who had been friendly with her in her mother's lifetime, and when she first married Rip. But there were few of the old friends left. She had made so many new ones after Rip died and she went to live in Florida.

She seldom, if ever, gave a thought to the man she called 'poor old Rip'. The awful accident that had robbed him of life had shocked her only so far as Petal was capable of being shocked, which wasn't far. She took everything so lightly. She was gay and frivolous except about the things that mattered to *her*, and then she acted with deadly precision, and with all the callous disregard for other people's feelings that she had shown as a child. (She had deceived Ripsdale and been his 'little angel wife' only for the first few months of their marriage, after which he had discovered how implacably hard she was—a ruthless egotist.) He had longed for children. She had refused him a son because she did not wish to spoil her figure or betray her age as time wore on. She knew quite well that he had been bitterly disillusioned before he died. She had driven him to other women with her coldness, her detestation of *giving* in any way. But she had not cared. And she had found it agreeable to wake up and discover that she was a widow with immense wealth—all Rip's possessions—and her freedom.

What had happened to her when she first met Laurence Moore, she did not quite know. It was just one of those things that occur in life and cause an inexplicable change of heart in the most unlikely fashion. She had really fallen in love with Laury Moore. Before she met him, she had been in a circle of adoring young men; old men, too. She could have married a millionaire in Chicago. She had at her feet an Argentine who wanted to marry her and take her to South America to his fabulous house and lead an existence of unparalleled luxury. But money was no longer of great interest to Petal. She had always had it, even when she was Vivien Laker. She had it with Ripsdale. Now, in her late thirties, she wanted something more; something she could not put a name to, but for which her lean ungenerous spirit craved in a curious way. She had found that something in Laurence. The distinguished serious-minded Englishman who had not only a shrewd business mind but a burning appreciation of beauty, fascinated her.

She had found him such a change from the others—particularly from the Americans who were supposed to make such wonderful husbands because they glorified the wife and mother in the home.

But to Petal they were exasperating—exhausting with their schoolboy humour, their relentless vitality. But Laury was smooth and cool, and charmingly lazy when he wished to be and *not* very easy to get. That, too, had attracted her. Added to which she liked the fact that he was a connoisseur of art. She knew the perfection of the beauty she, personally, had to offer. It excited her to feel that it would come under the trained eye of such an expert. She meant to join Laury in his search for wonderful pictures, for *objets d'art.* They would travel throughout Europe together. She had been so bored, *so bored* on Ripsdale's yacht or in one of his apartments in London, Paris or New York. But now she would become serious-minded, share this work with Laurence. She was quite ridiculously pleased when he praised her and told her that she had a flair for picking up the right thing. Even more pleased when he treated her as the most exquisite treasure of all.

She was more passionately in love with Laurence than with any man in her life, and she felt that fortune had smiled on her yet again. He had money but she had much more. They could have the most wonderful home in Rome or Paris, and fill it with their treasures; one day perhaps she would become quite famous; Petal Moore—the young, beautiful connoisseur. She grew starry-eyed at the prospect.

She would not have made this journey to Crans had Laury not insisted on it, but he seemed to want to visit his nephew, and the new, softer Petal who had fallen so much in love, was pleased for once in her life to do what somebody else wanted. She had never done anything for poor Rip.

She was charmed with Laury's nephew—such a brilliant young man. Late last night they had still been up, listening to him play tunes from *Summer Song.* They had all been so 'cosy' and happy, and just before Petal left the two men to their final whiskies-and-sodas, she had, in her gay intimate way which men found so enchanting (and which so completely blinded them to the real woman), asked Ashley about the young girl whom he had been entertaining.

"She looked so scared, and when she nearly fainted, so *ill.* But I suppose she has some fatal fascination for you?" she had teased Ashley.

He had answered rather abruptly:

"Oh—I don't think she's ill. I don't really know why she so nearly fainted. But there's no nonsense between us, you know, Petal. She's sweet—but *not* a girl-friend of mine."

Petal, being a woman, wondered. . . .

She wondered again this morning as she looked into the enormous dark eyes of the young girl behind the desk. She decided that her new nephew was probably just like all men—having a little fun, but that the poor girl had fallen for him. Rowan blushed bright red this moment when Ashley addressed her. Vaguely, Petal pitied Rowan but she just *could* not understand the way some women behaved. It was so stupid to become emotional and show it. Adopt a cool indifference and a man would eat out of your hand. *Never* give away *anything*; that was Petal's motto. On the other hand now that she, herself, was married to Laury, she was beginning to feel rather uncomfortably emotional about it. It was *he* who remained fascinatingly remote. For the first time in her life she was actually ashamed of her past, even afraid of it. She hadn't minded what poor Rip thought about her, but she wouldn't like Laurence to know everything. Oh, certainly not *everything*!

"Are you better this morning, Miss Gray?" Petal murmured to Rowan.

"Quite well again, thank you," answered Rowan. But her heart beat so fast as she looked into the amazingly violet-blue eyes of this woman, that she looked away hurriedly again.

'I hate her—I despise her,' she thought.

Yet all that was natural and human in her longed to say to this mother she had never known:

'Do you remember that little baby who was born in Montreux? Have you never given her a single thought? If *I* tell you that I am yours—Harry Treloar's daughter—would you feel one little spark of love or tenderness for me? Or would you turn from me in horror, in terror, in case I might ruin your life?'

But she never uttered those words aloud and Petal turned away, arm through her husband's.

Rowan heard her youthful voice as she walked off:

"Isn't this a *charming* hotel, Laury darling? We must come here for winter-sports one year."

Ashley lingered by the desk.

He made pretence of looking through the box of assorted postcards that were there on the bureau for guests to choose from. But he looked through his lashes at Rowan, instead.

"You're not *quite* fit yet—I can see it, my poor girl," he said in what was meant to be a friendly, sympathetic fashion.

Rowan felt as though her whole heart leapt in response to his voice.

116

"I'm all right, I assure you," she said.

He turned and glanced at the trim graceful back of his 'new aunt'. Then with a little laugh, he turned back to Rowan.

"Mercy me, as they say in Scotland—Uncle Laury has found a dream of a wife, hasn't he?"

"Do you admire her?" asked Rowan, trying to control her breathing.

"Don't you?"

"I think she's very—very beautiful."

"Yes. Although I admit she's not exactly my style. Too shallow. No great depths, would you say?"

"I really don't know," said Rowan, feeling agonized.

Ashley found himself looking at Rowan's sensitive curving lips, those lips which yesterday he had kissed so much more passionately than he had intended. And then into the dark eyes that were strangely full of pain and distress. He could not make her out. Something had happened to Rowan but he didn't know what. The girl was beginning to be a nuisance, he told himself angrily because he could not forget her quite as easily as he had meant to do—nor forget the passionate warmth of her surrender. It was damned silly, he decided, but he would really rather have snatched Rowan out of the office and taken her off somewhere up the mountains, and helped her to relax and be happy, than join Laurence and Petal. Then he remembered Frances. His lips tightened. He had almost forgotten Frances. He really must not get himself involved with one woman and then another or it would put paid to his work; it was too disturbing.

As he walked through the village just now, he saw a tall mannequin-figure strolling down the street and darted into a shop, dragging his uncle and Petal with him until Frances had passed. Fran had looked like a thunder-cloud, he thought.

Rowan suddenly said:

"It may be giving away official secrets but I thought you'd like to know you will soon have your friend, the lyric writer, to work with you. He's coming out here. I've just got him a room."

Ashley's pulses jerked uneasily.

"This is news indeed. When is he coming?"

"Tomorrow."

Rowan saw that troubled expression in Ashley's eyes. She thought:

'He's upset—I can feel an undercurrent. I know Mrs. Cottar is going to make trouble.'

But she dare not say anything of what she felt. She watched him walk away. Later she felt weighed down by the thought of her mother coming to The Valdana.

Should she go down to Sierre and pour out her story to Uncle Jean? He was kind and good; he was Mummy's brother—surely he would advise her wisely. Yet what could he do? What could anybody do in such a sensational affair? It was all so incredible. She just must learn to control herself and her feelings or pack up and run away.

Why didn't she go?

There were so many reasons. She had no right, for instance, to let the Garniers down and quit her job at the hotel's busiest time. And she had nowhere, really, to go. She did not want to upset the Garniers in Sierre or have to return to Blackthorn Farm and admit defeat. She had only just come here to face the world alone. Above all she knew that what really held her in Crans was her feeling for Ashley. She was so much in love with him now that she was quite devastated by her youthful passion.

To add to all the disturbance, Simon Cottar was flying out here at his wife's request. Rowan was afraid there was going to be trouble.

There was somebody else who was sure of it.

Ashley had felt quite unnerved by the news Rowan had given him. During lunch, Frances, moving with her incomparable grace, entered the restaurant and he introduced her to Laurence and Petal to whom she was all smiles and charm. But he fancied he saw a cool menace in the green long-lidded eyes that she turned on him.

Immediately after lunch, Ashley left Laurence and Petal to drink their coffee out on the terrace in the hot sunlight and walked with some determination up to Frances who had settled herself in the lounge with a new novel.

"What brings Simon out here in such a hurry?" he asked.

She smiled up at him, closing her book. He did not trust that smile. When she made no reply he questioned her again in a rough voice: "Is Simon coming of his own accord or did you send for him?"

"Why should I send for him? Don't you think he just hates being separated from me and can't keep away?"

"That may be but I also know he had no intention of coming out here for a fortnight. You said so yourself. I have a definite feeling that you want to make trouble."

"You must have a guilty conscience, my dear," she drawled.

Ashley lit a cigarette. He was aware that his fingers shook. How crazy could a man be, he wondered to lose his head even for an hour over a woman like this one. She was little better than . . . then his mind swerved to the present. He sat down beside Frances.

"Fran," he said, "what happens to you or to myself is of no very great account. What happens to Simon is something quite else. He is my friend. We've known and liked each other since we were twenty. He loves you—no—don't interrupt me. I'm well aware that your recent conduct may have disillusioned him. But I think he still loves you. Simon's like that. He's a faithful chap. I'm not going to have him hurt. I don't know what you intend to do or say—but I warn you. I will not let you take his best friend away from him as well as his wife."

Now Frances dug her white teeth into the bright scarlet of her lips and laughed. This time her laughter held a note of uneasiness.

"You needn't speak to me in such a fierce voice, Ash. And why all this? Who says I mean to make trouble?"

"*Don't* you?"

Her lashes flickered nervously. She pushed a cigarette into the long holder which she always used. She thought she knew Ashley pretty well but she had never encountered him quite in such a dark mood. She could see that he was not, like Simon, to be either hoodwinked by her charm or intimidated by her cruelty. Ashley was 'tough'. But neither would she let him off. She said in her low voice:

"You can't have it all one way. You started an affair with me, you got me to respond, and now you want to slide out of your commitments. I am not the sort of girl to stand for that type of male cowardice."

"The only cowardly thing I did, my dear Fran, was to make love to you on that evening when Simon was away."

"And 'the woman tempted you'?" she jeered.

"I don't deny that I *fell* for the temptation but I regretted it bitterly and, as you know, I put an end to things before they went too far. I told you at the time that I didn't wish to re-open the episode. Not only because I am too attached to Simon to play around with his wife but because I don't happen to like you any more. Is that straight? I am sorry if I have been brutal—but you've asked for it."

She was white now with her chagrin, her sense of humiliation. It was the first time Frances had ever suffered from it in her life. Suddenly she hated him.

"It's all very well for you to say that you wanted to end it. *I* didn't!" she cried. "Why should you think you can just kiss and run away?"

"It wasn't at all admirable of me and I am not proud of myself, but I *do* intend to run away—so that is that."

"Then you must take the consequences because I intend to tell Simon the facts."

"So you did send for him? And you *are* going to make trouble." She shrugged her shoulders.

"Of course there's still time, my dear, darling Ash. I can always put Simon off if you choose to be a little more co-operative."

He stared at her half in contempt, half in astonishment.

"You really are amazing."

"So men tell me," she laughed.

"Look, Fran. This doesn't call for jokes. If you tell Simon what happened between us—it'll more than upset him. He'll feel that his best friend behaved badly while he was away. You'll destroy his trust in me. But it won't help *you* any. It isn't as though you've anything to gain."

"Oh, but I have."

"What do you mean?"

"I'll gain a co-respondent for my divorce."

Ashley went scarlet.

"That wouldn't be possible. There was nothing like that between us."

"But I could always tell my fond husband that there *was*!" Frances said softly.

He looked at her for a moment as though he could not believe what he had heard. He had never been so angry or so disgusted in his life. But even then his fear was not for his own skin but for Simon's. Simon, who was married to this beautiful fiend. Poor chap!

Then Frances added in a changed voice:

"I'm not saying that I *will* make that sort of trouble. I just say that I *could* if I wanted to. But I'd so much rather that you and I got together in a more friendly spirit and that Simon didn't come here at all."

After a pause, Ashley got up. He said:

"This, my dear girl, is sheer blackmail. But you've chosen the wrong chap to threaten. Let Simon come, and do your worst. I shall tell him the truth and ask him to believe me. If he prefers to believe you, that's too bad. But there can't be any question of divorce for there's no justifiable cause for it and you haven't the slightest proof that there is. My last words to you are—lay off Simon. If you hurt him any more, I'll fix matters so that your life's not worth living. Think that one over."

She looked up at him, shaking. She didn't quite see how he could carry out such a threat but she was slightly demoralized by his attitude. She had not thought that Ashley could be quite so brutal. As he turned to leave her, she flung a few words at him which were calculated to hurt (she had no grounds for what she said, her one idea being retaliation).

"And I intend to warn that poor innocent girl in the reception that you are the sort to kiss and run away, and that *she'd* better be careful!"

Ashley stopped a moment as though those words were like arrows that found their mark and transfixed him. He was still shaking with anger when finally he walked away. He certainly had no intention of being scared by Fran into a continuation of their brief and disastrous love affair. And he had every intention of trying to spare Simon if he could. But Fran's last words hit him in a raw spot. They haunted him for the rest of the afternoon while he tried to get on with the operetta. Laurence and Petal had gone out for a walk.

Needless to say, no work was achieved. The ash-tray on the piano was soon filled with stubs of cigarettes. He kept remembering Rowan. How dared Fran bring her into it—that girl who was so innocent, so young and deserving of a man's respect? What incalculable harm a woman like Fran could do if she talked to Rowan as she had threatened. But it was against himself that Ashley directed the main force of his disgust that afternoon.

'What sort of chap am I?' he asked himself helplessly again and again through the long wasted hours. For he knew that he *had* taken Rowan in his arms and he knew it had not left her undisturbed. Frances Cottar, no man could hurt. She was the predatory ruthless female. But it was different with Rowan. He wished with all his heart that he had not taken that kiss from her inexperienced lips. Alongside that wish (in paradox) ran the surprising thought that he did not wholly regret it. Also, that he would like to hold Rowan in his arms again.

Could it be that he was just a bit (if only a little bit) in love with her?

He asked himself that question and could not find the honest answer.

13

Two days later, Rowan wrote one of her long detailed letters to Ann and Bill.

She could no longer keep the facts from them. She told them how she had come face to face with her own mother.

It's done something so strange to me, she wrote, *I can't seem to reorientate myself. Every time I see her come towards me or catch sight of her in the distance, I feel almost sick with nerves. I can't explain how I feel because it can't be love. One cannot love somebody one has never known and who behaved badly—just because she is one's mother. Yet the pull is there, deep down. The tremendous urge to reveal myself to her and see how she takes it. Sometimes I think she is the most beautiful person in the world and that it would really delight me to see her look at me as a mother should look at her daughter, and be drawn close to her. Then I remember the facts. I remember Mummy who suffered so much to help that other one—and I dislike her. I try to avoid her when she comes into the hotel. But it's all difficult and dangerous and I know that I ought to tell M. Paul that I can't stay in Crans. But I must stay—because of Ashley.*

Somehow it does me good to tell you both who know me so well, the truth. I want to confess everything. I'm in love with Ashley Moore. Desperately. I can't give you all the facts about his life because it would take too long and it is too complicated, but it does seem there has been something between him and Mrs. Cottar. I don't think he loves her any more, whatever he used to feel. I even think he hates her now. But she's pursuing him like a kind of snake. She really is evil under all that beauty. And now she is trying to make trouble for him, just when he wants to get on with his work.

Sometimes I think of Ashley with a burning resentment. I wonder if he's just the sort of man who likes to make women fall in love with him and then loses interest in them? Sometimes I tell myself that I don't really love him at all; that I am just a stupid, infatuated school-girl. Then I meet him again and one look from him and I'm lost. I feel myself tremble. It's ridiculous to be so much in love. But I can't help it. I just go on and on thinking about him—wishing I could die because he doesn't love me. I don't really come into his life. Yet that isn't true. I have come into it. He has taken me into his arms and kissed me and that can never be wiped out. When a thing like that happens to you it's as though a hot branding iron has been put on to your very heart and you bear the mark for ever. It can never be eradicated.

I go about feeling that I have a mark on my heart—and that Ashley is responsible. How different life has become for me since I said good-bye to you both and left Jordans. Everything seemed so simple before. It is as though when you know nothing, you imagine you understand all things. But when you begin to gain some knowledge of life, you find you know nothing at all.

Yesterday was rather dreadful. Simon Cottar arrived. That woman sent for him. She means mischief. He came to the hotel to ask for his wife. I spoke to him. He looked very tired and pallid next to all the bronzed men who have been ski-ing out here. He has none of Ashley's vital looks or personality. In fact you'd think he was a nonentity. A thin, pale man with straight brown hair growing rather far back and near-sighted eyes behind horn-rimmed spectacles. But when he smiled, his face was transformed and he looked suddenly charming. He certainly has a clever look. He is a quiet, deep man. But I could see at a glance that he had none of Ashley's strength and that he is too gentle for a woman like Frances.

He looked so worried that my heart went out to him. While he was talking to me, Frances came out of the lift. I saw the expression on his face when he turned to her. I assure you it was the most tragic, unhappy look—as if appealing to her. But she gave him her cruel icy smile and drawled: "Hallo, Simon." And when he made a movement as though to kiss her, she drew back. While I stood watching them walking together across the hall in the direction of the bar Ashley came into the hotel. He barely said "hallo" to me. He looked harassed, stern. He just asked Henri where Frances was and Henri directed him to the lounge.

What passed between those three I shall never know. It must have been a full half-hour later that I saw her come out alone, looking terrible—in a sort of blind fury. She came straight to me, because Henri wasn't there and said:

"Give me my keys and cancel my room. I shall be leaving Crans tomorrow morning."

I must say that did not displease me and I suppose I must have

123

shown what I felt (although I tried not to) because, looking like a serpent, Frances spoke to me in a voice that held all the venom in the world in it.

"You remember, my dear girl, that I once warned you not to disturb Mr. Ashley Moore when he was working. Now I'll give you a second warning. Don't believe one single word he ever says to you. He has no sense of honour and he wouldn't be above making a fool of you. Just keep away from him. That is my friendly counsel."

I didn't feel that there could be much friendliness about Mrs. Cottar and yet her warning naturally disturbed me. I found myself blushing. That awful habit of mine gave her the clue to my emotions. She clenched her long fingers over the keys I had just handed her, and spoke to me again.

"Oh yes! I know how you feel already. Ash Moore has quite a fascination for women. He would like a young innocent girl to blush at the mention of his name——"

I felt I had to interrupt her. My heart was palpitating.

"Mrs. Cottar——" I began, but she did not let me finish. With a dramatic gesture she suddenly beat her clenched fist against her breast.

"I can blush too—here in my heart—for what he has done to me. And now he has made trouble between me and my own husband. There was trouble before Simon came out but Ash has added fuel to the fire. Perhaps he's tired of me. Perhaps"—Frances fixed me with a baleful eye—"he thought someone very young and ignorant of life would be amusing for a change. Innocence is rather the subject of the new composition, isn't it? No doubt he wants 'copy' and hopes to get it out of you!"

I can't tell you how those words affected me. With all my soul I wanted to disbelieve them, to strike back at Mrs. Cottar in the way she was striking at me. But for the moment she had all the weapons on her side. I was helpless. I only knew that I wouldn't have been human if I hadn't believed some of these things she said. She was so clever, so apparently sincere in that moment that I did begin to wonder whether Ashley had been a cad to her. Well, I thought, I wouldn't let him behave like a cad to me. I didn't care what had happened between him and this woman and her husband—I just wasn't going to be the meek little fool they seemed to think me—ready to sacrifice myself on the altar of a man's ambition to find a model for the main character in his operetta!

In a flash I remembered the 'Snowbird'—the story he had told me about her suffering and betrayal by the man she loved. I felt deeply troubled and confused. I even began to identify myself with the

'Snowbird'. Because I love Ashley so terribly and long so much to be with him, I wondered whether I would not be wise to go away as soon as possible and never see either him or that woman who is my mother, again. Somehow I managed to answer Frances Cottar. I told her that I did not know what she was talking about. I laughed. And finally she turned away and went up in the lift to her room. I made a note on my pad to tell M. Paul that Mrs. Cottar had cancelled and that we had a single room and bath free now, should somebody else wish to take it.

Then Ashley and Simon Cottar came out of the bar. They passed by my office to which I had fled. Ashley called to me. I went to him unwillingly. My throat felt dry and my lids were burning. I didn't want to look at him. But like one mesmerized, I raised my eyes. I saw that he seemed calmer—less harassed than when he had come into the hotel. His expression was guarded. But he said in an ordinary voice:

"Meet Simon—my friend and the author of the book of the Summer Song."

"I have already had that pleasure," I said stiffly.

Ashley turned to Simon.

"Miss Gray is very musical, Simon, and a darned good critic. She has been helping me with The Snowbird."

"That's an exaggeration," I said, quite angrily, and saw that Ashley looked surprised at the tone of my voice and the fact that there was no soft friendliness in my eyes. But I didn't care. I was filled with a passionate desire not to be numbered among his conquests—even if there was only half a grain of truth in what that awful Mrs. Cottar had told me.

I tried to concentrate on Simon Cottar.

"Will you be staying in Crans for any length of time?" I asked him.

I thought that he looked terribly unhappy. He answered me in an expressionless voice.

"No, I only came on—business. I leave tomorrow morning."

"Yes, of course—Mrs. Cottar is leaving tomorrow morning, too," I said, trying to behave as though it were all normal. But I perceived the extraordinary bitterness in those weak yet highly intelligent eyes of his, as he said:

"Exactly." Then he added: "Has my wife gone up to her room?"

"Yes," I said.

He spoke a few low words to Ashley which I did not hear but Ashley nodded and said in his clear voice:

"I quite understand. Look in and see me later on tonight. Anybody will tell you where the chalet is. I'd like just to work with you for an hour. I'll explain to my uncle and his wife. They'll probably come and have coffee here after dinner. They won't mind."

Simon moved off. I wished that Ashley would go away too. I felt so terrible, and so much in the dark, not knowing what had passed between those three. Ashley had been smoking a cigarette. He stubbed the end on an ash-tray on the desk that separated us. Then he drew a deep sigh and looked at me through half-shut lids.

"You may not know it, my little one," he said in a voice half mocking, half serious, "but I've just come through a very unpleasant cyclone. I feel slightly uprooted."

I found myself answering rudely:

"I can't imagine any cyclone uprooting you. I think you have both feet planted quite firmly on the ground."

Now his eyes opened wide. He paused in the act of lighting a fresh cigarette.

"What's come over you, Rowan? You're not usually so sardonic."

"Maybe I feel sardonic," I said with a laugh that I had to force, but I was beginning to shake as I always did the moment I was near him. Looking up at that strong bony face which was burnt a dark brown now by the sun and the reflection of the snow, looking into the depths of his grey, far-seeing eyes, I felt pitiably lost. If only he would go away. But to my concern, he leaned nearer to me and said in a low voice:

"Don't change, Rowan. Don't become anything other than what you are. Don't let anybody or anything turn you into a 'belle dame sans merci'."

"I don't know what you mean," I said wildly.

"I don't suppose you do, honey," he said. (Oh the enchantment of Ashley's voice when he used that foolish name—like a caress.) "But just stay as you are."

As I remained speechless, he put the cigarette between his lips, lit it and through a cloud of smoke looked at me.

"Let me tell you I've been skating on thin ice and it nearly cracked," he said with a short laugh. "But even a dangerous woman can't break the trust that two men who are real friends have for each other. Does that make sense to you, Rowan?"

"No, I don't know what you're talking about," I repeated in the same wild voice, "and I don't want to know. What you do is not my affair."

Now, gently, he smiled and shrugged his shoulders.

"So I've upset you, somehow. I must be a damned awkward fellow. I seem to be upsetting everybody. Don't be cross with me, little Rowan. I value our friendship."

Then I shook so that I could hardly stand. Deliberately I turned away from him without saying good night. I went into my office and shut the door which was usually left open.

When I came out again, Ashley had gone. Of course being me—and stupid—I wished I hadn't been so rude and angry and that I could see him and speak to him again, and tell him I was his friend—even if it cost me all my pride to do so. I didn't care what poison Frances Cottar had tried to instil into me or who was to blame for the tornado that Ashley had spoken of, or what triangular drama was taking place—here under my very nose. I just loved him with every pulse-beat, with every particle of my being. And for the rest of the evening I felt dreadful and in a daze. And do you know, I also felt that I wished I could go to her, my mother. She was so experienced with the ways of men. She had seen so much of life. She was loved and cherished now by Ashley's uncle. She seemed to see her way so clearly. She didn't walk in a fog like I do, blindly, groping, knocking into all the things I want most to avoid. I wanted to beg her to look after me and impart some of her knowledge to me. I felt even a greater need for her than for poor Mummy, who lies dead and buried at home.

Oh, everything seems such a muddle. Tonight I almost wish that I had never been born!

And that was the letter that she wrote—but never posted. For she knew that she could not allow even Ann and Bill, who were her friends, to look quite so deeply into the secrets of her heart.

Alone in her little room at the top of the hotel, where she could only faintly hear the drift of the tinkling piano from the bar, Rowan read all that she had written, then with flaming cheeks tore the pages to pieces and threw herself on her bed, and burst into tears.

Ashley went home feeling curiously tired. He could not face cocktail time and the frivolous chatter of the beautiful Petal, nor talk to his uncle. He didn't think it would matter to his guests. They appeared to be still in the honeymoon stage. They would not mind being alone.

Ashley hadn't quite fathomed what the former Mrs. Ripsdale was really like. Having had time to recall numerous incidents about her when she was married to Rip, he had felt a as to whether Uncle Laury had done what so many confirmed bachelors of his age were apt to do—and married one of these diamond-hard women who were the 'takers' of this world, rather than the 'givers'. He couldn't really imagine Petal belonging to the 'giver' class. On the other hand, it couldn't be said she had married Laury for his money; with the Ripsdale fortune behind her. But on one occasion during a chat alone with Laury, Laury had actually told Ashley (with rather touching embarrassment) that they hoped in the future to have a child.

"Petal has altered my whole outlook on life," he said. "I don't suppose you'll believe this, Ashley, but I've begun to feel that one can waste an awful lot of time making a hell of a lot of money, then working equally hard to find new, amusing ways of spending it. And Petal feels the same. We've both had more or less everything we want, and done everything. Now we mean to tour Europe and buy some beautiful things for our home. But we'd *like* a settled home—say in a year's time—and an heir. Petal's nearly forty, I know, but that's not too old and she seems quite willing to try."

Those were the words he had spoken to Ashley who had received them without comment. He was prepared to believe that Petal had found her 'Waterloo' in Uncle Laury. Laury was not the chap to be turned into the sort of foolish slave that poor old Rip used to be, when Petal was Vivien Ripsdale. And she certainly must have changed a lot because it had been common knowledge in the society circles in which she moved that old Rip had wanted a child but that as far as Vivien was concerned, there was nothing doing.

Anyhow, it was no business of his, Ashley reflected, and soon forgot about it. He had other things more closely connected with himself to think about. But since Laurence and Petal had arrived at the chalet, he had once or twice found himself wondering whether Laury had not hit on the solution to the riddle of life. A loving wife, a nice home and children.

Yet Ashley shivered at the idea.

Perish the thought! Anyhow, there was plenty of time. He was ten years younger than Uncle Laury. He needn't get himself tied up and settle down just yet.

Leaving Petal and Laurence to their drinks, Ashley lay on his bed with arms folded behind his head. He knew that the exhaustion he felt was as much a mental as a physical thing.

That hour spent with Simon and Fran had really shaken him. He had never believed that even Fran could be so venomous. He had tried to stop her from spitting out that venom—much more for poor old Simon's sake than anybody's—but out it had to come. It had stupefied Ashley and completely spoiled any pleasure that Simon might have felt in being out here with his wife and his friend. After the first drink, Fran had come to the point, without subtlety, and with only one ambition—to bring about a divorce from the husband she was tired of, and put him, Ashley, into the position of having to do 'the decent thing', and marry her.

With icy indifference to Simon's suffering or Ashley's righteous anger, Fran had uttered one cold lie after another, weaving a story for the astounded Simon that was like a spider's web, until Ashley had thought Simon and himself were like two flies, caught and tied up, helpless, waiting to be eaten alive.

But as Ashley had told Rowan just now, it wasn't easy even for a human female spider to break the trust of two men who had been friends in their university days, and afterwards had worked together for years.

Fran had been cunning enough to produce the ready tear and whisper the words: "*You must try to forgive us, it was stronger than we were, dear, dear Simon——*" Simon, looking bleak and pinched had then turned to Ashley and asked him if it was true. Then Ashley had looked him straight in the eyes and answered:

"No—not altogether. I *did* take Fran out. There was—and I may say I am heartily ashamed of it—a somewhat amorous session in your drawing-room, and afterwards, once more, I weakened and took Fran out for an evening and made love to her. But I never meant it to happen and I absolutely deny that I ever betrayed you in the way that Fran seems to want you to believe."

"You unutterable cad!" Fran had said with a beautifully timed sob.

But Ashley continued to look into the eyes of the man he respected and admired.

"My humble apologies for what did take place, Simon. But cad or not, I do not intend to back Fran up even if she bamboozles you into believing it. She has no proof because there isn't one. I am *not* in love with her and I haven't the slightest wish to take her away from you. I want to make that quite clear—to her and to you."

Fran had then seized one of Simon's hands and looked at him with her wonderful green cat's-eyes magnified by her tears. She had spoken in a voice husky and seductive enough to get blood out of a stone (so Ashley had thought at the time). But funnily enough she got nothing out of Simon. She had thought him still her slave, but she had mistimed her attack. It came too quickly on the heels of all the countless minor cruelties that she had practised on him during the last few months of their marriage. Simon had loved her once and he was a weak man. But this evening he gained sudden strength. He was upset and sickened by the whole affair, but when he spoke, it was not in his wife's defence and neither did he take her hand.

"Please sit back in your chair and don't make a scene, Fran," he said coldly.

Ashley put in:

"I'm more sorry than I can say, old boy, I am not trying to wriggle out of my commitments. There just aren't any. What I did, I own to—but it went no farther than I've told you. Do you believe me, Simon?"

There had been a slight dramatic pause, then Simon had answered:

"Yes I do."

"*Thank God*," Ashley said under his breath. "All the same, I feel damn' badly about it."

Then Fran sprang to her feet. The tears had dried. Her face was a mask of fury as she looked from one man to the other.

"You're a fine pair. Neither of you has the guts to stand by me. You're despicable."

Ashley was the first to answer the accusation.

"I may be. I certainly despise myself for going as far as I did while Simon was away. But you've known for a long time how I've felt about it, and I see absolutely no reason why I should remove myself as a friend from Simon just because you're tired of him as a husband."

Simon spoke then—looking grey and much older than his years. Once he had loved Frances more than any woman in the world. But he smiled at Ashley.

"Guts or no guts—I'm glad you had the courage to be honest about the whole thing, Ash," he said. "I feel sure you would have preferred to spare me this. Well—just let me tell you straight away, it isn't going to make any difference to *us*."

"And what about me?" came from Frances in a suffocated voice.

"You must do as you like," Simon answered her. "You see, Fran, I *know* Ashley. If he had really been the cad you're trying to make him out, I'm positive he would have owned to it, not only now, but right away, when I first got back from Scotland."

"And what am I supposed to do about that?" she demanded.

"What you like," had been Simon's weary answer. "Only leave Ashley alone, and me, too, if it comes to that. I can't stand any more of the scenes we've been having lately."

"You can't turn me out of my home—you've no cause," she began furiously.

Now Simon's short-sighted eyes stared at her over the rims of his glasses and he gave her a smile that held a good deal of caustic humour.

"*Exactly*, my dear Fran," he said, "that's what we're *all* agreed upon."

After that, Frances had rushed off declaiming hysterically that she wouldn't stay in Crans another moment.

Now, reviewing the whole unhappy, rather sordid scene, Ashley wished for the hundredth time that he could wipe out that episode with Fran. A few moments of hot passion that had done no lasting harm, yet had proved to him that even a man of strength and character must watch out for the weaknesses in his armour. No one was invulnerable. But thank God even Fran Cottar had been unable to come between him and his friend.

Ashley worried about Simon as he thought what lay ahead. For what could there be but some sort of miserable end to his marriage? Fran wasn't the kind to go back and turn over a new leaf. And he would never trust her again.

'It is a lesson I'm not likely to forget,' Ashley reflected, and got up to look for aspirin because his head was splitting. 'How I hate women,' he muttered. 'Particularly Fran. She hasn't finished with Simon yet. He ought, of course, to leave her but he never will because he's the faithful kind.'

And then he remembered Rowan and the strange abruptness of her manner towards him.

He had a sudden memory of her embittered voice saying:

"*I can't imagine any cyclone uprooting you. I think you have both feet planted firmly on the ground. . . .*"

Why this sudden cynicism from little Rowan? The withdrawal of the friendly sympathy and understanding which he had begun to find so charming?

'Oh—I hate women!' Ashley muttered again.

He lay with shut eyes waiting for the aspirin to work, conscious that in a moment he would have to get up and dress and go down to join Laury and Petal for the evening meal. But although the pain in his head subsided, the stormy trend of his thoughts did not. He kept seeing Rowan's dark expressive eyes. Accusing eyes. Accusing him of *what*? He hardly knew, and he tried to put the whole thing out of his mind but those eyes continued to haunt him for the rest of the evening.

"You're not looking yourself—what's happened to you?" the new Mrs. Laurence Moore asked Ashley during dinner.

Once again he blamed his headache, assuring Petal that nothing was wrong. But he was somewhat relieved when she and Laurence took the hint and went off to The Valdana to have coffee, and later to the Sporting Club to dance. Petal adored dancing.

Never had he wanted more to be alone and throw himself into his work. And seldom had it meant more to him to have Simon up here with him in this quiet warm room, shutting out the white world of snow and ice, while they concentrated on their new united effort.

The name 'Fran' was not mentioned between the two men. It was possible, Ashley reflected, that it never would be again. And if he had failed Simon in even a small degree, that failure had obviously been forgiven, and wiped out by this evening while they discussed *The Snowbird*. Simon listened to some of the numbers Ashley had composed and had never been more friendly or companionable.

"It's terrific, Ash," he said as the young composer finished playing, and turned to him.

"You think it will be as popular as *Summer Song*?"

"I hope so," said Simon and added with his sweet smile: "We seem to be doing well enough with that, my dear chap."

"You like my 'Snowbird' theme?"

"You've made a beautiful song of it, Ash. Quite touching—that bit—*I fall, I fall, I shall not fly again.*"

"Good," said Ashley, feeling more enthusiastic and content than he had done since Simon's arrival in Crans.

"All the same, I don't see Greta playing the part."

"Nor I," agreed Ashley. "It wants youth and innocence, as well as heart."

"Difficult to find," said Simon.

Ashley frowned.

"Damned difficult."

And then Simon said, surprisingly:

"Do you know, I see our 'Snowbird' in that little girl up at The Valdana—Rowan, I believe you called her. Don't you think she has a 'Snowbird' quality about her? The right physical type, anyhow. Although of course one never knows with women—she may be as hard as nails. I don't know the girl."

Silence a moment. Ashley got up, poured out a drink for Simon and then one for himself. Then he said:

"I wouldn't say Rowan is hard and I, myself, when I first saw her, felt that she *was* the 'Snowbird', incarnate."

"Ah!" said Simon.

"But of course she can't sing and isn't on the stage. There it ends."

But as Ashley drank his whisky and continued to talk about the operetta, he had a strange and uncomfortable feeling that it wasn't the end. And after Simon left, once more he began to remember Rowan's eyes—and the warmth of her lips.

14

OUTSIDE the café-restaurant up at Cry d'Err, a crowd of enthusiastic skiers ate lunch and afterwards, watched by those who did not take part in the sport, skimmed down the white shining slopes back to Crans. Most of them had come up by the *téléférique*; a few travelled back by that fascinating overhead cable route. Because it was an afternoon of hot, dazzling sunshine, the mountain wastes were alive with skiers, and to travellers from the *téléférique*, they looked like toy figures, moving this way and that, leaving behind them a criss-cross of lines. A colourful collection, in their gay sports-outfits—blue, scarlet, yellow, black and white. The still pure air was full of the echo of laughter and voices and the constant drone of the motor working the cable-railway.

Rowan sat alone. She had come up alone, to try her luck from this dizzy height as a change from the nursery slopes. Three miles down to Crans. A good way for a novice. But she was eager to do it—and without Marc. She had been thankful when he rang from Sierre to say that he had to go into Montreux on business for his father and could not join her until tomorrow.

She had no wish to be with Marc; or with any man. She had been invited to ski with a party arranged by the nice Norwegian. She could, too, have had a pleasant gay afternoon with the elderly Englishman who seemed to admire her and hovered so often around the Reception. But she wanted to be alone. It seemed a pressing need—as though the constant surge of people in the hotel, and the necessity to talk and laugh with clients had caused a revulsion of her spirit.

Besides, Rowan had a great deal on her mind. Up here on the mountain-tops, in such magnificence, in the vast silence of the eternal snows—and during the ski-run—she might find an answer to the problems that harassed her.

She had been unfortunate enough to run into the Laurence Moores as soon as she reached the Cry d'Err café. There, at a table, they sat. At once, Rowan's heart was stabbed; her breath quickened as her mother looked at her, smiled, and beckoned. Rowan went unwillingly to her table. The Moores were eating omelettes and drinking red wine. Petal was exquisite, as usual, in black and white, but she was careful not to expose her transparent skin to the sun, like most of the healthy-looking women with their oiled tanned faces. She wore a huge peasant's straw hat on her rose-gilt head, and dark glasses. Rowan, herself, was hatless. Her face was well-creamed and glistening.

Said Petal:

"You haven't seen Ashley—have you, Miss Gray?"

"No, I haven't," said Rowan. Actually she had not set eyes on Ashley since yesterday when he had met the Cottars in the hotel. Petal seemed to be thinking of the Cottars, too, because she added:

"I think he sat up most of the night working with his friend, Simon. Is that wife of his ill? She didn't show up at the chalet?"

"I couldn't tell you," said Rowan. "I only know that Mr. and Mrs. Cottar left Crans this morning."

Petal's big lovely eyes threw a triumphant look at her husband.

"I told you there'd been trouble between those two—I couldn't get a word out of Ash at breakfast beyond the fact that he had done quite a good job with Simon, but he shut up like a clam when I mentioned Mrs. C. I can't say I liked the little I saw of her. I think she was after Ashley."

Laurence Moore smiled indulgently at his beautiful wife.

"Petal, my sweet, careful!"

She gurgled with laughter and glanced over her glasses at Rowan who was standing so straight and stiff in front of her.

"My husband pretends he doesn't like scandal. I think everybody does, don't you, Miss Gray?"

"Oh yes—of course," Rowan stammered, but felt that there was something constricting her throat. It was so utterly ridiculous, she thought but she could not stop trembling when in close proximity with this woman. She could not stop staring at her—

as though trying to find some answer to the baffling problem which was her own deep agonizing secret. *What was* Petal Moore —otherwise Vivien Ripsdale—made of? Had she a heart? Had she one single human generous instinct, or was she as soulless as a gorgeous butterfly—a winged creature with a single desire—to skim radiantly over the surface of things and extract the ultimate honey from existence, with no thought or expectation of immortal life?

Petal lowered her gaze. She frowned a little. How this girl looked at her! She *probed* with those big dark eyes of hers. Petal was not sure that she liked Ashley's musical friend, Miss Gray; yet she was strangely fascinated by the girl—by her extraordinary coldness. She was unfriendly and Petal was used to adoration from everybody she met.

"If you'll excuse me——" began Rowan.

But suddenly Petal felt an obstinate wish to alter this girl's outlook and extract homage from her as well as from others. She prided herself that nobody could resist her fascination when she chose to exert it. She wasn't going to have this silly little thing looking at her with such chilly indifference. She suddenly took off her glasses, blinked her long lashes, gave Rowan a ravishing smile and said:

"Come and sit down and have a cup of coffee with Laurence and myself."

Rowan felt hot and uncomfortable.

"I—I've already had a drink, thank you——"

"Then you can have another," beamed Petal. "One can never drink enough of this delicious Swiss coffee, with cream on it. I *never* take cream anywhere else, but in Switzerland I just do. It's fattening, but *you* don't have to diet. You're so deliciously slim!"

Laurence, who had got up when Rowan first approached, now found another chair and placed it between his wife and himself.

"Do let us order you a coffee," he said with his charming smile.

Rowan still felt horribly nervous and ill at ease, but could not get away without being rude. So she found herself pinned here, beside the very woman whom she had every reason to avoid—to love—*or to hate.*

Petal had a gift for conversation. She liked to believe that she was very sympathetic, and could win all kinds of confidences from people. She knew they always called her 'adorable and kind'. She had decided to be kind to little Miss Gray. She plied her with questions about herself.

"Where do you come from? Which part of England? Ash tells us you are quite alone in the world. How terribly sad. . . ." And so on, hardly drawing breath or waiting for Rowan's replies. It was as well. When Rowan did speak it was with confusion, with none of her usual tranquillity. She had to weigh every word—terrified lest her answers should wake some chord of memory in her mother (if indeed 'Petal' remembered anything about that infant to whom she had given birth, nineteen years ago. She looked so ridiculously young. It wasn't possible to imagine her as a mother of a grown girl).

Mary Gray's diary had not mentioned whether or not Vivien ever heard what had happened to Marie Garnier and the child. But Rowan was scared of mentioning even the name of the village in which Mummy had taken refuge. She said: "I live in Buckinghamshire with friends . . ." and spoke of the Jenkins and their children at Blackthorn Farm.

"Did someone tell me you were half-Swiss?"

Rowan flushed a burning red.

"No, I'm quite English—I was adopted——" she blurted out the words without meeting Petal's gaze.

Laurence, arms folded, had been staring through his dark glasses at the vista of the mountains in front of them. Now he turned with a slight smile to the young girl:

"You poor little thing," he said. "Tough, I call it—not having parents of your own."

"Dreadfully sad," Petal seconded in her flute-like voice.

Rowan sat speechless, thankful that her black glasses hid her eyes. She had meant to remain calm, but she was shaken by a positive storm of emotion. This conversation was dangerous. She knew it. She knew, too, that she dared not show what she was feeling. But when Petal added that she thought it so wonderful that so many adopted children were given good homes and that these days there was much less need for 'horrid institutions for the poor deserted babies', Rowan gasped. She could not help turning to look at Petal now. How incredible that she with her past should be able to speak like this. The pity, the tenderness, which she wanted them to believe that she felt towards what she called 'deserted babies' was utterly hypocritical. Or could it be that with the passing of time, she had almost blotted out the memory of her own 'deserted' infant?

"Did you like the people who adopted *you*? Did you have a happy home?" Petal went on, little knowing how deeply she was becoming embroiled by this artless endeavour on her part to show kindness to Rowan. Rowan clenched her hands and forced herself to speak calmly.

"Yes—my—Mummy—was the most wonderful woman on earth. I adored her," she said in a husky tone.

'Dear me,' thought Petal, 'she is rather *emotionée*.'

Now Laurence spoke:

"I happen to be particularly fond of children," he said. "I can't say that I regard this business of adoption with very great enthusiasm. Of course, I mean, that it's splendid from the child's point of view and from the adoptive parents' too—if they are doomed to be otherwise childless. But I've never been able to understand the attitude of the mother. How can any woman bring forth a son or a daughter and just hand it over to strangers without a backward look? There's something unnatural about it. Even wild animals don't desert their young until they are able to fend for themselves."

There followed a deathly silence. Neither of the women—the young one or the older—heard the sound of laughter and voices from the crowd in which they sat, nor the echo of those more distant voices from skiers skimming down the sunlit slopes.

Rowan, scarlet to the tips of her ears, no longer dared look at her mother—but she wondered what must be the thoughts passing through her mind in this moment. Almost she could pity her. For surely, *surely*, no matter what manner of woman she was, she could not sit here and listen to such things being said by the man she was supposed to love so dearly, and remain unashamed or unmoved.

In actual fact, the woman who had been born Vivien Laker, knew no shame but only a nameless fear. She clenched her small delicate fingers inside their thick fur-lined gauntlets. She felt a little sick. It was the first time she had heard Laury talk on this subject. And it was the first time for many many years that she had been brought face to face with her past in quite so unattractive a manner.

Yes, not since her girlhood had she allowed herself to *remember*. There had never been any need. Things had been made easy for her, at the time, by her doting mother and governess and she had never been found out. Why worry? Well—she didn't worry now, but the opinions expressed by Laury were something of a shock. They quite disturbed her. Of course she knew that he loved children and she had toyed with the idea of settling down at last and having a child by him. Certainly she had never wanted one with Rip, but she *was* in love with Laury (as far as she was capable of loving any man) and it might be amusing to have a son. Little Petal as a 'mama'—that would give everybody in her circle a thrill. But she had only *played* with the idea. She was still not anxious to ruin her figure or go through the miseries of pregnancy, and the subsequent pain of bearing a child. *She knew only too much about that.*

Petal shivered. The colour faded from her enchanting, heart-shaped face. She muttered:

"I think it's getting cold up here!"

Laurence did not hear. He was talking to Rowan.

"You say you were adopted. Did you ever discover anything about your real parentage?" he was asking her.

Before Rowan could answer, Petal said sharply:

"Oh, I expect this is rather a sad conversation for Miss Gray, Laury darling. Let's change the subject."

Laurence had not the slightest idea of the sudden chaos that whirled like an eddy of wind through the mind of his newly-made wife, raising a cloud unpleasant as dead, dusty leaves. He persisted—this time questioning her:

"I can't understand a woman ever giving up her own baby can you, Petal?"

Now Rowan looked in a kind of anguish at her mother. But whatever Petal Moore felt she did not show it. She was a past mistress of camouflaging her emotions. She answered:

"I dare say there are extenuating circumstances, Laury."

"None in my mind," said Laurence, "even if a woman has an illegitimate child and is deserted by the man responsible, I don't think she should give the child up. I think it's a sin against the greatest of all human instincts—the instincts of a mother."

Petal sat frozen. Rowan thought:

Oh, my God! . . .

Then Rowan sprang to her feet.

"I *must* go. I've got to get back to the hotel, and I haven't been on my skis yet. I won't wait for the coffee if you don't mind. Good-bye—thank you for—for asking me."

And she walked away before they could stop her. Laurence looked a trifle uncomfortable.

"She seemed a bit upset—was I tactless, darling?"

"Very," said Petal in such a queer strangled voice that he stared at her.

"Darling, you *do* look cold," he said. "I think you ought to let me take *you* down. The wind can be very treacherous up here, despite the heat of the sun."

Without a word Petal rose, zipping up her sheepskin-lined coat. She was quite astonished to find herself shaking. Really, this was quite absurd. She had never allowed herself to think about *that* . . . since it happened. Why on earth had Laurence got to say such things to that girl, and bring back such hateful memories? And how dared he be so censorious—so pious—so ready to condemn? Yet when he took her hand and began to walk with her towards the *téléférique* station she clung to his arm in a way that Petal had not clung to any man in her life before. She smothered an hysterical laugh. Certainly she must be growing old—losing her grip or something—she thought. Or letting herself fall too much in love with Laury. She minded in quite a devastating fashion what he thought of her. It would be an appalling disaster if he ever found out what *she* had done. He put her on a pedestal. But now she knew what he thought about women who abandoned their children.

Oh, thank God the past was dead and buried and could never be resurrected! she told herself.

Laurence threaded his way with her through the little tables and over the hard, caked snow.

"Splendid sight, Mont Blanc," he said. "I've enjoyed this. We must come up here again. What has happened to Ashley, I don't know."

"Don't let's stay too long in Crans," Petal suddenly said wildly. "It's too cold for me. Let's go on to Rome—soon."

"My sweet it'll be just as cold there at this time of the year."

"Then let's go down to Cannes."

"But, darling, the shopping is so frightful there from our point of view. I'd rather set my heart on a tour of the antique shops in Rome with you."

"All right—Rome—but don't let's stay much longer in Crans."

"I thought you were enjoying it here," he said, in a surprised tone.

She bit her lip. She *had* been enjoying it. But that unexpected conversation up here had shaken her to the foundations. She had a quite inexplicable desire to run away from the district. She felt, also, an equally inexplicable resentment against Miss Gray, the girl who had been the cause of the unhappy discussion. Petal said:

"I think Ash would rather we left him alone so that he can work in peace."

"Anything you say, darling. We'll push off tomorrow if you like."

"I don't mind another few days here," she said hurriedly, not wishing to appear unreasonable. Then just before they entered the *téléférique* station she turned and lifted her face to Laurence. "Love me?"

He stared. He had never known Petal to be quite so emotional. She was usually cool—very much in command of herself. He answered by catching her in his arms and kissing her on the mouth.

"You know I love every hair on your head."

"You always must," she said under her breath.

"I always will," he said.

"Even," she said with sudden daring, "if you found out that I——"

"That you—what?"

"Oh never mind, I was only being stupid," she added, losing courage.

But she was very silent on the return journey as they slid on the *téléférique* cable across the tops of the snow-powdered trees, down, down to the green valley, thousands of feet below.

15

ASHLEY had also meant to go up the mountains to ski that morning but he had suddenly found a tune that he liked and, once he started working, didn't want to leave his piano. He told his uncle and Petal that he would follow them. At luncheon-time, however, he was still working. Not until afterwards did he take his skis and trudge out into the snow towards the *téléférique* station.

He was rather pleased with what he had just done. It had also sprung to his mind quite automatically that he would like Rowan to hear it. Then, a trifle grimly, he reminded himself that he was not going to amuse or interest himself at Rowan's expense. Better leave her alone. He had only just got himself out of the waters that had boiled round his head—heated up by Frances Cottar.

Ashley had worked more light-heartedly this morning than he

had done for some time; feeling positive relief because Frances had gone. So far as he was concerned, gone out of his life. Simon, poor devil, had yet to cope with her.

Ashley was glad he'd had that evening's work with old Simon and they had shared their drinks and cigarettes afterwards, like the old friends they used to be. Simon hadn't allowed Fran to come between them. That, for Ashley, was a matter for rejoicing.

It did not, however, prevent Ashley from feeling ashamed of his brief fall from grace. But such a thing would never happen again. He had told himself that a dozen times since the Cottars left Crans.

By the time Ashley reached Cry d'Err, Laurence and Petal had already gone down. Ashley put on his skis and stood on the summit for a moment, breathing in the crisp air. He let the sun ravish his face, and the grandeur of the mountains delight his soul—then he propelled himself forward.

He chose a more remote way than usual, being a good skier, and anxious not to follow in the wake of the crowd. Three-quarters of the way down a narrow path through the pinewoods, he stemmed —took off his gloves and paused to light a cigarette and watch a little red squirrel claw its way up one of the tall slender trees and disappear in the dark foliage.

"Good luck, my friend," he called to it. "Yours isn't a bad way of life! I think I envy you."

Then he thought he heard a cry in a feminine voice. It was repeated.

"Hullo there, *hullo* . . . I need help!"

Ashley moved forward.

To his utter surprise, as he reached a small clearing, he found Rowan. She was sitting on the ground, dabbing at her forehead with a handkerchief which was red-stained. Her skis were beside her and one boot was off.

When she saw the man who reached her side, her face brightened perceptibly, but she looked pale and shaken.

"Oh, Ashley, thank *goodness* it's you," she said, with a laugh. "I've had such a stupid accident. I've been waiting for the next skier, but not many people seem to choose this route."

"But you must be mad!" exclaimed Ashley. "Nobody as inexperienced as yourself would dream of coming this way. It's tricky even for an expert. Very few use this path, in fact, but I always rather like the trees. But *you*—good heavens Rowan, what *induced* you——?"

"Oh, I know I was an imbecile," she broke in, "but I just wanted to get away from the others."

"So did I, but *you*——" Ashley stopped, shaking his head. "Oh, you silly little thing! What have you done? Broken your ankle? Or better still, your leg?" he ended with some sarcasm.

Now she looked up at him appealingly.

"Don't be cross with me. I've got an imperial pain in my head, but I don't think I've broken any bones. In fact I know I haven't. I just sort of tripped and fell and caught my head against a tree. It knocked me out for a minute or two."

Ashley shook his head reproachfully. Bending, he unbuckled his skis, stepped out of them and knelt down beside Rowan. He passed his hand over the slim ankle from which she had removed boot and sock.

"You're *frozen*," he said, "this is too bad."

Ten minutes ago, when the accident occurred, Rowan had thought so, too. She had felt a fool having chosen the most difficult route and proved herself incapable as a skier. She had been moving at some speed when she hit the tree. After she recovered she had felt sick and shaken. But now, suddenly, everything seemed better—even wonderful. All that had happened up at the Cry d'Err café—the things that had been said by her mother and Laurence Moore no longer seemed to matter. She was alone in the pinewoods with *him*. Of all the lucky things to have happened! How marvellous that Ashley should be the one to find her. Her heart beat fast and the colour returned to her cheeks, as his hand touched her ankle. Then she drew the foot inward and reached for her sock.

"It's all right really, just a bit twisted, but I am quite sure I can get up on it and walk home. I might even ski——"

"You'll do nothing of the sort," said Ashley, "even if you *can* walk it must be slowly, and hanging on to me. Let's look at that head."

Kneeling beside her he examined Rowan's forehead. She had taken off her ski-cap. The smooth fair hair tumbled about her neck. She looked so remarkably young and pathetic, he thought, with that slight gash just below the hair-line, and its accompanying bruise. His natural instinct of tenderness towards young and helpless things led Ashley astray again. He forgot all his good intentions. Taking out his own handkerchief, he gently wiped away a tiny trickle of blood and said:

"Poor little poppet—what a shame! Shall I kiss the place and make it well?" And before he could restrain the impulse, he had put his arms around her and touched her forehead with his lips.

She turned so pale and her eyes looked so dark and enormous that he immediately regretted what he had done. He heard her whisper:

"Oh—*don't*——!"

"Why not?" he asked curiously.

"Oh, I don't know—but just help me on to my feet," she stammered wildly.

And she drew on her sock and boot and struggled up. He helped her. Her breath rose like vapour in the frosty air. It was really cold here in the forest where no sun penetrated.

"Let's get out into the sun," she said, as though choked.

"I'm afraid you're angry with me——" began Ashley.

She was incapable of telling him what she really felt. She only knew that she wanted to run away from him—and from herself. She tried to step forward but her ankle twisted again and with a cry of pain she stumbled. It was only Ashley's arm that kept her from falling.

"Easy!" he warned. "Hold tight to me and don't use that foot any more than you can help. Would you like to sit here and let me send for a stretcher?"

"No, certainly not," she said, her cheeks hot and crimson with feeling.

He put his arm around her. How slender the child's waist was, he thought.

"I believe I could carry you——" he began.

"Oh, let's get *on*!" Rowan said so loudly that her voice echoed through the pine trees. He picked up both pairs of skis and shouldered them. They moved along but the ankle definitely hurt Rowan and she limped, lips tight-set, eyes mutinous. He could feel that she did not want him to touch her. She seemed to shrink away from him. After a moment of this difficult passage, he dropped the skis.

"Look—you're not in a fit state to go any farther. I'm going to get help," he said.

"No, don't leave me here——" she began.

And then, because she was trembling so violently—whether it was with cold or nerves he did not know—he put both arms around her. After that she was beyond making resistance. Warmth and passion seemed to engulf her frozen limbs. His lips came down hard upon her mouth. She shut her eyes, locking her small, cold fingers around his neck.

It was a kiss more passionate, more demanding than the others he had given her. She felt that she was awakened by it to a knowledge of the very life-force itself; to all the ardour that her womanhood could offer. There was no more child in her now. Woman incarnate, she offered her lips and received Ashley's kisses in return, while his hands, inside her ski-jacket, clasped the firmness of her young, straight back. Again and again, Ashley kissed her. When he drew back, he said in a shaken voice:

"You're a sweet thing, Rowan—much too sweet."

"I love you," she said. "I love you, Ashley, with all my heart and soul."

The flame of his own ardour died down. Deliberately he extinguished it. He still supported her with one arm, but he did not attempt to touch or kiss her again.

"You mustn't say such things, my dear," he warned her.

"But I *do* love you. Why shouldn't I say so?"

He turned from the sight of those big expressive eyes. He suddenly felt every kind of a cur. He tried to joke:

"You mustn't say '*I love you*' to any man until——"

"Until when?" she asked breathlessly staring up at him.

He clenched his teeth, struggling for mastery of himself, and to do what he thought the right thing for her.

"Until you meet the man you're going to marry, Rowan. Otherwise, darling—oh, *darling* little Rowan—you're so intense and much too sweet," he said again. He put his lips against one of her hands. "Just treat moments like this a little more lightly. You see, I don't want you to be hurt, darling Rowan."

She stood very still. The light had gone out of her eyes, the colour from her face. What he meant was plain enough. It left her with no doubt as to how *he* felt. She was conscious of bitter shame because she had let her own feelings run away with her. With a vain effort to regain lost dignity, she said:

"Really, Ashley, I didn't suppose you were going to propose to me just because you kissed me, you know. How silly you are!"

That reduced Ashley to silence. *Silly* he thought, furious with himself; more than silly. He was a damned fool. He did not believe that Rowan felt as flippant as she now pretended to be. She had not responded lightly to his kiss and he was disturbed not only physically, but mentally because that kiss they had exchanged had seemed like no other he had ever given or received. Here in the vast silence, amid the mountain pines with this young girl, could he have found the answer to life's problems, he wondered for a split second? Could this be an end to the journey of gay adventure that every man takes, and which must inevitably end with the great, mysterious discovery of *himself* as seen mirrored in the eyes of the woman he *really* loves? *Did he, Ashley, in fact love Rowan Gray?*

But there was no answer to that question, now. He only knew that he was not ready for a serious love affair—nor really wanting it to be that way. It was too soon after the unfortunate affair with Fran Cottar; and in the midst of his important work, too. He was almost thankful when Rowan hurried him on. She was laughing. If the laughter was strained, he did not notice it.

"Uncle Ash delivering lecture to silly little niece—you *do* make me giggle! But you needn't worry—little niece isn't as silly as all that. And what's the matter, anyhow? One kiss or more—who cares"—(more laughter)—"and why shouldn't I tell you that I love you? I do. I love Uncle Ash like anything, but all I really want is to get home and put this ankle up and stop my head aching."

She spoke gaily, frothily—punctuating every line with that meaningless laughter. If she had died of pain, she would not have let Ashley know it now. She struggled on down the path, clinging to him, limping and hopping. Almost he could believe he had made a mistake and that she had not been serious, after all. His respect for her deepened considerably. His respect for himself died.

Fortunately they were on the fringe of that green belt of trees. Soon they came out into the open—into the warm sunshine again. They were joined by other skiers; so that emotional episode was over. Rowan at once became the centre of attention from half a dozen young strong men who saw her plight. She was quickly taken to the hotel by two of the stalwarts who made a cradle chair of their linked hands for her to sit on. With arms round their necks, she was carried off. She laughed and grimaced over her shoulder at Ashley who followed, wearing a rather glum expression.

He went with her as far as The Valdana. There Henri came rushing out to help *mademoiselle*. Rowan turned to Ashley for a moment. He did not know why—but the look in her eyes seemed to stab his heart although her words were frivolous enough.

"Thanks for all your help, Ashley. Afraid I spoilt your ski run. And I bet *I* won't be able to ski for a day or two."

"I hope it'll prove to be nothing," he said.

Now Mme Garnier came into the picture. Her small pretty face was much concerned as she looked at Rowan's forehead. The cut no longer bled but the bruise was ugly and Rowan had two red patches on either cheek-bone.

"*Alors*—you've got a fever—you must go straight to bed and let the doctor come and look at you," said Vittoria.

"No, I'm all right," said Rowan, but her teeth had begun to chatter and she was really beginning to feel a little light-headed.

"It's delayed shock," Ashley said.

"We will take care of her," nodded Mme Garnier.

Ashley stood watching as they carried Rowan away and she disappeared into the lift.

He felt the strongest inclination to follow. He knew perfectly well that all the flippant remarks that Rowan had been making for the last twenty minutes meant nothing. He had just seen her eyes —those big, feverish wounded eyes.

'The Snowbird,' he thought. 'Oh God, she *is* the Snowbird!'

He refused the drink that the Garniers offered him. Skis over his shoulders, he walked through the intense cold towards his chalet. He went on thinking:

And am I to be the fellow who shoots her down?

Had his own story—his conception of the unhappy unrequited love of the Snowbird—become more than fantasy? Had it been prophetic? The forerunning shadow of the events that had taken place out here in Crans? Was there, in fact, some direct symbolism between his operetta and his meeting with Rowan Gray?

He did not know. He only knew that he did not find it easy to forget what had happened between Rowan and himself; nor his own cruelty. At the time he had meant to be kind, not cruel. He had thought it right to impress upon the young girl the fact that *he* was not to be taken seriously—that he was not in search of a wife.

But somewhere, somehow, he felt that he had blundered.

When the newly-married pair came back they found a note from Ashley saying that he had gone down to The Valdana for a drink.

What had actually happened was that he had been irresistibly drawn back to the hotel in order to hear the latest news of Rowan.

When he returned to the chalet he was curiously depressed. He told Laurence and Petal that Rowan was in bed suffering from shock and bruises. The doctor refused to let her get up for at least a couple of days.

Laurence was at once sympathetic.

"The poor child!"

This was where Petal liked to exhibit herself in the best light.

"What a horrid accident!" she murmured. "I'll go and see her tomorrow morning and take her some flowers and magazines."

"Yes, do," said Ashley, but he was frowning as he moved away from his guests.

That night they did not find him a very stimulating companion.

16

IN the morning Petal carried out her 'sweet idea' of visiting 'little Miss Gray'.

Laurence walked with his wife down to The Valdana. There were few clouds over Crans today. It was not so warm. Laurence had insisted upon Petal wearing her fur jacket and the little Russian fur cap which made her look charming.

"You really are adorably kind to everybody," was his comment as they walked through the village.

"Oh, one feels so sorry for girls like Rowan Gray who have nothing," Petal said in her most dulcet voice.

They stopped outside the photographer's shop to look at the boards on which hung photographs taken in the various hotels or clubs the previous evening. Sure enough, there was one of little Mrs. Laurence Moore with her tall handsome husband, snapped at the Sporting Club where they had been dining.

"We must order heaps of them. I want to send them to all my friends in England who haven't seen what a wonderful husband I've got," said Petal.

Laurence pressed her arm to his side. He studied the photograph a moment.

"I am always amazed every time I see your face, darling," he said. "Such amazing youth and innocence in it. Who could imagine you a twice-married woman with an international reputation for holding fabulous parties, and living such a full, exciting life!"

Petal hurried him on. She never quite liked Laurence's allusions to her 'youth and innocence'. As a rule she lapped up flattery, but perhaps, she reflected, she really did love Laury because she didn't want mere flattery from him. She genuinely craved for his approval. For a moment she remembered that other husband—the gay kind-hearted Rip to whom she had been so selfish and often so cruel; also of the mother whose devotion she had never repaid. And she thought, uneasily:

'I must have changed a lot. Well, it's because Laury brings out all the best in me.'

She left Laurence in the lounge of The Valdana, talking to Paul Garnier. Mlle Gray, Paul told them, was better this morning but he was sure she would appreciate such a distinguished visitor.

"Then don't announce me," said Petal, taking off her fur cap and running slim, manicured finger-tips through her exquisite hair. "I'll peep in as a surprise."

And as the small graceful figure walked across to the lift, Paul Garnier looked after Petal admiringly.

"*Comme elle est adorable, votre femme!*" he murmured to Laurence.

"Yes, I'm a lucky man," said Laurence, and took Paul off to the bar to order a coffee.

Upstairs in her small bedroom, Rowan was sitting up against the pillows, warm and snug in her bed, physically rested, although very stiff after yesterday's accident. The ankle was still a trifle swollen. The cut on the left side of her forehead was concealed now by a dressing. But she was no longer feverish, and she fully intended to get up and go back to her job tomorrow. She was not one for lying in bed. However, today she intended to write a long letter to the Jenkins. She had just had one of Ann's careless scribbles so full of homely bits of gossip about Blackthorn and the neighbours and the 'latest' from the children. The last paragraph had absorbed Rowan's attention:

You seem to have fallen hard for this composer fellow. I must say he sounds atttractive but a little hard, don't you think? Bill and I would like you to find a nice boy as sweet as yourself. Of course, I realize that Mr. Moore must be fascinating, and everybody at home is beginning to talk about his operetta. But do be careful. We don't want you to be hurt, duckie.

Rowan could almost hear Ann saying that. She looked out of the window that led on to her balcony, at the mountains which were obscured by mist this morning. There was no sun. Crans looked sad. And Rowan felt desperately sad, too.

We don't want you to be hurt.

Dear kind Ann and Bill. How right they were to advise her not to become involved with Ashley. Maybe they would have thought Marc Garnier a 'sweet boy', and decided that it was more suitable for her to attach herself to him. But life wasn't like that. One didn't necessarily fall in love with the most *suitable* person.

"One just falls in love. *Full stop!*" Rowan said the words aloud. Then she shut her eyes tightly because they were stinging. Tears had been close to the surface ever since she had last seen Ashley. No use, this good advice from her friends. It came too late. Rowan opened her eyes and gave a small bitter laugh.

"*I shall not fly again*," she quoted the line from *The Snowbird.*

(*Oh, Ashley, Ashley, if only I didn't love you so much. But all night I have remembered how you held me; and the touch of your hands and the warmth of your long, long kiss. Ashley, it's all too late. Whatever you say or do, I shall never be able to stop loving you now.*)

Somebody knocked at the door.

Rowan sat up, cleared her throat and rearranged the ribbons on her pale blue woolly jacket.

"Come in," she said in a high cheerful voice, thinking it was either Mme Garnier or the charming Swiss girl who served in the bar, or perhaps Maria, the pianist who sometimes came into the hotel to practise during the morning. It might even be Marc.

Rowan's state of mind can best be described as chaotic when the door opened and Mrs. Laurence Moore tiptoed into the room, carrying a huge bunch of roses, flesh and dewy from the Crans florist, and a pile of magazines. Rowan's heart seemed to turn over. Her young face set into mask-like lines.

"Oh! . . . good . . . good morning, M-Mrs. M-Moore," she stammered.

"Is it all right me coming in?" Petal smiled at Rowan. "Perhaps I should have phoned through to ask, but the porter said you weren't on the phone and I took a chance."

Now Rowan's face was crimson. *Her mother.* Her unknown, unknowing mother. The last person on earth she wanted to see this morning when she was already 'in a state'. But somehow she had to say:

"How very kind of you. Most awfully kind."

"Shall I perch here?" said Petal and sat down on the end of Rowan's little bed, loosening her fur jacket. "It's nice and warm in this room," she added, "you're in the best place this morning.

It's not a particularly nice day, although everyone says it will soon clear."

Rowan remained silent. She was trying so hard not to start trembling, or to show any agitation.

Petal went on with her affected, yet seemingly artless chatter. About the weather, the hotel, the people and, of course, Ashley.

"We've left Ash at work. He's a wonderful young man. I'm frightfully proud to have such a clever nephew. Laury says he knew Ash would make good one day. He always had talent."

Rowan nodded. Petal went on:

"Between you and me, Rowan—I must call you Rowan, it's such an unusual charming name—I'm glad that woman, Mrs. Cottar has gone. I think poor darling Ash was trying to get away from her clutches. She was one of these man-eaters. I know them. They're a menace!"

Rowan stared at her speechlessly. Listening to Petal's conversation, looking at her lovely little face, it did not seem credible to Rowan that it was *she* who had given her birth. What a hypocrite! To say these things—she who had been little better than Fran Cottar (at least until she married Ashley's uncle), for Mummy's diary had left no room for doubt that Vivien, nicknamed Petal, left a trail of broken hearts and quite a few ruined lives all over Europe. She had always been remorseless in her dealings with men.

'Look,' Rowan said to herself bitterly, 'what she did to my father. She must have destroyed all his belief in women before he was killed in that awful war.'

Petal was looking around the small bedroom. Her gaze lighted on a big leather-framed photograph which stood on the dressing-table. She rose and walked towards it.

"Can I be inquisitive? I do so adore other people's photos. Who is this—your mother?" she began.

Rowan's blood seemed to freeze in her veins. Her heart gave a jolt. Her face whitened. The thought flashed through Rowan's mind: *Oh God, dear God, she may recognize Mummy. . . .*

Not expecting a visit from Petal, Rowan had not bothered to put the photograph away. It was a speaking likeness of Mrs. Gray. And, unfortunately, one taken when she was younger. She had never had another done so far as Rowan could remember; she hated being photographed. This had been taken in Beaconsfield to please Rowan, about ten years ago.

Agonized, Rowan stared at Petal's back. She seemed to be

examining that photograph with the utmost intentness. Then Petal turned and looked straight into Rowan's eyes. *Now Rowan was sure that Petal knew!* For under the delicate make-up, the older woman's exquisite face was scarlet; curiously blotched. Her eyes looked stricken. In a low voice, she asked:

"Who is this?"

"My . . . my . . . mother," somehow Rowan managed to utter the words.

"Your adoptive mother. You told us you were *adopted.*"

Rowan clasped ice-cold hands against her breast.

"Y-yes."

"And your name is *Gray?*"

"Yes."

Petal looked at the photograph again. Rowan could see it shaking in her fingers. A terrible doubt had assailed Petal, otherwise Vivien. A doubt that was not really a doubt at all but a certainty. She said, hoarsely:

"I know this . . . this woman. There can't be any doubt about the face. I know it only too well. That pointed nose and the crinkles at the corners of the eyes when she smiles. That hair, parted in the middle and looped up in a sort of Edwardian way as she always did it. And the blouse . . . she used always to wear that sort of shirt with a highish collar and cameo-brooch at the throat. She never changed. My mother and I could never make her fashionable. She was always just *Marie.*"

"Marie . . . *who?*" came from Rowan faintly, with a last effort at stalling.

"Marie Garnier," said Petal in a slow queer voice. "This *is* Marie Garnier, isn't it? No, you can't deny it, because *I know.* Even that writing: *For my darling Rowan from her devoted Mummy.* Do you think I don't recognize that slanting fine hand? Marie taught me to write in the same way. People say even now that I've got a foreign-looking handwriting. Your name may be Gray, but this is Marie . . . and *you!* . . ."

Petal stopped. She came to the bedside. She looked down at the young girl who stared back at her in a dumbfounded way. The older woman's face was convulsed. The guard was down. This was not the lovely dewy-eyed Petal who looked so young for her age and who had fascinated Laurence Moore into marriage. It was a face that had sagged suddenly and grown old. For one split second, Rowan stared. Even in the midst of her own chaotic emotions in this crucial hour, she knew that she hoped to see love come into those violet-blue eyes. Love and remorse. But there was neither. There was only a terrible consternation.

"You . . . must be . . . the baby, Marie took away from me in Montreux. *You are my daughter*."

"Yes," said Rowan in a gasp.

"When did you find out?"

"Mummy left a diary which she had meant to burn—but she died suddenly of heart-failure. In the diary, it was recorded that you had become Mrs. Edward Ripsdale. You mentioned that name in front of me when we met in Ashley's chalet, and I nearly fainted."

"Why didn't you give me away then and tell the others?"

"I didn't want to," said Rowan. "I just couldn't."

"Wait a moment," said Petal, "I feel rather sick. . . ."

She dropped into the arm-chair at the side of Rowan's bed. For a moment she hid her face in her hands. Rowan did not speak. She, too, was beyond words. Life itself seemed to be spinning around her so fast that she had been caught up. She was spinning *with* it. She could not get back on to her feet. Yet she felt nothing, absolutely nothing in this moment. At last the woman in the arm-chair raised her face. It was still grey. The lovely limpid eyes that had charmed so many people seemed to beseech Rowan for compassion for herself, rather than offer an apology for the past.

"It wasn't my fault," she said. "I was so young. Only your age. I was taken advantage of . . ."

That did not tally with the story Marie Garnier had written in her diary. A story that Rowan knew must be true because *she* had been incapable of any distortion of fact. But she let Petal ramble on.

It would seem (according to Petal) that she had been the victim of passion rather than a willing participant.

"I married Harry because he insisted," she whimpered. "Can't you imagine how awful it was for me when I started to have you? My mother was heart-broken and so was Marie. They both loved me."

Now for the first time Rowan spoke.

"Yes, they both loved you," she said dully.

Petal tore her handkerchief to shreds between her nervous fingers.

"They made me have my baby in secret. I never thought I'd see or hear of it again."

"I don't know how you could have done it," whispered Rowan.

Petal looked into the reproachful eyes of the young girl in the bed, and shivered. *Her daughter.* She, Petal Moore, had a daughter of nineteen who was a receptionist in a winter sports hotel. It was catastrophic.

"What else could I have done?" Petal began to cry a little into her handkerchief. "It would have meant ruin for me, at that age. Nineteen years ago one had to be even more careful about what one did in social circles than one need be today. Harry was only a chauffeur. . . ."

"But he was nice, and he died a brave death. He was decorated in the war," came from Rowan, feeling a sudden need to defend her father.

"Did the diary tell you that?"

"Yes."

"I don't know how Marie could have been so indiscreet as to write it all down. She adopted you. You ought never to have been told."

Suddenly Rowan flamed in pure anger.

"Don't call Mummy indiscreet. Don't say anything against her. The diary was her one mistake. She just wanted to get it all off her mind. But I'm sorry that I found out. I don't want to think of you as my mother. I won't ever! Mummy took care of me from birth. I am *hers* and not yours!"

Now some kind of astonishment and awareness of Rowan seeped into Petal's mind which until then had been circling around her own dangerous and awkward predicament. She had even started to think that it had been a frightful blunder on her part to betray the fact that she recognized that photograph. But the shock had flung her off her balance. She stared at Rowan. Never in all these years had she given one wistful or tender thought to the infant which she had brought into the world after that brief, tempestuous love affair with Harry Treloar. It seemed utterly impossible that this should be her unwanted child. Rowan Gray, of all people in the world! *The long arm of coincidence,* some would call it. *Truth was stronger than fiction.* Yes—there were many sayings which related to this fantastic discovery. But now Petal began to see certain indisputable likenesses . . . between Rowan and her father, for instance. Those dark expressive eyes that she had inherited from Harry. He had been very handsome. It was his looks and his beguiling polished voice that had taken the young Vivien by storm. But the long fair hair tumbling to Rowan's shoulders . . . that was *her* hair . . . at least before she had tinted her own. Marie used to braid it and tie it up on top of her head with big bows, and everybody used to say how adorable she looked. Except for the hair, Rowan bore faint resemblance to her mother. Slim though she was, the girl was built on altogether bigger lines. But there *was* a look of Daddy about that resolute mouth and chin, thought Petal. Charles Laker, broken by the First World War, had been a stoic throughout all his sufferings and *he* used to purse his lips just as Rowan was doing now, in a sort of determined way . . . determined not to betray distress.

The years rolled back; to the time when Vivien Laker had danced her way through a débutante's season, and captured as many hearts as she had wanted. But she had never given her heart in return. Once, after she and Rip had started to lead separate lives, he had said to her:

"You've got something that beats, and pumps the blood through your beautiful body, but nothing that registers natural feeling. You're a tough nut to crack, Viv. I've never met a tougher. . . ."

Rip hadn't liked her a bit before he died, although nobody guessed. But now she was Laury's adored 'Petal'. And she *had* a heart. *He* thought so. Nobody could say she hadn't. It would be unjust.

At the very thought of Laurence and what he had said to her only yesterday on the subject of mothers and unwanted babies, the woman began to shiver.

"He must never know," she said aloud.

"Who are you talking about?" asked Rowan.

"Laury—my husband. He must never know about you. He'd never forgive me. You heard how down he is on women who have babies and get them adopted. I don't think he's right, mind you, but he's adamant on that subject. Besides, I mean to give him a child of our own. I want him to feel it is my first. What would happen if I suddenly produced a daughter of your age? It would make me look so ridiculous. . . ."

She broke off. Rowan sat very rigidly looking at her and the expression in those young dark penetrating eyes half alarmed Petal. It was so full of contempt. Then Petal put out both hands and seized Rowan's.

"Oh, my dear," she said, "my dear, don't hold this against me. Don't misunderstand me. I'm *not* as cruel and self-centred as I must seem. But this has been a terrible shock. I just cannot believe that you are my child. *I cannot.*"

For one moment Rowan had an irresistible desire to break down and beg her mother for the love, the tenderness that she so desperately needed, but that feeling passed. Contempt returned and with it a feeling towards this woman as chilly as the snow-peaks visible out there in the distance. She said:

"That suits me. Because I can't believe that you're my mother, and I repeat . . . I shall always think of Mummy as my real mother. She did everything for me. You needn't be afraid that I'll tell anybody about you."

She tried to draw her fingers away from Petal but the woman clung to them.

"You do see that it's better this way. It would never do for us to make the relationship known. It would ruin me and upset Laurence. It might even smash our marriage, and this is the only time in my life I've ever been truly happy."

Rowan tore her fingers away this time.

"Go on being happy, please. I shan't interfere with it."

Unspeakable relief showed on Petal's face. She said:

"You're really rather a wonderful girl. It's amazing the way you've taken this."

"Did you expect me to fall into your arms with a cry of *My mother*?" came from Rowan with a hard little laugh.

The older woman's cheeks flushed. Her gaze fluttered away from those inexorable young eyes.

"I . . . well, after all . . . *anything* might have happened."

Rowan repeated her laugh but now she was beginning to tremble.

"Yes, anything might have happened. You might have *wanted* your daughter."

"Oh, Rowan," said Petal, "I know you think badly of me, but my dear . . . I assure you it's better that we don't get worked up about each other. But I'm only human and I *do* feel a real desire to help you."

"In what way?"

"My dear, I'm a rich woman. There's no need for you to work like this in an hotel. Poor Marie would have wanted me to do something for you, I'm sure."

Then Rowan said in an ice-cold voice:

"I don't think Mummy would have wanted anything of the sort. She loathed charity. What she got from your people was hardly enough in the end to keep us going, but even if they had been alive she would have died rather than ask them for more. And I would die rather than touch a penny of yours."

Petal bit her lips and dabbed at her eyes with her handkerchief.

"You hate me. I can see it. I suppose I deserve it."

"I don't hate you," said Rowan. "I just don't feel I want to see you ever again."

"Then—you won't let me do anything for you?"

"No, thank you."

Mrs. Laurence Moore gathered up her fur jacket and rose to her feet. She was beginning to feel very uncomfortable in the presence of this girl who was her daughter. She was also feeling sorry for herself. Now if Rowan had been sweet and pathetic and begged for help, she would have been more sympathetic. She didn't see why Rowan should show all this animosity. Really, she was a peculiar sort of girl.

'Not a bit like me,' thought Petal. 'She's behaving just like Marie told me that Harry behaved when they offered him a cheque. I remember that, distinctly. I can't cope with these proud strong characters. They make one feel so *awkward*.'

Aloud she said:

"Please believe me when I say how sorry I am . . . about everything, my dear, but as you seem to have been very fond of poor Marie and you don't need me, or anything I can give you, we might as well call it a day and part as friends."

"Yes," said Rowan, clenching her hands very tightly on her lap and staring straight out at the mountains.

"Laury and I are leaving Crans tomorrow and I don't suppose we'll meet again."

"I don't suppose so," said Rowan.

At the door Petal hesitated.

"You would let me know if you ever wanted anything?"

"Thank you, but I shan't," said Rowan.

Petal cleared her throat.

"I—I hope one day you'll meet a very nice man and be happily married."

"Thank you," repeated Rowan in her frozen voice.

"And it is agreed that we neither of us ever disclose this incredible thing. I'm a little worried . . . I know you're rather friendly with my husband's nephew and . . ."

Now Rowan broke in and there was passion as well as resentment in her voice.

"Don't worry. I shall not tell Ashley if that's what you're afraid of. I shall only tell one person in the world and that will be the man I eventually marry, because nothing would induce me to start married life with a secret. *If* and when I marry, my husband will know—but I don't think you need be afraid that *he'll* interfere in your life any more than I will. I shouldn't, I hope, choose that sort of man."

'Oh dear,' thought Petal, 'she *is* difficult. I can't believe I ever gave birth to her. Not as sweet as I imagined.'

She gave a last look at her daughter and hurried out of the room. She shut the door, and made her way to the lift. Never had she been more in need of a strong drink.

Rowan sat quite still for a moment, her gaze still fixed on the eternal snows. Her heart beat so quickly that it hurt. She began to wonder if she was feverish again. The cut on her temple was throbbing. She turned her head and saw the expensive roses which Petal had left on the dressing-table. Rowan's lips tightened. She sprang out of bed and in a wild way, picked up the flowers, flung open her door and called to the *femme de chambre* who was coming down the corridor.

"Take these," he said, "I don't want them. You can have them."

Before the astonished girl could thank her, Rowan had shut the door again.

Then Rowan took the photograph of Marie Garnier from the dressing-table, climbed into bed with it, cuddling it against her, turned her face to the pillow and wept.

"You'll be my only mother always. Oh, I wish you could come back. I wish, *I wish you could come back*!"

Petal joined her husband in the bar. She looked so pale and distraught that Laurence was horrified.

"My *darling*—Petal, my *sweetest*—what on earth has happened?" he asked, taking her by the arm.

"Give me a drink," she said, gulping.

After she had finished the champagne cocktail he handed her, she told him to take her home.

"I'm not very well," she said. "I felt quite faint just now up in that . . . that girl's room."

Laurence truly loved this woman whose real character was entirely hidden from him. He insisted on ordering the local taxi and driving her that short distance to his nephew's chalet. Once there,

Petal, in an hysterical condition, flung herself into Laurence's arms and begged him to take her away from Crans immediately.

"But of course," he said without protest. "I'll see Ash and make the arrangements. We can go this afternoon if you wish."

She looked at him blindly. She knew that she had done many cruel despicable things in her selfish life and not the least despicable had been her reluctance to acknowledge her own child, known to the world as Rowan Gray. But she could not have borne it if Laurence had found out and turned against her. All her wealth, all that she had left of beauty and youth, would mean nothing if he did not want her any more. He had some strange control over her heart which no other man had ever had. Before leaving her lying there on her bed, he covered her tenderly with an eiderdown. As he reached the door she called him back to her side.

"Laury, you do really love me, don't you?"

He took her hand, kissed it and smiled, but he was startled. It was not the first time Petal had asked this question since she had come to Crans. She seemed so unlike herself here, he thought, so much more highly strung. He could only suppose it was the high altitude. The sooner he got her down to sea-level the better.

"I adore you, you know it," he said.

"And if I lost every shilling, if I had nothing—nothing of my own——" she began.

"I refuse to listen to such nonsense," he broke in. "Do you for a moment imagine I married you for *money*?"

She did not answer but held his hand against a cheek which was damp with tears. She kept thinking about her daughter—*her daughter*. The awful coincidence that had brought them together after nineteen long years. She whispered:

"I wonder what made you love me in the first place."

"Oh, darling, lots of things," Laurence answered, trying to speak gaily and bring her back to normal humour. "Don't worry your little head."

"Would you forgive anything I ever did?"

"Anything except preferring some other chap to me," he said with a laugh, and bent and kissed her. "But why such questions?"

She was silent—full of guilty, shameful thoughts. She had betrayed her infant after its birth. This morning she had betrayed it for the second time—in the form of that young girl up at The Valdana. She knew quite well that Laurence would not forgive her *that*. She knew that she was a coward. She had been lucky to find Rowan such a strong character—so dependable—someone who wouldn't give her away. Her secret would be safe with Rowan. But the shock of the discovery had shaken Petal to the core of her being, and for the first time in her egotistical life she knew what it was to be conscience-stricken. She also knew that nothing could justify her action. But all that she wanted now was to get out of Crans as quickly as she could, and never again meet that young, fair girl who had looked at her with such proud, scornful eyes this morning.

17

ROWAN spent a miserable day.
She had plenty of visitors, including young Marc who brought her flowers and appeared genuinely distressed by her accident, but she would not let him into her room and he had to be content with speaking to her through a half-opened door. He was followed by Mme Garnier. Rowan was forced to receive her employer's wife. Vittoria was kindness and consideration itself, and begged Rowan not to get up until she felt really well enough. They would manage without her down at Reception, she said.

Then later that afternoon, Ashley, himself, came and knocked on Rowan's door.

Her heart seemed to turn over when she heard his voice. He had been so much on her mind—he and that woman who was her mother. But she did not want to see him in her present state of mind. She was so bitterly unhappy—so disillusioned in life.

"Can't I come and smoke a cigarette beside you?" he called out, "or do you think it would be improper——" he added with a laugh.

Somehow she managed to echo the laugh.

"Not at all improper, but I just don't want visitors. I'm a bit dopey . . . and sleepy. . . ." (That was a lie but she had to say something.)

"I'm so very sorry, my dear," he called out.

She sat up in bed, her face white and strained, her big eyes fixed on that door as though she could see through it. She loved him so much that her heart seemed to hurt with the pain of hope-less loving.

"Thank you for coming," she said to him after a pause.

"Are you better?"

"Much better. I'm going to go down and work tomorrow even if I have to hobble."

"Good. Then in the evening I'll get you up to the chalet in a car and play you my latest. I've done quite a bit of work today."

She shut her eyes tightly. She told herself that she would not go to Ashley's chalet. She could not bear that he should take her in his arms and kiss her light-heartedly ever, *ever* again. All through this difficult day she had remembered him telling her that she must not love him. The memory made her feel cheap and wretched. She must just try not to see him any more than was possible until her job in this hotel was finished, and she could leave Crans.

Ashley lingered outside Rowan's door. He was curiously disappointed that he was not permitted to see her. He said:

"I don't know whether you know, but my fond uncle and his beautiful wife have pushed off——"

Rowan was thankful that he could not see the scarlet that burnt her face. So her mother had gone! She had run away—she had lost no time in going, Rowan thought bitterly. The utter cowardice —the lack of natural feeling—made her feel a little sick, but she spoke to Ashley in a voice that was meant to be casual.

"Why the sudden departure?"

"One of Petal's whims, I suppose. She's a woman of whims, don't you think? Uncle Laury said she'd been unlike herself and that the altitude was affecting her, so he rushed her down to Sierre. They caught the afternoon train to Geneva. They're going on to Rome. I can't say I'm sorry. I'll like having the chalet to myself again and I'm sure Hortense is as pleased as I am."

Silence. Rowan hugged her knees with her arms and laid her forehead against them. She wished Ashley would go away. She felt very lonely; very sad. Two big tears forced their way between her closed lids and trickled down her cheeks.

Ashley went on:

"Well, Rowan, sorry not to have seen you, but I'll look you up tomorrow and hope you'll be downstairs. Good night, my dear."

"Good night," she said and raised her head and looked at the door that was between them. It was symbolic, she thought; of the door that must inevitably shut him out of her life for ever.

Ashley went down in the lift, lighting a cigarette and feeling uneasy; not nearly as cheerful or self-confident as usual. He did not understand himself. He was working well. He had reached an understanding with Simon. Fran had gone. The honeymoon couple who had disturbed his peace up at the chalet had gone, too. What was troubling him? Nothing—except Rowan. And why worry about *her*? After all, she was of no great importance in his life. She was just a sweet, foolish child who had, in her inexperienced way, fallen in love with him.

Yet he could not get her out of his mind. He admonished himself:

'You're slipping, my boy.'

As he came out of the lift, he almost collided with the slim, pretty, French woman of the golden eyes, with whom he'd had one or two drinks in the bar.

"You are in a gr-reat hurry?" she said, smiling at him.

"Not a bit," he said, answering her in French. "Have a cocktail with me—will you?"

"*Merci*—but I am just going up to see little Miss Gray who had the accident."

"She doesn't seem to want to see people," said Ashley in a rather gloomy voice.

"Then I shall come and have the cocktail with you," said *madame*.

They talked of many things. She was, Ashley considered, quite definitely a charming woman. Ordinarily speaking, he might have been interested. But instead he kept thinking about the young girl upstairs. Strangely enough the picture that stayed in his mind was the one of Rowan as he had found her on the woodlands ski-run. Sitting there, nursing her injured ankle, looking so forlorn. The memory of Rowan's voice when she had said: "*I love you, Ashley, with all my heart and soul*," plagued him.

He had rejected her. He had done so believing it to be the best for *her*. She was far too like his 'Snowbird'.

'I'm damned if I'm going to be responsible for hurting her,' he kept telling himself and frowned as he sat at the bar listening to his companion's chatter.

Once back at his chalet, he went straight to the piano and tried, in an angry defiant sort of way, to work. But no inspiration came.

When darkness fell, he switched on the lamp and shut out the blue cold night. He smoked innumerable cigarettes. He continued to feel cross and restless.

The Norwegian skier from The Valdana, telephoned to him:

"There's a *bal masqué* at The Sporting tonight. Why not come with us, *mon cher*?"

Ashley refused the invitation. He was not in a gay mood, and a carnival with a lot of noisy youngsters wearing fancy dress held little appeal for him. But he could not shake off his restless mood. The chalet seemed quiet now that Laurence and his Petal had gone.

He thought of the woman Laury had married. From a masculine point of view, he could not deny her beauty but he had come to the conclusion that he did not like her. She was cold-hearted under that display of pretty appeal—he was sure of it. But he could see why Laury had fallen for her. The way she played up to him and his artistic side was wonderful. He only hoped that this happiness would last—for Laury's sake.

The thought of Rowan came back with a subtle persistence.

At last Ashley was driven to telephone her at the hotel. He was stupidly disappointed when Henri told him that Miss Gray's room was not connected with the phone.

"Can I give her a message, *monsieur*?" asked Henri.

"*Non merci*," said Ashley, and added casually: "Just say I rang to inquire."

That message was delivered to Rowan by the good Henri when he passed her door later that night.

It did nothing to lift the gloom that was suffocating her. She was not even comforted by Ashley's attention. It was, in her opinion, just another small twist of the knife in the wound. She didn't want to *have* to think about Ashley.

She spent the next day in bed—forbidden to put that bad foot on the ground. This, she found very frustrating. It was so difficult to stop brooding when one was lying in bed through the lonely hours of the day. In a way, it was a relief to know that her mother was no longer in Crans, yet she found herself thinking a lot about that small, beautiful creature who had given her birth. No doubt Mrs. Laurence Moore was having a wonderful time, somewhere, with her newly-married third husband; not giving a backward thought to her daughter. Despite herself, the idea of this hurt Rowan.

That next morning, she insisted on getting up and going down to work. Much of the swelling in the ankle had gone down. She hobbled to her desk in the office. She received quite a heart-warming reception from the rest of the staff and those guests who had heard about her little accident.

She plunged into arrears of correspondence. She even tried to show some enthusiasm when Marc came up from Sierre and brought her a big box of chocolates from his father. She agreed that he should take her down to Sierre to lunch at the Hôtel de Montagne on Sunday. He would drive her, he said, from door to door.

But there remained in Rowan's mind the certainty that sooner or later she would have to see Ashley again. He would come into the hotel some time this evening. She dreaded it.

It was another sunny day. Rowan spent most of her time off, during the afternoon, on the terrace in the sunlight; envying those who could ski. She hadn't had much luck coming down from Cry d'Err, she thought ruefully. Perhaps she wasn't going to make a first-rate skier.

She was just going back on duty when Paul Garnier, who had just finished a long-distance call from Geneva, came to her on the terrace with a shocked face and told her the news that he little dreamed would be of such personal significance to her.

"Terrible, terrible," he said, shaking his head. "A most terrible thing! That poor beautiful little lady and that charming man."

Rowan looked at him, uncomprehending for a moment.

"You remember," he went on, "only forty-eight hours ago they were here."

"But *who*, Monsieur Paul?"

"The uncle and aunt of Mr. Ashley Moore."

Now Rowan's heart plunged. Her hand instinctively went up to her throat.

"What's happened?" she asked tersely.

"My friend, M. Daponte from Geneva—you remember he was here last week-end—has just telephoned to tell me. One of the Geneva-Roma passenger planes crashed on the runway soon after taking off this afternoon. M. and Mme Laurence were on the passenger list."

Silence. Nothing to be heard but the distant lilt of music from the skating rink across the snow, and the drip of water as snow thawed on the sloping roof of the covered terrace and fell down into a little pool.

The shock to Rowan was intense. White, trembling, she stared at M. Paul. He took a handkerchief from his pocket and wiped his sun-browned face.

"*Quel désastre!*" he muttered. "All—*all* killed. Crew and passengers. Something went wrong. There will be the usual inquiry. It is such a sudden and violent end. And those two on their honeymoon. *Mon Dieu!* One can only be glad they died together.

But she—so tiny and sparkling and sweet—like an angel to look at—to think of it is horrible——"

Then Paul broke off with an exclamation. He caught little Miss Gray by the arm. He thought she was about to faint. He began to propel her towards her chair. But she recovered herself. She asked in a low, trembling voice:

"Is it—definite—that the two Moores were on that plane?"

"Quite definite," answered Paul. "My friend went down to the airport to inquire. He is a big business man in Geneva. Well known. He was afraid that friends of his were involved. They were not, but it was confirmed that Mr. and Mrs. Laurence Moore were on board. He met them here in the bar with me, a few nights ago."

At that moment Vittoria joined them. She, too, had heard the news. She began to talk rapidly to her husband in their own language. Rowan sank into her chair. Her heart beat violently. She felt sick. She covered her face with her hands.

'My mother is dead,' she said the words in a whisper to herself. 'Poor, poor little thing, *she is dead*!'

She heard M. Paul speaking:

"Somebody ought to tell that boy at the chalet about his uncle."

"We will go together to tell him," said Vittoria.

Rowan sat in her chair in the office, feeling stunned. She could not pretend that she had loved her mother. After their conversation that day up in her bedroom, she had felt an extraordinary coldness, even indifference towards the whole relationship. Nevertheless, to imagine Petal crashing to her death in so sudden and dreadful a way, did not bear thinking about.

What an end for Marie Garnier's beloved little 'Vivien'; and for Laurence Moore with all his charm and culture. He had been very kind to *her*, Rowan thought. It gave her a pang to remember how, physically, he had resembled Ashley. He had been more handsome perhaps, more sophisticated, but there had been a strong resemblance between the two and it was grim to know that so delightful a man had been wiped off the face of the earth. *Or was it a mercy that Laurence would never now be disillusioned in his wife?*

Within twenty minutes, the Garniers returned to The Valdana without having seen Ashley. He had gone out; Hortense did not know where.

Suddenly Rowan felt a frantic desire to see Ashley herself. Perhaps she would tell him the truth now. When she had promised her mother not to disclose the secret, things had been different.

Now it could not matter any more. Rowan's mind and heart were overflowing with torrential feeling. If she knew no grief, she knew at least a deep immeasurable pity for that beautiful woman still so youthful, who had died in the prime of life.

Rowan needed to talk to somebody—and it could only be to Ashley. A little while ago she had made up her mind not to see him alone again, but everything seemed to have been changed by the shocking news.

She half expected that he might come into the hotel as usual for an aperitif. But tonight he did not come.

At seven o'clock, Henri in his kindly way suggested that Mlle Gray should go and rest. There was little more she could do in the office tonight, he said. It was an hour earlier than usual but she accepted Henri's idea. Ever since the news of the disaster had reached the public, her nerves had been sorely taxed. So many of the guests had come up to discuss the affair with her—those, in particular, who had met and talked to the Moores while they stayed in Crans.

"She was so beautiful—so sweet," they kept saying. "*He* was so good looking."

"How dreadful these air-disasters are—I don't like flying," some had said.

Rowan had listened to it all and commented, and wondered ironically what else they would have said if she had told them that it was her own mother who had been killed in that accident.

The urge to see Ashley grew so strong that finally it became irresistible. She would go and find him if she could. No one would miss her. Dinner was beginning. The staff was fully occupied. Rowan did a thing which ordinarily she would not have dreamed of doing. She approached the attractive Norwegian who always had a smile and a word for her and had so often tried to include her in his parties. She knew that he had a car outside in the garage. She asked him if he would drive her to l'Étoile.

"My ankle is still weak but I can limp to your car," she said with an effort at a smile.

The Norwegian looked surprised but was too polite to express it.

"Of course I'll take you anywhere you like to go," he said.

She wrapped herself in coat and scarf, and drove with him over a road which was white and slippery with ice, tonight. Crans glittered under a full moon. The sky was fiery with stars.

"Can I wait for you or fetch you again?" the kindly Norwegian asked Rowan as he pulled up at the chalet.

Rowan said that she would not dream of such a thing and that Mr. Moore would see her home. Then with hot cheeks and a nervous fluttering of eyelids, she added: "Would you mind not telling them all at the hotel that you—brought me here?"

"I quite understand," said the man.

But he did not, and he returned to The Valdana, somewhat puzzled.

As Rowan waited for Hortense to answer the door-bell, she experienced a sensation of despair. Why had she come? Possibly Ashley was still out and would not be in the whole evening, in which case she had wasted the Norwegian's time and her own energies. She would have to ask Hortense to telephone for a taxi to take her back to the hotel at once. This was madness.

The door opened. But it was not Hortense who opened it. It was Ashley himself. In the old slacks, and polo-necked sweater, a cigarette between his lips, he stared at the young girl.

"*You*," he ejaculated. "*Bon Dieu!* What a surprise!"

She did not notice how genuinely pleased and relieved he seemed to be to see her. Her heart was too full. She began to mutter something. He put out a hand and pulled her in and shut the door.

"My dear child, for heaven's sake, come right in. You're letting in all the cold and you'll catch your death."

She looked up at him piteously. His brown rugged face with the strong bones, the strangely light eyes, looked so unmoved, that she knew that he had not heard . . . he confirmed this by saying:

"I've just taken a long walk—well beyond Montana. It was wonderful in the moonlight."

Her trembling fingers began to unbutton the collar of her coat. She whispered:

"So you didn't know that—Paul and Toria had been to see you?"

"Hortense has just told me. I believe I am supposed to ring them, but I haven't done so yet. Why did they want to come and call on me this evening?"

He was being very cheerful. He tucked an arm through Rowan's and led her into the lounge where a pine-log fire burned with frosty brightness. The piano looked as usual, untidy, littered with manuscript. Ashley nodded towards it.

"You see I've been trying—but I couldn't do a stroke of work. I am so glad to see you, my dear. I was a bit worried because I felt I had offended you or something. And I thought you weren't able to walk, either——"

He broke off, fully aware now of the look of strain on Rowan's face. She balanced on the arm of a chair and threw off her coat.

"What is it, Rowan?" Ashley spoke again, this time in a serious voice. "Has anything happened?"

And then for her it was as though the flood-gates opened. She could not stem the torrent of feeling that rushed through her. Death had changed everything. While her mother had lived, she had felt nothing but an icy contempt for her. Tonight, she wept bitterly for Petal—her face hidden in her hands—feeling as though all the anguish and loneliness in the world had descended on her.

"Oh, Ashley, *Ashley*," she sobbed.

Her complete abandonment to grief distressed Ashley. He did not stop to analyse his own feelings. Caution was flung to the wind. It seemed the most natural thing in the world for him to gather Rowan into his arms, hold her close and try to comfort her.

"Don't cry like that, don't cry, darling, *don't*!" he kept saying.

He strained the slight body against his and threaded his fingers through her hair with slow caressing movements. He tried to assuage a sorrow—the significance of which for the moment he barely understood. He only knew that she was dearer to him than he had imagined.

"My poor little sweet . . . Rowan . . . my honey . . . don't cry like that," he kept saying.

She clung to him as though her life depended on it, pressing her wet contorted face against his shoulder. After a moment she controlled herself and drew away. When he made an effort to take her back into his arms she shook her head.

"No. Let me alone. I'm making a fool of myself."

"A very darling fool," he said tenderly. "I really am glad you've come up to me. I swear it. Don't feel that you oughtn't to have come."

She knew, of course, that he did not understand why she wept.

Now she did what had to be done. Holding a handkerchief against her quivering lips, without looking at him, she said:

"I have terrible news for you, Ashley. Somehow I felt I must come up here and tell you, myself. Paul and Toria came to break it—but I think *I* ought to be the one."

He stared at her.

"What are you talking about?"

She drove herself to tell him. When he knew, his face grew a little grey. He felt shaken to the roots of his being. He stared at her, horrified.

"Good God!" he said slowly, "good *God*!"

"Yes—it's terrible," she whispered. "I'm so terribly sorry . . . about your uncle. You loved him."

"I just can't believe it," said Ashley, and pulled a cigarette from a packet on the table and lit it, his fingers shaking.

"Nobody could," Rowan said swallowing hard. "Everybody at the hotel—is horrified."

Ashley sat down heavily.

"Uncle Laury and that pretty charming creature he only married a few weeks ago. How grim! How unutterably grim!"

For a moment he asked her for more details. She told him all that she knew. He nodded once or twice, drawing in deep long breaths of his cigarette. After a pause, he said:

"This is a frightful shock. I must phone the airport at once. I am Laury's next-of-kin. I ought to go to Geneva and see them as soon as I can get there."

Rowan nodded. Ashley got up and poured himself out a strong drink.

"No good offering you one, Rowan?"

"No, thank you."

"It was good of you to come and tell me. Thanks," he added, clearing his throat. The muscles of his cheeks were working. He had not thought it possible to be so upset.

Another difficult silence then Rowan raised her head and looked at him. It was a long, rather tragic look. Now he was standing with arms crossed, staring at the fire. To utter words of sympathy would have been superfluous; besides they stuck in her throat. And the other news she had meant to give—about Petal being her mother—somehow she no longer wanted to tell him that now. It would seem purposeless except to re-focus his attention upon herself; to draw from him a sympathy which would not for that cause be justified. She felt bitterly unhappy, but her mother's death

168

was not the direct cause. She wept for Petal and also for Ashley. In his arms just now she had felt that she had reached the beginning and end of all things. She loved him with such a consuming passion; but he must never know. She would not make him feel in any way responsible for her.

Ashley, in his masculine fashion, began to turn his mind to the practical side of things. Rowan and his feelings for her were temporarily forgotten.

"I must ring up the airport," he kept repeating.

"Of course," whispered Rowan.

"Poor Laury——" Ashley bit at his lips. "Poor old Laury! And his Petal; all their hopes and schemes. What a hell of a life, Rowan! One never knows when one's turn is coming."

He walked towards the door. Rowan called him back.

"Will you please ring for a taxi for *me*? I can't quite walk properly yet."

"Don't go yet——" he began.

"I must," she broke in. "I must get back to the hotel."

"Then I'll come with you and make my arrangements from there. Anyhow I'd like to speak to Paul and Toria. I'll have to go away for a night or two. And perhaps," he added, "I ought to go back to London. I know I'm Laury's executor. There'll be his lawyers to see, and I'll have to look into poor Petal's affairs, too. I don't know if she has any relations in Europe—or even in America. There'll be so much to inquire into."

He had become frighteningly remote from Rowan again. Sufficiently remote to show her how little she counted in his life. That knowledge helped to restore her emotional balance. She was quite calm when the taxi came and she drove back to The Valdana with Ashley.

The steps leading into the hotel from the snow-whitened road were slippery. Ashley insisted on carrying Rowan. It was only as he picked her right up that he seemed to come mentally closer to her again, for he gave her a little hug and put his cheek against her cold one.

"Thank you for coming up to see me, dear. It was terribly sweet of you. It helped having you there," he whispered. "I'll have to come back to Crans after I've been to Geneva. I'll probably stay on and try to finish my score. I'll see you then, if not before."

She nodded but made no reply. Just for a moment she clung to him.

I shall never see him again, she thought in her despair. *He doesn't feel as I do—why should he? And I see no object in hurting myself by continuing to see him.*

She made up her mind even if it meant upsetting Uncle Jean and inconveniencing them all at The Valdana, that she would leave Crans at once. She would be gone before Ashley returned.

18

BILL JENKINS had hardly walked through the door of his home before Ann rushed at him and let out a stream of words about Rowan. He gathered that Rowan had unexpectedly left Switzerland and was back in this country.

"You could have knocked me down with a feather," Ann said, "when *this* arrived——" and she thrust a letter into his hand which looked so bulky that Bill blinked.

"Hold your horses. I can't digest all that literature before I've had a breather and a sherry, sweetie-pie," he said.

"Come into the kitchen; I'm cooking," said Ann.

"Shall I say good night to Scrap first?"

"No, she's been frightfully naughty all day and made to go to sleep, and she's not to say good night to you, as a punishment."

"What did she do?"

"Had that awful little girl up the road in to tea and they both put jam all over the wallpaper in the spare room. They said they were making a modern design."

Bill threw himself into a chair, watching while his wife put a pie into the oven. He alternated between laughing and swearing.

"The little so-and-so! All *my* work gone to ruin. Where's Jeremy?"

"He's in his bed and asleep too; or ought to be. He joined in when he got back from school, called himself the Human Roller and licked most of the jam off, and made a ghastly mess."

"Dear life!" said Bill rolling his eyes heavenwards. "Give me that drink. We might as well stop trying to make the home look attractive and live in a barn. It's all the children need and appreciate and *we're* supposed to lead our lives for them."

But the parents of the two delinquents smiled into each other's eyes as they grumbled and complained.

It was bitterly cold and raw outside, this February night. Inside, the kitchen with its arched timbered roof—the oldest room in the farm—was full of bright lights and the warmth coming from the cooker. Everything was spotless if a trifle untidy. Tidiness had never been Ann's strong point. But there was a delicious odour of freshly-baked scones which Bill liked and his wife seemed to him the most attractive woman in the world; with her flushed face, free of cosmetics, her curly hair escaping from its pins, and all the love and welcome in the world in her bright blue eyes.

This family of his, this shabby old farmhouse, were his pride and joy—his kingdom. He had had a hard day in the office. The train had been late due to fog on the line. He was cold and tired. But nothing seemed to matter now. He pitied the sort of fellow he had talked to in the train who had to go away on business for a couple of nights, and said he was thankful for what he called 'a break from home'. Nothing could ever mean a 'break' to Bill unless it included Ann and those young ruffians upstairs who made such a lot of work and cost such a lot of money. And of course there was the third ruffian, Luke, who had just scratched at the scullery door and been let in. He rushed at Bill, leaving muddy paw marks all over the clean floor, and two splodges on Bill's City trousers.

"Get away, you brute," said Bill, "look what you've done to me."

"Read Rowan's letter," said Ann.

Relaxing now in the warmth, sipping his sherry, Bill quickly scanned the long letter which, he saw, had been written in Crans but posted in Geneva. It was written, as Rowan always wrote—clearly and descriptively. She did not wish, she said, to keep any-thing from her friends because they already knew so much about her, and she wanted them to understand why she had packed up and intended to leave Crans in such a hurry. She knew that it would be a surprise to them and they probably wouldn't approve of her action, but she had reached the end of her tether and felt absolutely compelled to get away. She thought that the best thing she could do was to come back to England. First of all she told them of the catastrophe that had ended the life of the one-time Vivien Laker.

She went on:

Even though I hardly knew my mother, and what I did know had not endeared her to me—her death was a shock. And it all came on top of my unhappiness over Ashley. I am so terribly much in love. Things seem to be crowding down on me. I just can't take any more.

I can't go on working in the hotel, knowing that he means to come back to Crans and to the chalet. It means that I would not only see him at The Valdana every day but that he would ask me to go up and see him and I'm too weak to say no. I couldn't keep away from him. You see, I really do love him. He isn't like any other man in the world. But he's not for me. I seem to amuse and interest him a little but he always treats me as though I was a child. And he never stops warning me not to fall in love with him. You'll agree that the best thing is for me to get away from him.

I didn't want to upset the Garniers but the whole matter was made a little easier for me when M. Garnier announced last night that he had heard that my predecessor was very much better, and would be able to take over the job again if I could wait a week. I agreed to that.

Naturally, when I told Paul that I was going, he was upset and Uncle Jean seemed terribly sad and sorry about it. He was afraid, he said, that I hadn't been happy in Mummy's country. I told him that I had—very—and that I would never forget the mountains or my life in Crans as long as I lived. But I made up a story about being sent for because of sudden illness of a relative at home and that I had to go. Tante Elise did not seem sorry about it because I know she wanted to get Marc away from me. Poor Marc! He was genuinely upset, and proposed to me about half a dozen times in the hour that I spent down in Sierre. But I just couldn't love Marc that way, so that was that.

Yes, I'm afraid I've been an awful coward and just run away, but try not to blame me. I shall post this to you in Geneva on my way back. I'm not going to take an expensive plane back. I shall go by train to Paris and then boat. It's much cheaper. I expect to arrive in London on 20 February. Soon after you receive this I shall be in England again—probably in an hotel in London. I know of one where Mummy said she stayed once or twice and which the poor darling used to call 'very respectable'. From there I shall try to get a secretarial job. I must keep myself. I can't just sit around and spend Mummy's capital.

I long to see you and the children and Blackthorn, so you'll get a phone call from me quite soon. Good-bye for now.

Bill read the letter up to this point, then tossed it on to the kitchen table. His blue eyes looked solemn.

"How pathetic," he said, "how absolutely pathetic."

Ann pushed a wisp of hair back from her pink moist face.

"That's what I thought. Our Rowan just *had* to go and fall in love with the wrong man."

172

"I must say she didn't choose small fry. Moore's name is always in the papers in connection with that new musical."

"I know," said Ann, "and just imagine the drama of meeting her own mother out there and then of the poor woman being killed like that in a crash."

"All very dramatic," said Bill.

"And it makes her in a way semi-related to the very man she's fallen in love with, which is even more strange."

"It's all very complicated," said Bill.

"And a fantastic coincidence, but these fantastic things do happen," said Ann, sighing.

"Sit down a moment, darling, and let's talk," said Bill.

"I must get on with our meal, darling."

"But oughtn't we to do something about this poor child?" Bill asked. "Can we let her live in a miserable boarding-house in London and go out to a job? She must be so wretched."

"Well, of course, I want her to come down to us," said Ann. "I've been wanting it ever since I read her letter."

Bill twirled the stem of his empty glass between his fingers.

"You don't think there is any hope for her with this composer chap?"

"I shouldn't think so. He's obviously not in love with her. He's a successful young man likely to make pots of money, and he can have his pick of glamour-girls. You know our Rowan. She's a darling—but *not* glamorous."

Bill got up, put an arm around his wife's shoulders and dropped a kiss on her soft hair.

"It isn't all men who search for glamour," he said. "And I believe it's the other women who really like the so-called glamorous women."

"That's a very profound remark for you, dear," said Ann with her tongue in her cheek, her eyes twinkling at her husband. "But I have a sneaking feeling that you are suggesting that *I* have no glamour!"

"I hate the word," said Bill. "Anyhow, speaking of Rowan— when she does contact us, let's ask her down to talk things over."

He started to walk towards the door. Ann called after him:

"I have certain small tasks, none of them glamorous, which you might like to perform for me, my dear Mr. Jenkins."

Bill stopped.

"I knew it. A man never has a moment to himself. What now?"

"A bucket of coal for the drawing-room. The boiler to make up. The jam to wash off the spare room wall (or you can re-paper it if you prefer), and the vet says that Luke's got to be wormed."

"I'm darned if I'll worm Luke and I'll only see to the boiler because I want a hot bath," said Bill. "Otherwise I shall do none of those other things."

Ann seized a jar of jam from the cupboard.

"If you don't, I shall smear the contents of this over the paper in your dressing-room—just where it can trickle on to your chest-of-drawers and in on your new shirts."

"I consider," said Bill, "that I am a very badly treated man and——"

He stopped. The telephone bell was ringing.

"I'll answer it," said Ann. "You go and get the coal, my boy."

She lifted the telephone receiver, wishing as always that the telephone was not in the hall where there was such a howling draught.

She was delighted and surprised to hear the voice which she had been anticipating and so much wanted to hear.

"Rowan!" she exclaimed, "my *dear*, how lovely!"

"It's lovely to hear your voice again, too, Ann," came from Rowan.

"Where are you? How long have you been back?"

"I arrived yesterday, and I'm in a little private hotel not far from Notting Hill Gate. I'll send you the address."

"Rowan, you're to come down here at once—before we go any further. You're a very naughty girl not to have come to us immediately. You know I've always told you Blackthorn Farm is your second home."

"My one and only home, I have no other, darling Ann. But I didn't think I ought to land myself on you and Bill."

"If it's £ s. d. you're thinking of," said Ann, "I can surely offer such an old friend a bed for a week or two and then if you *must* be so proud, why not live here and do a job for me, instead of leading a wretched life which I know you'll loathe, in a London office, and going back to frightful food and no fresh air, in some dreary boarding-house."

A moment's hesitation, then from Rowan:

"Well, I've already been to several agencies about work and I don't think I'll have much trouble in getting a secretarial job, but I admit I'd love to come down for a day or two and see you and the old district. I've so much to talk to you about. It has been rather beastly and lonely . . .'' the voice broke.

Ann's motherly heart surged with feeling.

"You're to come by the first train tomorrow morning. Them's my orders. I'll meet you at Beaconsfield. You can catch that—whatever the train is—that gets you here about half past ten."

So Rowan returned to Jordans.

She was a changed Rowan. Ann Jenkins was swift to discover that. She did not even look the same. Ann was accustomed to a rather pale girl who rarely seemed to have colour in her cheeks. This Rowan was tanned to a warm golden brown which suited her. Whatever her state of mind might be, she had grown positively beautiful, Ann thought. But she was painfully thin. Her cheek-bones jutted out. She looked older too. She had a new maturity not only in her face but in her manner.

'This love business has hurt the poor child,' Ann thought, 'but she's sort of *come out* of her shell—she isn't nearly so inhibited. The poor lamb has learned a bit about life, I suppose. When she lived here with Mrs. Gray she knew nothing.'

Rowan stood in Ann's familiar kitchen and looked out at the garden that she knew so well, and through those trees towards the little cottage which had for so long been her home. Tears filled her eyes.

In a way it was wonderful, even comforting to be here again. Yet she knew that she no longer belonged in this place. She had left her heart out there in Crans; there where *he* was. By this time, he would surely have finished his business in London. He would be back in the chalet working on his score, playing his piano, taking a few hours off to skim down those glittering white slopes in the warm sun, under the blue, blue sky; or to laugh and talk in The Valdana bar.

How cold and raw it seemed here in England. Colder than Switzerland although the actual temperature was much higher. The countryside looked desolate, grey and bedraggled; soaking wet. She would miss the pure, piercingly keen atmosphere up in those mountains. She hadn't stopped shivering since she reached London. If that had been all, she thought mournfully, *if only that had been all*! But she had run away from the person who really mattered in this life. *Oh, Ashley, Ashley, when you find that I've gone, will you give me a single thought? Will you feel one pang?*

Her heart was breaking for him. She could really believe, now, that hearts could break. Suddenly she put her face in her hands, and struggled with an emotion too strong to control.

Ann's arms went around her. Rowan was led into the drawing-room where Ann had lit a wood fire. She sat there on the old sofa weeping against Ann's shoulder as she had sometimes done in the past.

"There, there, my poor darling. It's a shame! I could kill that man. He had no right to make love to you."

"He didn't really, I made love to him," came from Rowan with something that might have been a laugh or a sob. "I shall never blame *him*. It's just my silly self."

"Do you want to talk about him?"

"No," whispered Rowan, "it's no good. I've just got to stop thinking of him. The sooner the better."

"These things take a bit of time to get out of one's system," said the practical Ann. "When I was your age I was absolutely mad about a married man, and my parents shot me off to an aunt and uncle in Egypt—Army people. (In the days before all this Canal business.) I had the whale of a time, you know. In fact, I became the pride and joy of the regiment and then I got home and met my Bill, and you see how happy I am."

Rowan nodded, laughed and blew her nose forlornly. Somehow she didn't think that dear old Ann could ever have loved her married man as she, Rowan, loved Ashley. It just *couldn't* have been the same. Rowan was a one-man girl. There *were* people like that in the world. It was silly—but that was how it was, if you were built that way.

All the way back from Crans she had thought of Ashley's 'Snowbird'. Somehow the words of that song he had so often played to her, had haunted her all through the journey.

I shall not fly again. . . .

That was how she felt. So deep were her wounds she would never recover; never again spread her wings. It must be Ashley—or nobody.

She heard Ann's cheerful voice:

"Don't go back to London. Stay with us and do a job here, Rowan. It's not merely a matter of generosity on my part. I could do with your help, duckie. There isn't a soul to give a hand and I know you love the country, and the kids, and I'd give you a salary. I don't mean as a permanency. You must get away *some* time and try to make something of your life. But say for a few months, until you see how things are shaping."

Rowan turned to her. Her throat worked.

"You've always been so sweet to me. Mummy used to say that you were the nicest person in the world."

"Nonsense," said Ann, nevertheless deeply touched, "Bill and I like *you*. It's a mutual admiration society."

"I'd like nothing better than to have some home life with you," Rowan whispered, "I'm so sick of hotels."

"That will be wonderful news for Scrap and Jeremy!" exclaimed Ann. "Will you stay tonight?"

"No, I'd better go back and get my things and have one more night in Town. It'd look so funny if I didn't."

So the matter was settled and Rowan remained at Blackthorn until the late afternoon.

While Ann was busy, Rowan went alone to the little churchyard to lay some flowers on her adoptive mother's grave. The sun broke through the straggling clouds for a moment, offering a pallid light and warmth on the desolation of the wintry scene. Rowan's heart was very full as she stood there looking at the inscription on the simple stone which had been put up since she had gone away. Bill had seen to that for her.

There lay her true mother, she thought sadly. She wondered how to regain peace of mind. The trouble was that one could never go back; one must go forward—learn to be a fatalist.

As she walked back to Blackthorn Farm, Rowan met one or two people whom she used to know and who stopped to speak to her. Everybody said how well she was looking. Everybody said how much they missed her and Mummy. And it seemed so normal to walk up the path to the old farmhouse, be greeted first by the obstreperous Luke, who dashed out to bark at her; then by the children who hailed her from the schoolroom window. They had both given whoops of delight when they heard that their beloved Rowan was coming to live with them.

Things were the same on the surface but with a deep underlying difference—significant of the inevitable changes that must take place in life; the remorseless turning of the wheel of time.

She was made truly welcome in the Jenkins' pleasant home and lucky to be here; she knew it. But as she sat in front of a roaring fire, eating Ann's hot buttered scones with home-made jam, and listening to the children's chatter, she was almost ashamed of the fact that she felt so homesick.

Wasn't it Cicely Courtneidge who used to sing that song— *Home is the place where your heart is*? It was so poignantly true.

If *he* was out there in Crans at the chalet, *there* her heart must be. And she was torn with longing for him, and for the splendour of the mountains.

Just before she left Blackthorn, Jeremy switched on the television for the Children's Hour. A girl's voice was making an announcement about tonight.

"*At nine o'clock this evening, Angus McGlellan will be interviewing famous personalities who will include two young men who have just reached the pinnacle of success with their musical* Summer Song, *which is packing the Regal Theatre. Ashley Moore, the composer, and Simon Cottar, who wrote the lyrics . . .*"

The announcer went on to mention other celebrities to be seen in the same programme.

Ann looked at Rowan. She saw that the girl's cheeks were fiery red. After a moment Rowan returned her look and said:

"So he's still in England."

"So it appears," Ann nodded.

"He's probably had so much business to see to for his uncle, he's had to stay. But he'll go back to Crans in a day or two."

It thoroughly disturbed Rowan to know that Ashley was in Town. She could imagine what was happening. He had told her so much about the publicity and fuss that went on, once anyone becomes a success in the theatre world. They wouldn't have left Ashley alone until they got him on one of the programmes; and Simon, too. Rowan wondered if the famous Fran was still with her poor husband. How far away all that Cottar business seemed now!

Rowan returned to London before Bill got home. She would see him when she came back with her luggage tomorrow.

It was a raw, foggy night in London and hard to believe that spring was not far away. The little private hotel in which Mary Gray had once stayed was shabby and genteel, full, Rowan could not help noting, of dreary old people. Nobody young to talk to. Nothing to lighten her gloom. All a painful contrast to the gay, beautiful Valdana.

She was glad she was going back to Jordans tomorrow. Quite frankly she had dreaded living in a place like this and doing a secretarial job in some office in which she hadn't the slightest interest.

The evening meal was almost uneatable, but Rowan didn't care. She had no appetite, anyhow. She felt exhausted and decided to go to bed immediately afterwards. It was only when she got up from the table that a kindly-looking, if seedy old gentleman at the table beside her, gave the pretty young girl a smile, and said:

"Going to look at the television tonight? I hear there's a good play."

And then Rowan's heart gave a jerk and she remembered:

At nine o'clock tonight Ashley will be on. . . .

Hurriedly she told the old gentleman that she was not interested in T.V. She went straight up to her small, cold, little room. It seemed half filled with fog. She lit the gas fire and then looked at her watch. It was only eight. What an awful time to go to bed, and she had nothing even to read. She stared blankly at her face in the mirror. How tired she looked and how unlike herself. Was she going to bed? She kept thinking about the television downstairs. She felt weak and reproached herself for not being stouterhearted.

'You're such a little *fool*, Rowan Gray——'

That was what she kept repeating to herself. She began to take off her dress. But at five minutes to nine she put it on again, and clenching hands and teeth, left her bedroom and ran down the stairs in a fever of impatience and longing.

She knew that she *must* see him. She must hear his voice.

The old gentleman who had spoken to her in the dining-room made a place for her on a sofa beside him.

"You've missed the play, my dear."

"I don't mind, thanks," she said breathlessly.

In an agony of emotion she scrutinized the gleaming oblong screen on that small mahogany box which was about to produce for her a vision of lost delight.

She could hardly bear it when, at length, she actually saw Ashley. He was sitting beside the interviewer. Dear life, she thought, what anguish—yet what joy! He was the same Ashley, yet not quite so familiar in that smartly cut Town suit and dark tie. He had never dressed like that in Crans. The person who had tuned in the picture had not done so very cleverly It distorted somewhat the shape of Ashley's face and head; but it *was* him and as the camera showed a close-up, Rowan's throat constricted so that she could hardly breathe. For one moment Ashley seemed to look *direct at her*. Those bright, remarkable eyes that had such power to draw the very heart out of her body pierced her consciousness. He smoothed back his hair with a quick nervous gesture which was very characteristic. Now she could even see the signet ring which she knew so well; and she heard his voice; the beloved, charming voice. He was answering all the questions about his show. As she watched and listened, she wondered how it was possible to feel so acutely about anything or anybody in the world.

The old gentleman croaked in her ear:

"Nice-looking young chap, isn't he?"

Rowan wondered for a split second what the old man would have said if she had answered:

'Yes, I knew him well and I love him, I love him, *I love him*!'

She heard the interrogator ask Ashley how long he intended to remain in England. Ashley gave a quick smile and said:

"No longer than I can help. I don't like it in this weather. I intend, actually, to fly back to Switzerland tomorrow and work on our new operetta."

"May we ask what it is about this time?" asked the interrogator's quiet voice.

"If you don't mind, I'd rather not say just for the moment," was Ashley's answer.

'*But I know, I could have told everybody*,' Rowan thought, '*I could have told them it's *The Snowbird*, and when I hear it in the future, it will always mean something so terrific to me!*'

The camera moved away from Ashley. Simon Cottar, on the other side of the interviewer, came into focus now. But Rowan only gave a brief look at Simon's nice face, then got up and fled from the room, up the ice-cold staircase and into her room where the small spluttering fire did little to produce any warmth. There was a howling draught under the door that lifted the mat. The narrow windows rattled.

Rowan flung herself down on the bed and hid her face against the pillow. Her cheeks burned, although the rest of her body trembled with the cold. She had been mad ever to go down there and see him and hear him again, she thought. It had brought things back much too vividly.

For a long time she lay crying desolately.

19

THE first thing that Ashley did on returning to Crans—ten days after the air disaster which had wiped out Laurence Moore and his wife—was to walk along to The Valdana Hotel.

He had been enormously busy in London during his brief visit. He had, in fact, stayed most of the time in the house of his friend and collaborator. For Fran had left Simon. There had been a final scene. For once, it appeared, Simon had stood firm, whereupon Fran had walked out. Once it would have broken Simon's heart, but things had reached such a pitch that, he told Ashley, he couldn't just go on *giving* and never receiving. He had reached the limit. And now he didn't seem to mind any more, but rather welcomed the peace of his home once Fran left it.

Fran had a new Spanish boy-friend; a young man with one of those old titles and still older castles, in the Andalusian mountains. The glamorous ex-model appealed to him. He had money to spare, so Fran had gone away with him.

"Take my advice, Ash, and be a bit more cautious than I was when choosing a wife," Simon had told Ashley. To this Ashley replied:

"What I see going on all around me, scares me stiff. I don't think I'll *ever* marry. I think it's safer to have the odd girl-friend, and retain one's freedom."

That was what he had said.

And he had talked about sharing a flat with Simon once he had got back to Town for good. They were going to be comfortably off, as well as famous, if *Summer Song* continued to play to packed houses, and with another operetta on the way. And, as Ashley had said to Simon with some irony, "Once fortune turns her face upon you she seems to smile from all directions."

In addition, Ashley found that he had inherited quite a considerable sum of money, as well as a positive museum of art treasures from his uncle.

It hadn't been possible to attend to all the necessary business in one short week. The law works slowly and the winding up of an estate is a long tedious affair. Ashley did what he could; wrote to most of his uncle's friends and left the rest of his affairs to the solicitors.

Of course the newspapers had made some show of the sensational death of two such well-known people as the Moores. There had been a lot written about the ex-Mrs. Edward Ripsdale, and reference to Petal's former family, the Lakers. But, so far as Ashley had been able to find out, poor little Petal had no living relatives and she had died intestate. Ashley had only managed to find the firm of solicitors who had acted for her when she was married to 'Rip'. It seemed that after inheriting the Ripsdale money, she had never bothered to make a Will of her own.

"Like so many people in the middle thirties and forties, they think they've got plenty of time ahead," the solicitor had told Ashley sadly, "then this sort of sudden tragedy occurs and the result is chaotic."

It looked as though Edward Ripsdale's money would pass to distant cousins. These, Ashley had had no time to contact. He was anxious to return to Crans. And despite what he had said about appreciating his freedom—he knew that he wanted to get back to Crans *in order to see Rowan.*

He was astonished to discover how much he wanted it; how the last ten days away from her had increased rather than decreased his interest in her. He could not get her out of his mind. Her rather childish, touching devotion to him; her loneliness; that 'lost' look about her, had taken a decided grip of him. He kept remembering, too, her tears and her kisses; and the expression in her eyes when he told her she must not love him.

He was beginning to have a remorse complex, he told himself; afraid that he had encouraged her to fall in love with him. She was much too sweet. Pity was a dangerous thing. But now it did not seem that it was pity alone that drew him back to her side. It was some fundamental need that she supplied; and it was a need that he had never before experienced with any woman.

It was a considerable shock to Ashley when he walked into The Valdana and saw Suzanne, the former receptionist, in Rowan's place.

He complimented Suzanne on her recovery, then asked, casually, what had happened to Miss Gray.

"*Je ne sais pas,*" was Suzanne's unhelpful reply.

It was Paul's wife, Vittoria, who supplied the information.

"Paul and I do not really understand what happened. Maybe that accident upset her more than we imagined, but suddenly—like that"—Vittoria snapped her fingers—"Rowan announced that she must leave us. She went a few days after you left—as soon as Suzanne could get here."

"I see," said Ashley slowly and lit a cigarette.

But he didn't see. Frankly he was perplexed and disappointed. All through the journey from London Airport to Geneva, then on in the train to Sierre, he had thought about little Rowan; of his first meeting with her in that same train, and so much else.

He sat at the bar frowning over his drink. Paul had joined them.

"I was a little annoyed at first that Rowan left us so abruptly," Paul remarked. "After all, we had made her very welcome here and shown our appreciation for her good work. Then Toria told me she felt there was something much more behind Rowan's wish to get away. You know what women are, *mon cher*; they see things we men do not see."

Ashley glanced quickly at Vittoria.

"And what did you see?"

Madame Garnier looked a little uncomfortable.

"Oh, it's all guesswork on my part, but I think she was deeply upset about *something*, and it could not have been only the tragedy of your uncle's death, although that did seem to affect her. But it could not mean all *that* much to her, now could it? No—I am going to be indiscreet, and Paul will be cross—but I think *you* are the reason."

Now Ashley positively blushed. He could feel the blood surge into his face. However he laughed.

"Me? What nonsense."

"No, honestly," said Vittoria, "it is naughty of me but I do think little Rowan Gray was madly in love with you."

"Toria!" said Paul in a reproachful voice.

"Well, what do I do about it?" said Ashley in a rather rough voice, and finished his drink and got off the stool. "I doubt if it's true but thanks for telling me. And now I must get down to some work. It's what I have come back to Crans for. London was impossible. All that publicity ... enough to drive one round the bend. See you folks later tonight, perhaps. 'Bye for now."

He walked quickly out of the bar and out of the hotel.

It was the sort of evening that he had remembered and missed while he was in Town. The sky studded with stars, the moon shining radiantly over the majestic range of mountains; the diamond-caked snow scrunching under his boots. Henri said it was going to be fine tomorrow for the ski-ing.

Hortense had a real welcome waiting for *monsieur*, and one of her best dishes of veal with cream, wine and mushrooms. But Ashley had no appetite. After toying with the meal he went to the piano and began to strum the Snowbird theme.

He muttered the words: *I shall not fly again*, and thought of Rowan, lying on the woodland path as lately he had so often seen her in his imagination; like the wounded Snowbird, herself.

"Dammit!" he said aloud savagely, played a discord and got up from the piano, "anybody would think I was in love with the wretched girl."

It soon became evident that he was not going to be able to compose with ease, and that this journey out here had been wasted. When he stopped trying to work, he flung himself into a chair and took up a book of poems which he found in the bookcase—English poems of the eighteenth and nineteenth centuries.

He came to one by Thomas Campbell (1777–1844) who had written of the Battle of Hohenlinden.

Ashley became interested; it was such a dramatic pen-picture of that epic battle when the great Moreau had destroyed the Austrians.

The bitterness of that old winter campaign came to life in the peaceful firelit chalet, while Ashley read the words aloud; his cigarette burning to ash in a tray beside him.

> *"On Linden when the sun was low*
> *All bloodless lay the untrodden snow*
> *And dark as winter was the flow*
> *Of Iser rolling rapidly. . . ."*

He put down the book, leaned back and shut his eyes.

The untrodden snow. It was there, outside high above the chalet lying on those tall summits, shining in the cold light of the moon.

The untrodden snow, repeated Ashley.

Back in a flash, to haunt him came the face and the slight form of Rowan Gray; her cheeks wet with tears, pressed against his.

She was like the untrodden snow. There had been a strange purity about her. The enchantment of purity imperceptibly blended with passion.

In his careless way, he had dared to tread upon the whiteness. And once she had come to him here in her loneliness and grief and taken him to her heart. What had he done for her? Nothing but destroy her peace of mind. So much so, that she had run

184

away. She had left Crans because of *him*. Vittoria had said so, and in his heart, Ashley knew it to be true.

'Damn, damn, *damn*,' he said through his teeth and threw the book on to the table, went back to the piano and made a futile attempt to complete a song that he had begun while Laurence and Petal were here.

'My God,' he thought, 'I'm feeling pretty bleak tonight.'

It was not only Rowan he kept seeing in this room but poor old Laury and lovely, light-hearted Petal; those two who were now no more than dust; for ever lost and gone.

'I am famous and I am richer than I have ever been in my life and I have never been more miserable,' Ashley brooded.

That next morning, walking out in brilliant sunshine to buy something that he wanted, he ran into Marc Garnier. That meeting seemed to settle the whole matter of Rowan in Ashley's mind.

He stopped Marc and began to speak to him brightly, but the Swiss boy, unsmiling, gave him only curt monosyllables in reply. Then, as though forcing the issue, Ashley asked about Rowan.

"Wasn't it a pity that your *petite cousine* left so suddenly—it was doing her good here——" he began.

Marc, crimson-cheeked, burst out:

"Why didn't you leave her alone? Everything was all right until you upset her."

"I didn't mean——" Ashley began to speak.

But Marc walked on and left the Englishman standing there, alone.

Ashley, tight-lipped and resentful, made his purchases and returned to the chalet. It was only a matter of forty-eight hours before he decided that he had lost all interest in composing the music for *The Snowbird*—or being in Crans. It was not merely what Vittoria had said; nor Marc's impulsive outburst, but because he must face up to the truth which lay within himself. He knew that he loved Rowan and that he must find her and tell her so.

Once having made such a decision, a strange excitement seized Ashley. It drove him to swift action.

He rang up the astonished Garniers and told them that he was flying back to Town tomorrow.

"But you've only just returned!" they cried.

His answer was that he might return yet again and that he

would leave his luggage in the chalet, but that he had special business which necessitated a flight to London.

Only then did he realize that he had not the slightest idea where to find Rowan.

Nobody at The Valdana knew where she was. Not even Henri, who was the keeper of most addresses. *Mademoiselle* had told him, he said, that she did not expect any mail, so she left no forwarding address.

"But Monsieur Jean Garnier will know," Henri declared. "He is her uncle."

"Of course," said Ashley.

He paid a call at the Hôtel de Montagne at Sierre on his way to Geneva.

At first Jean Garnier refused to give Ashley the address. He received the famous young composer from England a trifle stiffly and coldly. Ashley's fame meant nothing to him, but Rowan was important and her sudden departure had upset Jean very much.

"I do not know that she would *want* me to give you her address, *monsieur*," he said. "And I did not approve of her friendship with you."

"Look," said Ashley with heightened colour, "I know what you're thinking. Your son also made it quite clear that I'm supposed to be responsible for Rowan leaving Crans. If it is so, I'm deeply sorry but I assure you that there was nothing between your niece and myself to warrant this—this criticism."

"*Monsieur*, I think that she loved you," said Jean with quiet dignity.

For a moment Ashley felt a deep embarrassment and then with a nervous gesture, running his fingers through his hair, he said:

"And I love her, Monsieur Garnier, only I did not know it when she was here. If you want the truth—I am going over to England to ask her to marry me."

Jean Garnier's blue eyes brightened. Looking at Ashley's strong unhandsome face which was yet so attractive and winning, he felt a sudden liking for the Englishman—a new sensation of trust.

"That is good news, *monsieur*," he said. "And I shall of course, be delighted to tell you where Rowan is to be found."

20

THAT same night, Rowan was sitting by the fire in the drawing-room at Blackthorn Farm, performing the unromantic task of mending Jeremy's socks. There were a pile of them in the basket. This seemed the perfect time to do them. Rowan was alone. This was her 'baby-watching' night. With her encouragement, Bill had taken Ann off to dinner and a cinema in High Wycombe where there was a film they particularly wanted to see.

It was horrible weather thought Rowan. A night of sleet, while a wild wind tore round the farmhouse and rattled the loose windows and doors.

As a rule Rowan did not mind solitude or stormy weather, but tonight she felt lonely and depressed.

Every now and again, with a big sigh, she stopped darning and bent to pat Luke who was stretched at her feet occupying the best position, almost on top of the grate.

She knew that she was lucky to have this home with the Jenkins family. But she hadn't felt very well since she left Crans. She had developed a cough. She could not get used to this climate again after the radiance of Switzerland.

Rowan could have put on the television, but there was nothing she really wanted to see. When she had turned on the radio for a moment she had heard music from *Summer Song*—music written so obviously in the Ashley Moore vein with which she was now so familiar—it had hurt. She could not bear it and she had switched it off.

"The trouble with me, Luke," she addressed the dog, "is that I feel things so dreadfully. I keep thinking about Ashley and about my mother crashing in that plane. I just can't stop it. It's stupid and I'm a coward! I wish I were you, Luke—just dozing and dreaming of a nice bone."

Luke raised his head, glanced at her out of the corners of his eyes, gave a long sigh to express his own feelings and then went to sleep again.

There was nothing now to be heard except the wind and the rain. Time passed slowly.

Suddenly Rowan looked up from her darning. She could hear the sound of car wheels. They came nearer, until it was beyond doubt that a car had pulled up in front of Blackthorn Farm.

'Heavens!' thought Rowan.

She hoped that some of the Jenkins' friends weren't paying an unexpected call. She was only wearing jeans and a 'woolly', her hair was tied back loosely with a ribbon and she hadn't any make-up on her face. She hadn't expected visitors.

When the rat-tat came on the front door, and she opened it, she could not for a moment see through the rain and the darkness, nor recognize the face and form of the man who was standing out there. He was bare-headed and wearing a thick Jaeger coat. Behind him, was a magnificent Daimler with a chauffeur.

"I'm so sorry——" began Rowan, clinging on to the door to prevent a wild gust of wind from slamming it; then the words stuck in her throat. The wild colour tore to her face and throat. She felt as though an electric current sparked right through her, till she tingled from head to foot.

"*Ashley!*" she cried.

And Ashley it was. Rowan drew back into the hall. He took a step towards her. In a casual sort of voice, he said:

"Hello, Rowan, honey—can my chauffeur come in? It's a bit stormy for him to sit outside."

"Of—of course," she stammered. "He can g-go into the kitchen. I expect he'd l-like a c-cup of tea."

"Thank you, miss," said the driver.

During the next few minutes Rowan behaved as though she was in a dream. A cyclonic dream; she was caught up in it and seemed to have no will of her own. She ushered the chauffeur into the kitchen; put on a kettle, showed him where to find tea and biscuits, and told him to make himself a pot; pushed a bundle of papers and magazines in front of him then went back into the drawing-room, her heart beating so fast that she gasped for breath. Ashley had taken off his coat. He stood with his back to the fire.

"This is very warm and charming," he said, "we had the hell of a drive down. I'm so rich I was able to hire a Daimler. Aren't I smart?"

"Terrifically smart," nodded Rowan, swallowing.

Despite her wild excitement and the unexpected delight of seeing him, she managed to note such details as the fact that he was wearing a dark suit, and a beautiful blue and wine-coloured silk tie, with matching handkerchief in the pocket; and that the hair which used to be so rough and curly in Crans was smoothly brushed. This was the immaculate man-about-town. The man she had seen on television. The famous Ashley Moore.

Speechless, she stood staring.

And Ashley stared back. A pang shot through him at the sight of her pallor. In so short a time she seemed to have lost her sun-tan. Her eyes were bigger than ever. In those close-fitting jeans, those thick woolly, boy's socks, she looked incredibly young.

He felt stricken with an unutterable tenderness and with the remorse that had been his ever since he faced up to the fact that it was he who had caused her pain and, perhaps, even despair.

"Rowan," he spoke her name in a low yearning voice.

Without understanding, her large eyes regarded him. She was beginning to tremble as she always did when Ashley entered the room. She whispered:

"I thought you were in Crans."

"I was but I couldn't stay. I just found it impossible!"

"Why?"

"Because you weren't there," he said abruptly.

She put two fingers against her lips.

"That can't be true," she said in quite a shocked voice.

"I must confess it shakes me, but it *is* true," he said with a short laugh. "As soon as I got back, I realized that I'd got to find you—*you*—and not just to carry on with my work."

Rowan found no answer. She felt as though she was choking. She felt as though the ground was opening up and she was falling through space. She felt as though she must be mad and that she was not really hearing these things at all.

Then Ashley gave her a long, deep look, and caught her in his arms, and held her close, pressing his cheek against hers.

"I love you," he said. "I knew it out in Crans when I got back. I told your uncle and your Cousin Marc that I was coming back to ask you to marry me. They gave me your address. That is why I am here. I love you, my darling little Rowan, my beloved little Snowbird. I want you to marry me."

Words came more easily to Rowan then; the tears came too, raining down her face; but it was a radiant face and her arms locked very tightly round his neck.

"I adore you," she said. "You know it. But I never dreamed in this world that you would ever want me. I thought you told me that I *mustn't* love you. Oh, Ashley, Ashley, that is what you said!"

"I was a fool. I didn't realize what it was I really wanted, but I do now, beyond all shadow of a doubt. My darling little Rowan —you're so young and sweet, and I'm all kinds of a heel, as the

Americans would say. But I think I can safely promise that I'll be a good husband to you. Will you take me on?"

"I'll love you a lot," she said, "but I don't know if I'll make a good wife for a successful composer."

"That's where you're wrong. You'll make an absolutely ideal wife. You'll be a wonderful help to me in my work. We'll work together. And if I go on being successful and getting rich, I'll buy you a chalet in Crans and we'll live there among the mountains where it is even more beautiful in summer than in winter. You'd like that, wouldn't you? To see the gentians come out in the sun —millions of them, all over the mountainside."

"Oh, Ashley," she said. Her voice broke and she pressed one cheek against his coat in silent ecstasy. He went on caressing her hair, covering her face with kisses. He said things that he had never said to any other woman in his life and would never say again. He gave her all that he knew of tenderness as well as those long, passionate kisses which seemed to draw the very soul out of her body. He mentioned things that she barely understood, such as *the untrodden snow* and his wish to preserve, for ever, that child-like quality and simplicity that set her apart in his mind from all other women.

And finally, of course, when they had both calmed down, she told him about her mother. She described that final unhappy meeting with Petal.

"I did say then that I would want to tell the man that I was going to marry, so I'm telling you now," she said, "I feel somehow it might draw us even closer together than we are—if that's possible."

Ashley was shaken and amazed by her story.

"Petal was your mother, *she*—Uncle Laury's wife! But how fantastic!"

"Yes," nodded Rowan, "but it's true. You shall see poor Mummy's diary and read about Petal—when she was *Vivien Laker*."

"If she was still living, I should hate her for what she did to you, my darling," Ashley said in a low voice.

"I almost hated her myself. I thought she was terribly callous. Yet one had to acknowledge her charm and now she's gone for ever, I must try to forgive her," said Rowan in a low voice.

Ashley nodded.

"But what a story. God! We must never let anybody know. If the Press got hold of this, they'd have it all over the papers.

He flung off his coat, sat down on the stool and ran his fingers over the keys.

"A frightful tone, but better than nothing."

"What have you thought of?" she asked anxiously, leaning her arms on the open lid, looking at him with her shining eyes.

"A theme for a song in the last act of *The Snowbird*. One for him to sing to her; when he picks her up in his arms after the shooting. Look here—Simon will have to re-write these lyrics. I'm damned if I'm going to let my Snowbird die of her wounds. Not now. *Not now.*"

"Oh, Ashley," she said, "I'm glad. I didn't want her to die."

"She won't," he said, and grinned at his Rowan in the old familiar way, while he broke into a sudden melody. "There's going to be a new song. She shall spread her wings and fly again. I'll *make* her fly! Just as you and I are going to fly, my darling, straight into the sun!"

He was still playing to Rowan when Ann and Bill came in.

really *is* a drama. Your mother and my uncle—and now *we're* going to get married."

Rowan, who had been sitting on a stool at Ashley's feet, lifted her face to him—a very different one to the one he had seen when he first came in. It was rosy, glowing.

"Darling Ashley, it isn't a dream? You really *are* here and I really *am* going to be your wife?"

"As soon as I can get a special licence and fix it up," he said.

"I'm terribly scared of all the publicity. You're so famous."

"You'll carry it off, honey, and soon I'll carry *you* off. I think we'll go straight back to Crans and finish *The Snowbird* together."

"Won't the Garniers be surprised?"

"Somehow I don't think they will," said Ashley and put his arms around the slight figure and drew her right up into his arms. She leaned against him and gave a long, contented sigh. Lifting one of his hands, she put it against her burning cheek.

"You'll wait till Ann and Bill come in and tell them the news?"

"I wouldn't dream of leaving until I've told them."

Another sigh from Rowan. She shut her eyes, savouring to the full, the splendour of this thing that had happened—of his arms—of his lips—of the thought of the mountains and the sunlight; of all that awaited her.

For a little while longer, Ashley held her, marvelling at the length of her lashes, playing with the silk of her hair, profoundly contented that this love had come into his life. It meant so much more than all the other good things. It was, as he was fast learning, the *only thing* of real importance to a man, except his work.

Suddenly his eyes lit on a huge and rather elderly looking piano at the far corner of the room.

"You've got a piano here!" he exclaimed.

Rowan sat up.

"Yes. It belonged to Ann's mother. It's an old thing but it's in tune. Ann kept it for the children, in case one of them was musical."

"I want to play," said Ashley. "I've got an idea. It came to my mind just now as I saw you here in my arms looking as though you were asleep."

She stood up, the flame of his excitement setting fire to her. Walking to the piano with him, she switched on more lights, and he opened the lid.

"Oh, Ashley, this will seem like old times!" she breathed.